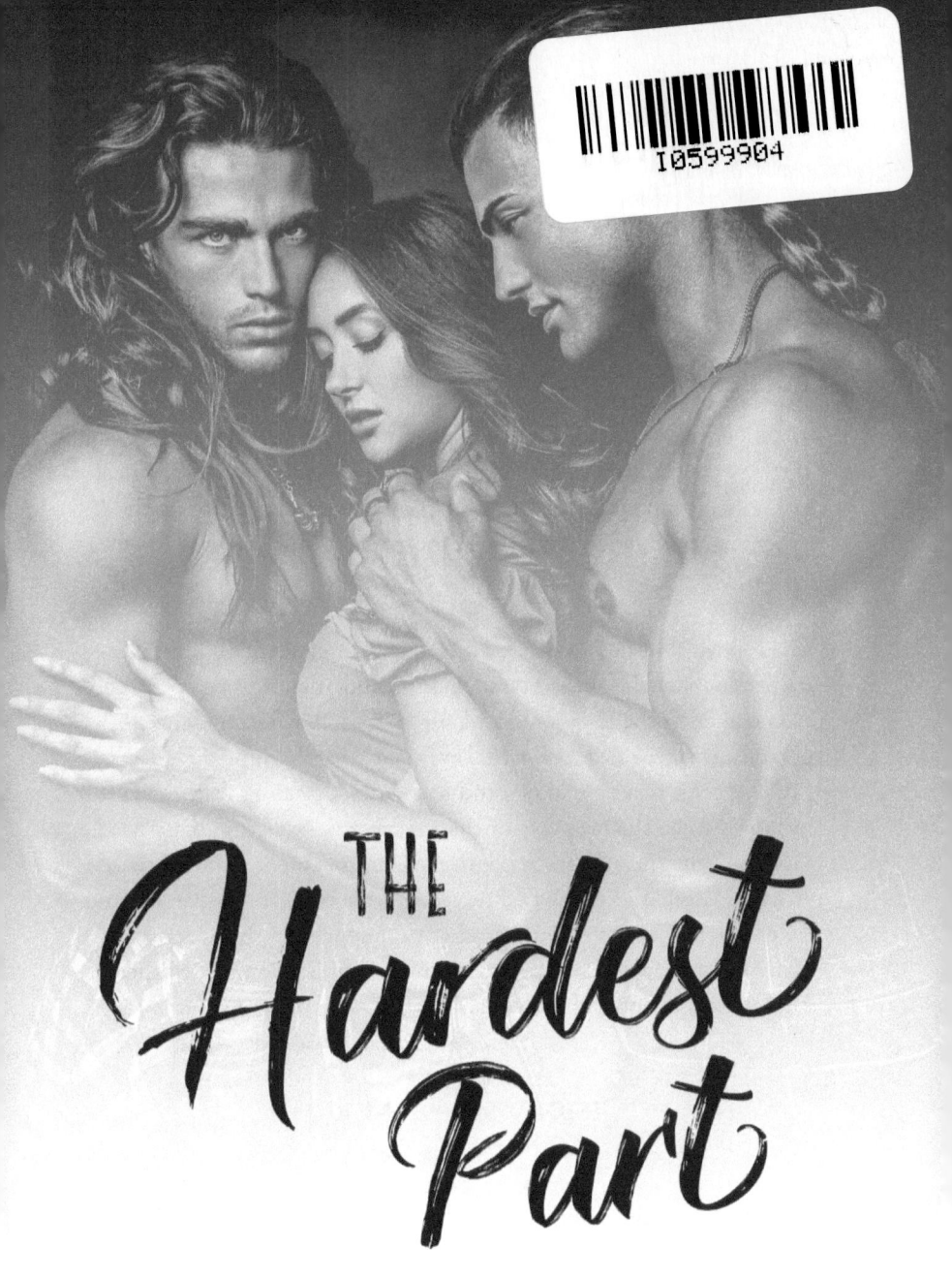

THE Hardest Part

DYAN LAYNE

ISBN: 979-8-9923243-0-3
ASIN: B0DCSZSZRK

Cover photography: Michelle Lancaster, @lanefotograf
Cover models: Andrew Murray, Tristan Pons, and Verity Runje
Cover designer: Lori Jackson, Lori Jackson Design
Formatting: Stacey Blake, Champagne Book Design

Playlist

Tom Petty and the Heartbreakers | *The Waiting*
Scotch & Brandy | *All American Dream*
Ruel | *Kiss Me*
Mackintosh Braun | *Made for Us*
Ghost Hounds | *Dirty Angel*
State of Mine (feat. Drew Jacobs) | *God's Country*
dArtagnan | *Hey Brother*
Stevie Nicks | *Edge of Seventeen*
Sam Smith | *Fire on Fire*
Sleep Token | *Mine*
Radio Company | *Sounds of Someday*
Tyler Childers | *House Fire*
††† (Crosses) feat. Robert Smith | *Girls Float † Boys Cry*
Extreme | *More Than Words*
Steven Rodriguez | *Like You Mean It*
Grace VanderWaal | *Burned*
Benson Boone | *Hello Love*
Clejan | *The Way That I Fiddle*
Written by Wolves | *GODDESS*
Amber | *Wherever You Go*
Nothing More (feat. Eric Vanlerberghe of I Prevail) | *HOUSE ON SAND*
Palaye Royale | *Morning Light*
Lana Del Rey | *White Mustang*
Lainey Wilson | *Wildflowers and Wild Horses*
Thousand Foot Krutch, Citizen Soldier | *Be Somebody - Reignited*
Sleep Token | *Take Me Back To Eden*
First Aid Kit | *My Silver Lining*
Steven Rodriguez | *Love Me Harder*

The Castellows | *Cowboy Kind of Love*
Parmalee | *Gonna Love You*
Lana Del Rey | *Ride*
Tim Montana | *Be A Cowboy*
State of Mine | *In The Air Tonight*
Cory Marks (feat. Ivan Moody, Travis Tritt, Mick Mars) | *Outlaws & Outsiders*
Written by Wolves | *PLEASE, JUST BREATHE*
Dean Lewis | *How Do I Say Goodbye*
Jamie Bower | *Heaven In Your Eyes*
Benson Boone | *In The Stars*
Ruelle, Fleurie | *Carry You*
Dasha | *Even Cowboys Cry*
The Lumineers | *Ho Hey*
While She Sleeps | *TO THE FLOWERS*
Sleep Token | *Rain*
Bring Me The Horizon | *Kool-Aid*
The Devil Wears Prada | *Ritual*
Bring Me The Horizon | *YOUtopia*
Yungblud | *I Was Made For Lovin' You*
Taylor Swift | *This Love (Taylor's Version)*
Forest Blakk | *If You Love Her*
P!nk | *A Million Dreams*
Nightwish | *Perfume Of The Timeless*
The Plot In You | *All That I Can Give*
Warren Eiders | *Sin So Sweet*
Myles Smith | *My Home*
Nation Haven | *Our Home*
Ashes & Arrows | *It's Alright*
Parmalee | *Take My Name*
Lee Brice | *Love Like Crazy*
The Outlaws | *(Ghost) Riders In the Sky*
Ghost | *The Future Is A Foreign Land*
Ashes & Arrows | *Wild Horses*

Author's Note

This book contains subject matter which may be sensitive or triggering to some readers and is intended for mature audiences.

While it isn't necessary to have read the previous book in the series, as this is a standalone novel featuring a unique romance, it is _highly_ recommended. *Brookside* is a series of interconnected standalone novels. All of the main characters reappear and some storylines connect from book to book. For the best experience, the series should be read in order.

If you are following the series, **The Hardest Part** begins shortly before, and overlaps, with events in **The Third Son**.

For my girls over at The Ridge. May you all find a cowboy (or two) of your very own.

Thanks for being the best humans ever.

Love y'all.

The mountain is a living, breathing thing.
If you listen very closely you can hear its deep, low hum.
—Carrie Sawyer Gantry

THE Hardest Part

Prologue

I n all his twenty-two years, he'd never seen a more beautiful girl.

An enchanting vision, sunlight warmed her sable hair as she washed clothes in the river, crouched at its bank. Caught up in her task as she was, the girl didn't notice him. Good thing too, since he couldn't tear his eyes away from her.

A day's ride out of Fort John, having come to the end of the great plains, they stopped the wagons to rest for the night here—what remained of them, anyway. There were thirty in their traveling party when they left Missouri and civilization behind, full of dreams for a new and prosperous future in the unclaimed West all those weeks ago. They'd lost six of them already.

One wagon turned back.

The river claimed two.

And three to a deed most foul.

He shuddered to think of it, closing his eyes to squelch the burning rush of saline.

Camped just east of the steep foothills ascending into the Rocky Mountains, the most arduous leg of the journey to California lay before them. So, after sixty-seven days of pure hell, and a good hundred more of them to go, this ravishing creature washing clothes in the river was a most welcome sight indeed.

"Levi?"

He turned to peek over his shoulder. Boots caked in dust, wiping the sweat and grime from his brow, Elijah Brooks approached him.

"Supper's near ready." A hand landed on his shoulder. "What you lookin' at?"

Levi tipped his chin toward the water's edge. "Who is she?"

"One of Josiah Walker's girls, I reckon."

"And who in the hell is Josiah Walker?"

"Mountain man who knows the trail. He's to be our guide now." They'd lost the one they'd hired on in Independence to the dreaded cholera. "Jacoby met with him yesterday. Promised to take us as far as Fort Bridger."

How'd he not know that? One too many whiskeys with Archer last night, he'd wager. The trading post having been the closest semblance to the world Levi knew before they ferried across the Missouri River, he drained one glass after another. The spirits numbed his grief for a time and he slept without the images of bloodied corpses haunting his dreams.

"I see."

"You thinking of bedding her, good brother?"

Elijah might not be his brother by blood, though he would have been by law had Caleb and Amelia not met their tragic fate, but he was kin nonetheless. Like their parents and grandparents before them, they'd been a part of each other's lives for as long as Levi could remember. All of them gone now, both he and Elijah were left with no choice other than to see this through and care for their younger siblings.

"Does she look like a whore to you, Eli?"

"No, but if I didn't assume her to be Walker's daughter, I'd swear she was a—"

Levi stopped him before he could say anything more. He didn't care to hear it. "She's beautiful. The kind of girl you take to wife before she warms your bed, not after."

"You have need of a wife, Levi Gantry," he said, mirth rising from his throat.

As if he didn't. Left with a six-year-old sister to raise, Elijah's plight was much greater than his. Young Elizabeth required the tender touch only a woman could provide, whereas, at nearly sixteen, his twin sisters were considered women grown.

It's not that Levi didn't intend to marry and start a family of his own someday. He hoped to find a suitable wife when they reached California and had dreams of fertile pastures, a large house, and many children to fill it with.

"As do you, brother."

With a solemn nod, Elijah squeezed his shoulder. "Come now. You know how Victoria and Mary Alice don't like to be kept waiting."

Jacob Gantry closed his great-grandfather's journal, the fragile pages brittle and yellowed with age. His vision blurred, eyes weary from hours spent deciphering the faded ink, he rubbed at them. Call him a historian, a chronicler, an archivist, to him preserving the origins of Brookside, and its history, was an important task, and a role he enthusiastically took on.

Weaving together the rich tapestry of their stories he'd

found documented in leather-bound journals, long-forgotten letters tucked inside dusty, old trunks in cobweb-laced attics, and timeworn cemetery gravestones, future generations would always understand who they were and how they came to be so favored. The blood, sweat, and tears of those who came before them.

The abundance.

The absolute love.

The purest joy.

Jake's greatest fear was that with the ever-changing world outside their gates, they could lose favor, their culture, traditions, and their land. The community everyone worked so hard to build for nearly two hundred years. But with full knowledge and understanding of their past, his generation and those who came after them would do everything in their power to protect what they shared here. And that's why his work was so important.

Smiling to himself, his fingertips traced over the worn leather cover of Levi Gantry's journal. Fortunately for Jake, writing things down was commonplace then. It made his job easier. *So many stories.* Detailed and vibrant, the past came alive on the pages.

He loved all the Brookside stories and treasured every last one, but there were two he held especially dear to his heart, though one had yet to be written.

The story of Levi, the bluebird, and the butterfly.

And the greatest love story of all.

His own.

One

His kiss was everything.

The taste of a crisp fall apple on his tongue, tart and sweet, he held her face in his hands, thumbs caressing her cheeks, and took her lips with his. Emily loved how Billy kissed her, the way he made her feel. Beautiful. Worshipped. Adored. His mouth on hers soothed like a warm summer rain while fireflies twirled in her belly.

She recalled the first time Billy got up the nerve to kiss her finally—a real one, and not some misplaced peck on the cheek, though it kind of started that way. The month after her sixteenth birthday, at the community cookout Brookside held every year during the last weekend of May, he took her for a walk. They sat together on the grass alongside the stream, sharing a glass of Grams' fresh-squeezed lemonade.

"This is nice," Billy said, plucking at the tender green blades between them. He seemed nervous. "Just me and you."

With the straw between her teeth, Emily smiled into her lemonade and took a sip. "I think so too."

"Do you wanna go to the bonfire tonight?"

"Sure, if you want to." Her hair lifted in the breeze, a piece of it sticking to her lip. "Shiloh and Griffin said they're going."

"I know." Looking down at her mouth, Billy freed the strand. His head dipped, lips ghosting along her jaw. "I've been dyin' to kiss you, Em."

Do it, then.

She'd only been waiting for what felt like forever.

Playmates from the time they were toddlers, Billy was her best friend, and Emily his. Though they hadn't made an official announcement or anything yet at the time, even then it was already a foregone conclusion they'd end up together at the stones.

"Can I?"

Turning her face toward his, Emily nodded as Billy's mouth connected with her cheek. Threading his fingers in her long, brown waves, with the brim of his hat shielding them from the glare of the afternoon sun, he lowered his lips to hers and the fireflies took flight.

And they'd been flying ever since.

Even now, more than a year and thousands of kisses later, they had that effect on her. Maybe it's because Billy was the first boy, and the only boy, who'd ever kissed her. Maybe it was because she loved him so much.

So, on this cool, blue Sunday morning in November, Emily lay with Billy in the field behind the converted Dutch barn she lived in with her mother, pulling him closer. Loving the feeling of his belt buckle digging into her skin as he pressed his hardness into her softness through their clothes.

If she positioned herself just right, the center seam of her jeans would rub on her clit and give her enough friction to come.

"Let me use my fingers, Em."

God, she wanted him to. Billy's fingers were magic.

"My mom is home."

"But I wanna make you come." Reaching for her nipples, his hands slid beneath her sweater.

Then she heard the patio door slide open.

"Emily?"

Billy pulled away with a groan.

Fuck.

"Yeah," she answered as he helped her up.

Holding her hand, Billy led her back to the house. Her mom sat at the kitchen table, ledgers open, papers spread out, and her laptop in front of her. She kept the books for the ranch.

"Miss Kim." Cheeks flushed, Billy tipped his hat.

"I'd ask what you two have been up to, but goin' by the odd bits stuck in your hair, I think I already know."

"Mama." Side-eyeing Billy, Emily ran her fingers through it and plucked out a twig.

"Uncle Matty just called. Wants us up at the house for supper at six."

Same as every Sunday, but...

"Isn't he in Denver?"

"Got back last night," her mom said, scribbling away in the ledger. "Says he's got some big news for us."

"What do you think it could be?"

"Don't rightly know." And with a shrug of her shoulders, she put her pencil down and turned to Billy. "He wants you and your brother to come, too."

Jake drove.

The distance to the main house wasn't all that far—just a few miles up the stream. An easy ride on horseback, and she'd done it often enough. Holding her hand on his lap, Billy stared out the window. Emily glanced up at Jake. His arm bent over the steering wheel, he hummed along to a tune playing on the radio. Long hair flying with the breeze coming in through the window he had cracked open, she reached out and touched it. His face turned to hers and he smiled. Taking her hand from his hair, he lowered it to his thigh and gently squeezed.

"Have you spoken to Kellan or Tanner?" she asked him.

He answered with a nod, "I have."

"So, what's this big news?"

Did Uncle Matty score a prize Limousin bull or a sought-after Wagyu? He went to Denver on business all the time. Emily wasn't exactly sure what he did there, but he'd been going a lot more often lately.

"I didn't ask, and they didn't say."

Course not.

"Could be a wedding," Billy offered, rolling his head away from the window.

Emily burst into a fit of giggles. "Whose?"

"I saw Tanner talkin' all friendly to Samantha Quigley in town a few weeks ago." He shrugged. "I know they're hellbent on waitin' for their dream girl to appear, but my dude's turnin' twenty-two. How long do you expect him to wait?"

Looking down at her, Jake winked. "As long as it takes."

"It's not that," Emily said with a tsk. *At least it better not be.* The butcher's daughter was nice, but far too docile for Kellan. Her cousin needed someone who'd challenge him, someone who'd bring out the loving man she knew he could be. Samantha was not that girl. "Tanner is friendly with everybody."

"Well, I ain't got a clue, then." Jake pulled in behind her mother's truck and Billy put his hat back on his head. "It's prob'ly a whole lot a nothin.'"

Billy might be right about that, but as Jake helped her down from the truck, she felt it—a distinct energy to the air. Something was about to change. Something big.

"Hey, Ems." Tanner was waiting at the door with his arms open, ready to wrap her up in a giant bear hug. He was good at those. "How's my favorite cousin?"

"I'm the only cousin you got." Standing on her tiptoes, Emily kissed his cheek.

"So?" He ruffled her hair, making a mess of it. "You're still my favorite."

"Where's Kel?"

"With Dad." He hitched a thumb behind him. "They've got steaks going on the grill."

She headed into the kitchen. Sure enough, her cousin and Uncle Matty, beer in hand, and her mom and Grams, were outside, deep in conversation. Judging by the looks on their faces, it sure wasn't a prized bull they were talking about. Kellan saw her through the glass, and with a tip of his chin, alerted the others to her presence.

He turned his back on her, taking the meat off the grill. Three heads turned toward her, their strained expressions giving way to weak smiles that didn't quite reach their eyes. His mother and sister coming along behind him, Uncle Matty walked in and squeezed Emily to his side.

"Here's my girl." The sweet scent of hickory smoke lingering on his flannel shirt, he kissed her crown. "You been doin' your schoolwork and mindin' your mama like I told you to?"

Twice a widower, Matthew Brooks was the closest she had to

a father growing up, being hers died when she was only three—killed serving in Afghanistan. She remembered little of it. But Uncle Matty filled in as best he could, teaching her to ride, and taking her to all the daddy-daughter dances at school. He was always there for her, the same as her mom was for Tanner and Kellan. Their mothers died when they were just babies.

"Course, I have." Her smile building, Emily tilted her head to the side and glanced up at him. "So, did you have a good trip?"

"Sure did." With a short nod, he smiled back. "And I'm gonna tell you all about it."

"Sweetheart, help me with this, would you?" Grams handed her a big bowl of mashed potatoes. "As soon as Kellan brings the steaks in, we can all sit down and eat."

Matthew took his place at the head of the table, her mother at the foot. Emily sat with Billy and Jake, Grams and her cousins on the other side. Smirking to himself, but then when wasn't he, Kellan passed around a basket of biscuits looking like the cat that swallowed the canary.

Her curiosity in overdrive now, she nudged his shin under the table with the toe of her boot. "Why're you lookin' like that, babes?"

"Like what?" He licked his lip, the corner of his mouth ticking up.

Like you've got a secret you're dyin' to let out, but you won't.

"Never mind." Her gaze darted to the basket in his hand. "I'll take one of those."

"Help yourself."

Jake got a biscuit for her, and buttering it, put it on her plate. He shifted closer, their thighs touching. Warmth infused her cheeks, and Emily smiled up at him. He was always doing little things like that. His countless simple gestures showed her how much he cared. She already knew it, of course. Even so, she appreciated the reminder.

Once Grams made sure everyone had a glass of sparkling hard

cider in front of them, her uncle cleared his throat. Her lips twitching, Kimberly fiddled with the napkin on her lap, and exchanging a glance with his brother, Tanner cracked a grin. Unlike Kellan, he displayed his heart for all to see.

With a tilt of his head, Matthew Brooks expelled a breath as a smile crept onto his ruggedly handsome face. Wrapping his fingers around the glass, he rubbed its smooth surface as if carefully weighing his words. "This is probably the last time we'll be sitting at this here table like we are right now."

Her mind racing, Emily looked first to her cousins, then to Billy, and lastly to Jake. He took her hand, and giving it a comforting squeeze, held it on his lap.

"There's gonna be a wedding."

"Samantha Quigley," Billy whispered in her ear. "Tellin' ya."

No way.

"Who's getting married?" Emily asked.

His face lighting up, Matthew puffed out his chest. "I am."

Oh.

"I've been seeing a lovely lady in Denver."

Breathing a sigh of relief, she elbowed Billy's ribs.

"We're expecting a little one end of May."

And her eyes widened. *Ohhh.*

"The wedding's on Friday."

Friday's for crosses. Wasn't it bad luck to get married on a Friday? Though most weddings are held on a Saturday, Emily supposed, and that's not so lucky either. Wednesday is the luckiest day to have a wedding, but she held her tongue.

"I'm taking the boys back with me." His gaze landed on his sons. The brothers bumped shoulders, and with a nod, Tanner threw his arm around Kellan. "We'll get the girls all packed up and moved in before Thanksgiving."

"*Girls?*"

"Jennifer has a daughter. Her name's Arien." Matthew winked. "She's a senior, same as you."

"You're gettin' a new cousin, Ems." Tanner nearly bounced in his seat.

Kellan leaned across the table, intense dark eyes boring into her green ones. "And you're gonna be her new best friend."

Their grandmother reining him in, Melinda Brooks pushed Kellan back into his chair. "Coming from Denver, Brookside is going to be quite a change for Arien, honey. She's going to need looking out for, especially at school."

"I know, Grams. I'll have her back, don't worry. Billy will, too." Emily scrambled from her seat and, skipping over to her uncle, she wrapped her arms around his neck. "I'm so happy for you, Uncle Matty. I've always wanted a sister, and this is almost like getting one."

"Thank you, sweetheart. We've been favored." Hugging her against him, he kissed her brow. "You and Arien are gonna get on real well. I just know it."

"And a new baby," she said with a sigh. "It's all so wonderful, ain't it, Mama?"

"Babies always are." Biting her lip, Kimberly glanced at her brother. "Does Jennifer know about us, Matty?"

"She does." With his eyes downcast, he bobbed his head. "Explained it to her as best I could."

"And Arien?"

"Not yet." Matthew gulped his cider down, then raked his fingers through his hair. "Might need some help with that, but me and Jennifer want to get her settled first."

Oh, boy.

Brookside was a place like no other. They lived their lives a different way. *The best way.* Her new cousin was in for quite a surprise, but she'd surely come to love life here.

"Arien's your dream girl, ain't she?" Sitting back in his chair,

Billy looked at her cousins, a smirk rising on his face. "The one you've been waitin' on."

Tanner nodded, and Kellan, who hardly ever smiled, grinned.

From the time they were little, their father told them she was coming. He saw it.

Emily glanced at Jacob, and with a wink, he kissed her crown.

Everything that comes in threes is perfect.

And they were meant to be.

She closed her eyes, happy knowing her cousins would be just as loved as she was.

Two

The Shoshone believed visions were of great importance. A gift given by the spirits, these dreams often granted wisdom and power to the recipient. Not that he'd ever experienced it. Sure, Billy dreamt like most folks did. Crazy, mixed-up shit that never made a lick of sense. Heck, most of the time, he couldn't remember them when he woke up in the morning. He tried to, though.

Like Matthew Brooks, his father had inherited the gift. But Billy didn't need a dream to tell him Emily was his future. He'd always known it, just as he'd always loved her, even before he understood what loving somebody meant.

He glanced at Emily beside him, then at Jake beside her. They were one of the lucky ones.

His brother turned onto the gravel drive that would take them to Miss Kim's Dutch barn house, its timeworn wood weathered and gray. Pots of vibrant flowers he'd helped Emily plant this past spring, all but dead and gone now, flanked the front porch. Once calving season was done and over with, when the weather warmed up again, they'd plant new ones. Emily loved her flowers. And anything she loved, Billy loved, too.

"Goodnight, wild one." Taking her hand in his, Jake raised it to his lips and kissed it. "Sweetest dreams."

"Night, Jake." Smiling up at him, Emily went to kiss his brother's hand in return, but he moved away before she could.

Idiot.

Her smile frozen in place, Billy felt her limbs tense up beside his. She bit into her lip, and rubbing them together, turned to him. He took her by the hand, offering a gentle squeeze, and opened the door. "C'mon, babe. Let's get you inside."

They stood on the front porch, the cold November wind blowing through her long chestnut waves. Taming it with his fingers, Billy tucked it behind her ear and held her body snugly against his. "I love you."

"And I love you."

He kissed her. "Jake loves you, too, you know."

"I know." Her fingers rubbing the front of his jacket, she sighed. "But sometimes it sure don't feel like it."

A touchy-feely kind of girl, Emily craved physical affection. And his brother couldn't give her that. Not for now, anyway.

"It's hard, Em, but Jake does the best he can." Taking her chin in his hand, Billy bent to kiss her gently on the lips. "Five more months and you'll be feelin' it. You won't have any doubt how much he loves you then."

"And then I have to go without you." Pained green eyes looking up at him, she swallowed hard. "I don't know how I'm gonna survive it."

Truth be told, he didn't either, but those were the damn rules. If they failed to abide by them, they risked losing favor, and Billy wouldn't allow that to happen. Come her eighteenth birthday, Emily couldn't let him kiss her anymore. Or touch her the way he loved touching her. Not until he came of age, too, when he and his brother would meet her at the stones.

"It's our test, baby." He rubbed his hands up and down her arms to soothe her—and himself. "Just one year of our whole lives together. For Jake, it's been a helluva lot longer."

His brother, being almost twenty-three, hadn't so much as kissed her yet.

"Well, it's stupid."

Billy couldn't disagree. They loved each other, and they were going to be married, for chrissakes, so what difference did a year make? *None.* But the rules said it did. And so, they would endure the senseless waiting, just as every other triad had before them.

"But we'll appreciate what we share even more for it, Em." That's what Jake always told him. "Now, give me a kiss."

Her luscious lips, soft and full, melted into his. Sliding his fingers into her hair, Billy slipped his tongue inside, tasting her as if his life depended on it. Because it did. His dick stiffening in his jeans, he groaned, and holding her even closer, he kissed her until the need for air forced him to stop.

"We love you, Em. This is from the both of us," he murmured, out of breath, pressing a parting kiss to her forehead. "G'night."

Thumb tapping against the steering wheel, looking straight ahead, Jake stared at nothing through the windshield. Even after Billy got back inside the truck, his gaze did not waver. "Let's go."

"Right." As if clearing his thoughts, he gave his head a quick shake. "Emily get in okay?"

"Yeah." And he looked his brother square in the eye. "You gotta love her more."

His brow furrowed, but otherwise, Jake didn't respond.

"Show her, I mean," he said as the truck turned toward town.

"What the hell? You sayin' I don't?"

"You do, but…" Scraping a hand through his hair, he cleared his throat. "Could be I said it wrong. You gotta let Emily love *you*, brother."

"Heh. I think maybe you had too many glasses of Grams' cider."

"And you're supposed to be the older, wiser one." With a furtive glance at Jake, Billy crossed his arms. "You pull away from her all the damn time."

"I do not."

"Yeah, ya do." His voice rose a notch. "I ain't blind. Our Em's an affectionate girl, Jake. She needs hugs and kisses."

He didn't even pull over. Jake stopped the truck and then turned to look at him. "I can't."

"You can," Billy insisted. "It's not breakin' the stupid fucking rules to hold her. You can let her kiss your cheek or play with your hair."

"Believe me when I tell you, I can't." His hand curling into a fist on his thigh, he dropped his chin. "Come April, you'll understand."

Maybe so, but Billy didn't care to think about that right now. While he could only imagine how difficult this must be for his brother, it was Emily's feelings that mattered here.

"You gotta at least try. For her."

He put the truck back in gear. "I know."

The upperclassmen made a beeline for the stairs at the sound of the bell. Emily, Shiloh, and Griffin were waiting for him, the same as they always did since the senior classrooms were the closest to the stairs. At least they got to have lunch together this year. Last year, when Billy was a sophomore, he only passed them in the hall.

He hooked his arm around Emily's waist, and drawing her closer, kissed her on the cheek. "C'mon, I'm starving."

"You always are."

True, but then he'd woken up late and barely had enough time to wash down a pop-tart with some orange juice, so he was extra hungry today. To make up for it, he loaded his tray with a double cheeseburger and an extra-large order of chili-smothered cheese fries.

"That's a heart attack on a plate there, Billy."

"So good, though," he said, his mouth still full. "My mom wants you and your mom to come over for dinner one night this week, so y'all can start makin' plans."

"Already?" With a lift of her brow, Emily's pretty green eyes widened. "The wedding's a year and a half away yet."

"It's never too soon to start, Ems." Shiloh nodded, drowning her French fries in ketchup. "You have no idea how much work goes into it."

"That's only 'cause you and Cassie can't agree on nothin'." Archer tipped his head back, and staring up at the ceiling, he sniggered.

Ignoring their friends, Billy took Emily's hand in his. "You want our day to be perfect, don't you, baby?"

"Course, I do, and it will be." Her smile beaming, she kissed him on the lips. "Let me ask my mama when's a good day. She and Grams are doin' up a room for Arien and we might have to go to Jackson for some things."

"Arien?" Shiloh put the ketchup down. "Who's Arien?"

"Shoot," Emily muttered, clapping her hand over her mouth. "It just slipped out."

"It's okay, babe. No one said it was a secret."

"Okay, so spill it." Shiloh's gaze riveted on Emily, she reached for a soggy red French fry.

"Uncle Matty met a lady in Denver and they're having a baby," she all but squealed, bouncing in her seat. "The wedding's Friday."

"Oh...wow...wait...how come y'all are doin' a room for her?" Shiloh asked, her face scrunched up all funny. "Won't she be sleepin' with your uncle?"

"The room ain't for her, silly. It's for her daughter." And Emily grinned. "Arien's seventeen. She'll be finishing her senior year here with us."

"Well, I'll be damned." His mouth falling open, Griffin tossed his shaggy blond mop and grinned along with her. "Their old man called it, didn't he?"

"He sure did," Billy agreed.

"The Brooks boys got themselves a girl," Archer announced to everyone in the dining hall. Then, chuckling, he glanced over to the girls at the next table. "Sorry, ladies."

"Sit your ass down, Griffin Archer." Shiloh tugged on his shirt. "She's an outsider. It will not go over well."

"Those bitches wouldn't take kindly to it even if she weren't," Emily said with a shrug.

"What if it don't work out?" Shiloh's question was valid, especially considering this girl knew nothing of their ways. "She might not take a liking to 'em."

"Are you kidding?" Emily disregarded her concern. "Arien's gonna fall head over heels for Tanner the minute she lays eyes on him. Everybody loves Tanner."

"And Kellan?" Archer raised a brow. "Look, I love the guy, but y'all know he can be a moody motherfucker."

"He is hot, though. My sister said—"

Griffin cut Shiloh off with a scowl. "No one cares, girly."

"We're puttin' her in the room right across the hall from him." Emily giggled as if their scheming were the answer to everything. "Kellan's been waitin' for her forever. I think he loves her already."

"You can't know that." Shiloh tsked with a dismissive wave.

"Yes, I can. I know my cousin and he was smilin'. Big."

Shiloh mouthed a silent *ohhh.*

But lunch was almost over and Billy had more important things on his mind. "Wanna go by the barn after school?"

"Yeah." Emily kissed him. "I do."

The old red barn stood by the stream, within walking distance of the school, near the edge of town. Belonging to the ranch, the structure had been empty for a very long time. It had become the place to throw a party and dance, to sit around the fire with your friends and a beer, or just hang out with your girl.

Under a warm afternoon sun, they took advantage of the picture-perfect day, watching crystal-clear water tumbling over the rocks as it made its way downstream. His chin resting on Emily's shoulder, Billy wrapped his arms around her middle, breathing in the scent of her hair. Herbs and sweet wildflowers. Winter was coming, and soon, there wouldn't be any days left like this.

"I think we'll be seein' snow before the weekend."

"I can almost smell it." She turned in his arms, her pretty green eyes gazing up at him.

His lips brushed over hers. He pulled her in close, her softness pressed against him sending blood coursing to his dick. *Holy fuck.* This girl made him crazy.

Kissing Emily as they went, Billy backed her into the barn's rear door, a hand firmly planted on her ass. Without having to look, he released the latch and staggering into the very first stall, they fell onto a nest of straw that reeked of the stench of stale beer from the last bonfire party.

It didn't matter. Because his body embraced hers, fingertips stroking warm, soft skin. For one stolen, precious hour, it was just the two of them.

Emily hooked her leg around him, pushing the aching bulge in his jeans into her belly. With a grunt he couldn't contain, clutching the fabric of her long-tiered skirt between his fingers, his hand swept up her thigh. Silky panties greeted him. Billy let the skirt go to slide his fingers inside.

He felt for the patch of curls and parted her lips, skimming his knuckles along her slick folds. Emily pulled at his shirt, a squeak coming from her mouth. Sweet, warm breath fanned his neck, the beat of her heart galloping against his chest.

"You're so beautiful," he whispered, teasing her with his finger.

Billy circled the hole, and taking a dip inside, brought it to his nose. "Yeah, baby."

She stammered, a flush of pink creeping across her cheeks.

"You smell so damn good, I gotta have me a taste." His mouth watering, he sucked the digit into his mouth. "Divine."

He'd never done this before and wasn't sure how to go about it. The only thing Billy knew at this moment was that he had to have her in whatever way he could.

The denim jacket she wore eased down her arms. Tossing it to the side, he pushed her shirt up and kissed the creamy swells of flesh spilling out from the ivory silk. He nipped at her nipples through the fabric, smiling at her whimpers and the stiffened buds he left behind on his way down her tummy.

With the skirt bunched around her waist, he removed her panties, and caressing her thighs, Billy positioned himself between them. Her cunt on display before him, he stared at it in awe. He reached out, the tension leaving his body, and swiped his fingers through her slit. Maybe he couldn't fuck her with his cock just yet, but he could with his tongue, dammit.

"I'm gonna eat this pretty pussy up, baby," he said and threw her legs over his shoulders, Emily's cowboy booted feet dangling behind him. "Make you see stars."

At least I hope I can. I don't know what the fuck I'm doin'.

He'd seen videos, heard his friends brag about it—couldn't be that hard, right?

Her ass cheeks cupped in his hands, he breathed her in and

took the first tentative lick at the crease of her thigh. Dainty fingers grasped his forearms. It was his own heart galloping now. His stomach fluttered and his mouth was too dry. But Billy inhaled her deep, and determined, his tongue sought her smooth pussy lips.

He took his time. Long, delicious strokes up and down, his nose grazed her clit with every lap. Her head thrashing on the straw, he glanced up at her. Was he doing it right? Did she like it? It seemed so. Billy relaxed then, licking and suckling on every part of her pussy, caressing her thighs, along her sides, and her nipples.

Emily's sounds made him confident. Breathy pants and soft whimpers became moans. He traced her hole with his tongue pointed. She seemed okay with that, so Billy pushed it inside, and fuck. Succulent. He couldn't think of another word to describe it. A pussy that tasted like salted honey. He twitched, his breath easing between his teeth.

She tangled her fingers in his hair, holding him to her cunt.

He answered with a breathless chuckle.

Wishing his throbbing dick could be inside her, he fucked her with his tongue. Then, with a torturously slow lick up her slit, he brushed over her clit. Just barely. Billy did it again and again until she shimmied her hips to get his tongue right where she wanted it. Slow circles. Quick flicks back and forth. He experimented to see what would bring her the most pleasure.

Addicted to the taste of her now, Billy nibbled at her clit. He suckled on it, and sensing she was close, slid a finger inside her.

He loved watching her unravel.

But it was the sound of her cries as she tumbled over the edge that was his undoing.

Hot, sticky semen filled his underwear.

"You were right, Billy." Emily panted, her fingers raking through his hair. "I saw the stars."

He kissed her clit and smiled.

Three

Twenty-four wagons formed a circle in a dusty clearing some sixty paces from the river's edge, a campfire burning at its center. Oxen, horses, and cattle grazed, oblivious to the evening din of a fiddler. Boisterous card games. Children playing tag. Where did that energy come from after walking all those miles? They'd gone another twelve today, Levi reckoned. Could've done fifteen, maybe, if they hadn't had to prolong their nooning to repair Quigley's wheel.

He gazed over at the mountain range that loomed up ahead. The setting sun appeared to melt into the rocky, snow-capped peaks. To reach California, they had to cross them before winter

set in or perish. It was going to take a miracle, some divine intervention. August was nearly gone.

"We shoulda listened and left in May."

Hell, April would have been even better if anyone had bothered to ask him, but no one did. It would've fallen on deaf ears,
anyway. To his father, Levi was just a kid—seen and not heard—
when it suited him.

"Couldn't. We had to wait for them spring rains to let up."
Elijah threw an arm around his neck. "Imagine the wagons get-
ting stuck in all that muck. Swollen rivers, rising waters churning.
I doubt we'd have gotten everyone across 'em."

"Not to mention whirlwinds."

Levi pivoted to stare blankly at an unfamiliar leathery face.
Golden eyes. Long wiry hair, more silver than brown, with a beard
to match. His shirt and britches sewn from deerskin.

"Twisters." Chuckling under his breath, the man's lip quirked
up on one side. "My woman called 'em storm horses. I've seen a
herd of buffalo swept up into the sky until they were nothin' but
wiggling black specks. Consider yourself favored you ain't run into
one of those yet."

"You must be Mr. Walker."

"Josiah." He tipped his hat, hitching his thumb behind him.
"These here are my daughters, Lucy and Fallon."

Her name is Lucy.

The girl from the river. She was even more beautiful up close.
Golden eyes like her father. A hint of a smile. Neither she nor her
sister would look at him, though, their gazes downcast.

"Pleasure. Levi Gantry," he said, shaking Walker's hand. He
proudly turned to the twins who'd come to stand beside him, having returned from bathing little Elizabeth. "And my sisters, Mary
Alice and Victoria."

"Ladies." His gaze lingering on their like visages, he offered
them a polite nod.

"And I'm Elijah Brooks." Stepping forward, he extended his hand.

Josiah shook it, looking down at the child who clung to Elijah's knee. "That your little girl there?"

"Elizabeth? No, she's my baby sister."

"Where's your mama and papa, child?" he asked, getting down on his haunches.

The little girl didn't blink an eye. "Dead."

Elijah patted the long, wet hair dripping splotches on the muslin of her dress. They all fretted for Elizabeth. She had yet to cry for her mother. "We lost them, and our sister, back in Nebraska territory. There was cholera and—"

"I know. Seen it," Josiah said, cutting Elijah off, then abruptly he turned to him. "Lost yours, too, didn't ya?"

Drawing his sisters close, Levi nodded. "And our brother."

"My condolences to you all. Goin' on six years since their mother's been gone." His lip trembling, he pressed them together. "It's damn hard tryin' to raise my girls right out here without her. This ain't no kind of life for 'em, ya know?"

"I s'pose not." Levi's gaze went to Lucy and her sister.

Josiah oddly grinned. "I seen it comin'."

"What's that?"

"All good things." The mountain man winked, nodding along as he spoke. "Every good thing in the world is born of something not."

Jake read the words once more and transcribed them onto his laptop. They resonated with him, and not just because Levi underlined them three times.

His phone signaled an incoming text message. Not wanting to be distracted from his work, he'd set the damn thing to silent, but even the slightest vibration was jarring to him.

Two words. *They're hitched.*

"Kel." Jake chuckled with a shake of his head.

Before he could tap out 'congratulations' in reply, two photos appeared. Matthew Brooks with a pretty blonde in a short ivory dress and another of a girl holding a camera in her hand. *The daughter.* Seeming to be lost in her thoughts, she had a far-away look in her eyes.

The new Mrs. Brooks and the future Mrs. Brooks, the caption read.

For Kellan's sake, and Tanner's too, he sure hoped so.

Jake closed his laptop. He had a future of his own to get ready for. A house to build. A wedding to plan.

Emily and her mother would be here for dinner soon. Another evening of looking on, pretending to be unaffected, when he was dying to touch her the same way his brother did.

And taste her.

Yeah, he saw them together in the barn the other day. Jake hadn't meant to spy on them, but when he noticed Emily's convertible sitting in the school parking lot, long after the dismissal bell rang, he grew concerned.

Her lips parted, breasts exposed, holding Billy's head to her cunt. She looked so beautiful. Jake couldn't tear his eyes away. However, upon hearing her coming for his brother, he hurriedly retreated to avoid being discovered as the sick voyeur he knew he was.

He ran home and went straight to his room. With the image of the girl he loved half-naked on a bed of hay, Jake lubed up his dick. Slippery, hard flesh sliding between the circle of his fingers, it was him she held onto. Him she cried out to. Him she came for.

It's not that he was jealous. There was no reason for it. They were a triad, after all. Meant to be before they were ever born. Emily was his as much as she was his brother's.

Envy?

Perhaps. While the feeling is similar, it isn't quite the same, is it? Yes, Jake loved her, and yes, he deeply desired what he couldn't have yet, but there was no maliciousness behind his discontent.

This was *his* test.

Five more months and Emily would be eighteen.

And in eighteen months, she'd be his wife.

He just had to wait.

Until then, Jake resolved to give Emily what she needed to feel loved by him. Billy might be only sixteen, but he was keenly astute and so very wise for his years. Their circumstances dictated his brother knew her feelings better than he did.

Jake had the power to change that, though. He could talk to her more, be with her more. Meaningful conversation and showing affection weren't against the rules—so long as he didn't let it go too far. That right there was the problem. He didn't trust himself not to. And he certainly didn't trust her.

"They're almost here, bro," Billy said, poking his head inside his room. "Em just texted me."

"She texts me too, you know."

"Yeah, but I also know how good you are at forgettin' to turn your phone back on." He plopped his ass down on the bed. "Just lookin' out for you."

"Appreciated." Smiling to himself, Jake buttoned up his shirt. "Want to go over to the site with me tomorrow?"

Billy grinned up at him. "Sure do."

"I just want to set out some stakes. Get a feel for where we want to put the house come spring."

A home of their own. For Emily. And he and his brother were going to build it.

"I wish we didn't have to wait 'til then."

"Me, neither." Tucking in his shirt, Jake let out a loud breath.

Sometimes, it seemed like waiting was all they ever did. "But we'd never get the framing up before it snows."

"We're supposed to get some flurries tomorrow." Impeccably dressed as always, their father, Justin, appeared in the doorway, a mischievous grin on his face. "Your mother asked me to come for you."

The Gantry family dynamics differed from most. Their father's husband and their mother's brother, Justin Sawyer was their uncle biologically, but he was as much a dad to them as Victor. And more like a mom than their mother was. He was the one who got them ready for school, helped them with homework, and tucked them in at night with a bedtime story.

"Well, what she actually said was, it would be rude if you weren't downstairs when Emily and Mrs. Keough arrived." With a click of his tongue, his hand swirled through the air. "Appearances. You know how she is."

Jake exchanged a glance with his brother. Oh, they knew.

Carrie Sawyer Gantry needn't have worried.

Her hair half up, Emily looked so beautiful. Rich, deep hues of red and brown framed her features, with long, loose curls flowing down her back. His fingers itched to pull the clip from her hair and run them through the silky strands while he kissed her senseless. But Jake itched to do so many things he couldn't. Instead, inhaling her wildflower scent, his lips brushed across her cheek. He let them linger there a moment as he brought her in for a hug. It was the most he could do right then.

Emily sat between them at the dining room table, he on her right and Billy to her left. While her mother complimented his on the herb-crusted sirloin medallions, the pearl onion red wine sauce, and garlic mashed potatoes, only to learn it was Justin who deserved all the accolades, Jake allowed his palm to rest upon her thigh. Fingertips unfurling over the smooth fabric of her skirt, he imagined the warmth of her flesh beneath it.

"Matthew did it then?" Carrie asked Kimberly, dabbing a napkin at her lips. "He married her?"

"They're going to have a baby."

"That's no reason to get—"

"Carrie." Across the table, Victor's golden eyes widened, his tone a warning.

"My brother loves Jennifer. He told me so, and that's reason enough."

"But…"

"Carrie." His father glared at his wife, then turning to Emily's mother, his features softened. "Matt is my dearest friend. You know that, Kimberly. I want nothing but love and happiness for him. He deserves it after everything he's gone through, as do you."

Jake squeezed Emily's knee beneath the table. Victor's gaze may have lingered on his future daughter-in-law's mother just a bit too long.

"We have our children's wedding to talk about, now, don't we?" Clearing her throat, Carrie changed the subject. "Let's go have some coffee. What did you make us for dessert, brother dearest?"

"Cheesecake, sister dearest," he said, rising from his chair. Winking at Emily's mom, he offered her a hand. "Trust me when I say, Mrs. Keough—"

"Kim."

"All right, then." Justin's tongue swiped across his lip and he smiled, his somewhat effeminate voice just above a whisper. "It's almost better than sex."

On the way to the family room, or the parlor, as his mom liked to call it, Jake clasped Emily's hand in his while his brother held on to the other. He noticed the drop in her shoulders, her neck tipping back as she studied Justin's paintings and the photos of them as children displayed on the walls, a tender smile lighting her face as if she'd never seen them before. She had. Countless times.

"I'm only gonna insist on one thing." Billy paused, tugging on her arm. "We get hitched on the very first Saturday after I turn eighteen. Ain't waitin' longer than I have to."

"Nope, not Saturday. Wednesday is the luckiest day for a wedding."

"Fine, the first Wednesday then." In a quick, fluid movement, his brother pulled Emily to his chest and he kissed her.

When their lips unlocked, she bit her lip, fingertips rubbing his pec. "Why is your mama so…I dunno…out of sorts over Uncle Matty getting married?"

"C'mon, Emily, you know the answer to that," Jake said, tucking a glossy curl behind her ear.

Justin came up behind them. "He married an outsider."

"So? Plenty of folks have. My grams was an outsider once."

True, but then that wasn't the actual issue here.

"Melinda Brooks is one of a kind. It takes a special person to embrace our way of life. It seems as though your uncle has cast aside what we hold sacred—to my sister, at least." Justin squeezed Emily's shoulder. "She fears he could lose favor, and that, as you well know, would affect every last one of us. I don't believe so, of course."

Bingo. That's what Jake feared, too.

"Finding love again, Arien, *and* a new baby? He saw all of this, you know. So, the way I figure, he's gained favor, if anything." Emily glanced up at him. "Right, Jake?"

He wanted so badly to agree with her, but he couldn't.

"I think so, too, dear girl." Justin opened his arms wide and wrapped her up in a great big hug. "After all, is there any greater gift than that?"

Jake couldn't think of one.

Every good thing in the world is born of something not.

Yeah, maybe she was right.

Four

She blamed John Jacoby.

If it hadn't been for that miserable old coot showing up on Thanksgiving like he did, the talk with Arien wouldn't have gone down the way it had. Emily was sure he didn't come by to wish Tanner a happy birthday. More likely, he wanted to check out Uncle Matty's new wife and determine if her daughter was worthy of his grandsons.

Probably wanted to start trouble, too.

Which, of course, he did.

"You've broken tradition, yet you have been greatly favored," Jacoby told his one-time son-in-law.

Innocuous enough, right? But that seemingly innocent

statement was loaded. Her new cousin picked up on it right away, questioning the meaning behind the man's words.

They'd talked it over together beforehand. Uncle Matty, his new wife, Jennifer, and the boys had decided an honest but gentle approach with Arien would be best. Emily, Billy, and Jake would extend their support and provide backup if needed. Because understanding life in Brookside wouldn't come easy to someone who hadn't been raised here.

"Me and your mama discussed how to explain our ways to you. Planned to sit with you tonight and do just that." Clasping his wife to his side, Uncle Matty came forward. "I know you're probably wondering how it is Kellan and Tanner are so close in age, especially their mothers being sisters and all."

The boys were born three months apart, so Emily had a pretty good idea of what Arien must be thinking. She was wrong, though. And while she'd only known her since Sunday, she already liked her and wanted her to be happy here. Her arm linked with her step-cousin's, Emily glanced down to see Tanner holding the girl's hand so tightly that the whites of his knuckles showed.

"Our customs, how we live, the reason we prosper, goes all the way back to when Brookside was founded. I think you've already figured out we don't do things the same here, and here..."

And here we go.

Emily watched her uncle's chest rise as he paused to take a breath. "...marriage is between a man and two sisters or a woman and two brothers."

"Huh?"

Arien wore the same expression on her face Emily often had during trig class.

Jake got down on his haunches in front of her. "Our unions are triads. There is a universal power in three. The nature of the world is tripartite—heavens, waters, and earth." Then he took Arien's other hand in his. "As are human beings—mind, body, spirit. The triad is the whole, you see. It is all. The beginning, middle, and end."

Emily saw Arien's hazel-green eyes flick over from Tanner to Kellan. Arms folded across his chest, he stood by the fireplace, the look on his handsome face inscrutable. Not even a smirk. She knew his tells, though, and the nervous tick in his jaw gave him away.

"Anthropologists call two brothers married to the same wife, fraternal polyandry, and two sisters married to the same husband, sororal polygyny. We call it the trinity, and to us, it is sacred."

Arien drew her head back, shaking it rapidly. "You can't do that. It's not legal."

"Not out there, no," Uncle Matty said, his fingers running up and down his wife's arm. "The elder sibling is on the marriage license at the courthouse…"

Emily squeezed her step-cousin's shoulder, glancing again at Kellan. His usual smirk returned, and sliding his hand down the front of his jeans, he winked at Arien.

"…but what we do inside our gate, how we live inside our homes, is no one else's concern."

"You were married to them both at the same time," Arien said softly under her breath.

Ding, ding, ding! Now you're getting it, girly.

The Jacoby sisters, Heather and Amanda, the aunts Emily never knew, tragically died shortly after giving birth to Tanner and Kellan. And the animosity between their grandfather and her uncle that followed their deaths still lingered.

Arien turned to her then, pointing at Jake. "He's your boyfriend too?"

How do I answer that? "Yes and no."

With his index finger beneath her chin, Jake turned Arien's face back toward him. "We're to be married when Emily and my brother come of age."

"I'm a junior." Leaning forward, Billy grinned with a shrug. "So not this summer, but next."

Then Arien laughed and said they were all fucking crazy.

Well, of course, she did.

They couldn't ease into the conversation, regaling her with the stories of Brookside's history as they'd planned to. If she'd gotten the chance to hear them, then maybe Arien wouldn't have reacted so harshly.

But thanks to John Jacoby, she got slapped in the face with it. So, yeah, this was all his fault.

As soon as Tanner finished blowing out the candles on his cake, Arien stood, and excusing herself, disappeared up the stairs.

Her lips pursed, Emily glanced over at Jake. "That went well."

Not.

"I should go talk to her," Jennifer said with a sigh, extricating herself from her husband's embrace.

"Give her some time, honey." His hands massaging his wife's shoulders, Matthew's gaze settled on Tanner, who looked gutted, and a surlier-than-ever Kellan. "She'll come around. You'll see."

"Believe me, I know how she's feeling, and Matthew is right, my dear." Grams spoke in that reassuring tone Emily knew all too well. With a toss of her pale-blonde curls, she lightly clasped Jennifer's forearm. "You look exhausted."

"I am." She rubbed the back of her neck with a heavy sigh. "I don't remember being so tired all the time with Arien."

"Go on and get some rest, dear." Grams gave her arm a gentle pat. "We can take care of the kitchen."

With Uncle Matty and his wife tucked away upstairs, they went to work setting the kitchen back to rights while Jake and Billy remained with Kellan and Tanner. Emily could see the four of them talking in a huddle by the fire from her position at the sink.

"Those boys need to relax," Grams said, handing her some dirty plates to load into the dishwasher. "Arien just had a bomb dropped on her head. What's normal to us isn't to most folks. I remember what it was like to be in her shoes."

"An outsider?"

"Your granddaddy brought me up here to meet his family. Hell, I'd never been on a horse in my entire life, let alone seen heifers dropping calves." She nodded, a soft snort coming from her nose.

Emily giggled at the sound of it. "Yes, for spring break. It was calving season."

"Paul saddled up a mare for me." With a far-off look in her paisley-blue eyes, Grams' voice thickened with emotion. "Her name was Rosie. Such a sweet, gentle thing. He took me up to the lake, told me he loved me, and that he saw a future for us together."

"How romantic is that?" Emily sighed. She could see it in her head, like a movie.

"Hmm, yes." Grams chortled, her tone changing. "Then he explained the trinity and informed me that for that to happen, I'd have to love his brother, too."

"Oh, Grams, what did you say?"

"I told him he was out of his ever-loving mind if he thought for one second I could ever love anyone else besides him."

"But you did."

"I did indeed." A smile crossing her face, Grams took hold of both her hands. "Garrett was something else, let me tell ya. There was just no resisting that man. The three of us were married at the stones a few months later. It was the 70s—free love and all that. Our generation was more…open-minded, I guess you could say, so opening my heart to them both was easy for me." And choking on a breath, she let go. "God, how I miss 'em."

"I know, Mom. We all do," Kimberly said, hugging her.

Grams kissed her daughter's cheek and turned to Emily, her smile back in place. "Arien is going to need some time, and a lot of love, patience, and understanding from all of us."

"Matthew should have never shared his vision with the boys." Her gaze darting to the fireplace, Kimberly shook her head.

Uncle Matty must've told them from the time they were little. Tanner and Kellan had always known of it. They'd been waiting for their dream girl to come along for a very long time.

"Why not?"

"What's meant to be will be of its own accord," Grams replied, patting the top of her head.

Huh?

"But Victor shared his vision with you."

"With me. Not with you, your mother, or Jake and Billy, either." Squeezing her shoulder, she smoothed a lock of hair behind her ear. "So as not to influence the choices the three of you made, Victor Gantry kept the future he saw to himself."

And they'd chosen each other, exactly as he'd seen it, all on their own.

"Billy and Jake are my everything."

"And you're theirs, my dear girl." Grams drew her into a warm embrace. "Never doubt it."

With the dishwasher loaded and running at last, Emily strolled back into the living room to find her boys in front of the TV all alone. "Where'd everybody go?"

"Kellan took off." Billy got up from the sofa and kissed her. "Don't know where to."

Jake lifted his chin. "Tanner's talkin' to Arien."

"Oh." Her gaze traveled up the stairs. "What do we do?"

"Nothing." Jake took hold of her hand, pulling her to sit down beside him. "Arien, Kellan, and Tanner have to find their way to each other all on their own, same as we did."

"I can't not do something." To stand idly by went against her very nature.

The corner of his mouth twitched up because Jake knew that, of course. "You can be Arien's friend. She's going to need one. Look out for her at school, answer her questions. She's going to have plenty of them, I'm sure. There's a lot *we* can do, but we cannot push them. Understand?"

"*What's meant to be will be of its own accord.*"

Free will. She got it.

"I just want them to be happy like we are, Jake."

"I know you do." Her hand in his, he brought her knuckles to his lips and kissed them.

Encouraged by the gesture, Emily chanced running her fingers through his hair. For once, he didn't stop her. "I was going to take Arien to Jackson tomorrow. She probably won't want to go now."

"Show up. Take her anyway."

"She'll go." With a wink, Billy clicked his tongue. "There's a Starbucks in Jackson. Tanner told me she's always goin' on about them fancy coffees they got."

She'd resort to bribery if she had to. Suddenly elated, she grinned. "You're right."

Jake chuckled. "We better get goin'. Take a walk with us, Emily."

Tucked tight between them, they strolled outside to Jake's truck. Leaning back against the passenger side door, Billy pulled her into his arms to kiss her goodnight. Fingers tangling in his hair, she slipped her tongue inside, while Jake pressed in from behind her.

He'd never done that before. Most often, when Billy kissed her, Jake would look away or get in the truck to give them a moment, but not this time. He swept her hair to the side. Cool air grazing her neck, Emily felt the warmth of his breath at her nape. His velvety lips brushing over her skin made her shiver.

Made her want them even more than she already did.

Emily reached behind her and, holding onto Jake's hair, kissed Billy harder. His cock, granite in his pants, dug into her belly. She could feel his brother, hard and thick, against her ass. God, she couldn't wait for them to be inside her.

Together.

Emily dreamt of it all the damn time. One in her ass, another in her cunt, or both in her pussy at the same time, stretching her wide open. *Fuck.* Would it hurt? Maybe. She didn't care if it did. She wanted them that badly.

At the thought, Emily whimpered and yanked on Jake's hair. He kissed her neck, his teeth nibbling on her skin. Billy's fingers slid beneath her sweater to squeeze her breasts.

"More," she squeaked.

He grabbed hold of her nipples between his fingers, flicking and pinching them the way he knew she liked. His teeth grazing her neck, Jake pushed his cock against her, grinding himself on her ass, while Billy thrust at her front.

"I think our girl needs to come."

Yes. Yes, I do.

"Then, by all means, make her come, brother."

Billy's fingers went to the button on her pants. As the zipper came down, Emily held onto Jake's hair with both hands, keeping him there against her. She glanced down to see Billy pulling her jeans to her knees.

"Tell him what you want, wild one." Smiling against her skin, Jake crooned the words in her ear.

"I want to come."

"How do you want to come? On his fingers?" He licked up the side of her neck. "His tongue?"

Loving this side of Jake she'd never seen before, she said, "Both."

"Good girl." He sucked on her earlobe. "Now, tell him how many fingers you want inside that pussy, baby."

With Billy running them through her slit, Emily answered, "Three."

"Perfect, my love," Jake whispered. "You're fucking perfect."

Licking her clit, Billy fucked her with his fingers. Jake held her, rubbing his dick against her ass while whispering how much he loved her and all the ways he was going to make her come once he could.

She came so fucking hard.

"Told ya so, sweet cheeks." Billy sipped more kisses from her lips as Jake licked her cum off his fingers.

You sure did.

"Night, baby. I love you." He kissed her once more. "Call me when you and Arien get home from Jackson." Then he got in the truck and shut the door.

Jake turned her around to face him and held his lips to her forehead.

"I love you with every breath, *michante*." My heart. "You know that."

Spent and speechless, Emily could only nod against his chest.

"Say it," he commanded, gently lifting her chin with his finger. "Tell me you feel it in your bones."

"I do." She wet her lips. "It's just that sometimes…"

"I know. You need to feel my hands on you."

And your lips. The taste of your tongue.

Not daring to say it, she closed her eyes and basked in the feeling of his fingers tracing her spine. The heat coiling between her legs. Without a coat, the November air was frosty, but in his arms, she was burning.

"I need you, too, wild one." His dick poking at her belly, he pressed in. "We just have to wait a little while longer."

"But it's so hard."

"I know it is." Threading his fingers in her hair, Jake bent her head and kissed her crown. "It's the hardest part."

Five

nother six inches of snow fell during the night. Buried in it, Billy could barely find the stakes he and Jake set out a couple of weeks ago. He walked along the icy creek, an offshoot of the stream that tumbled down the mountain, imagining the view from their back window. Children playing in the meadow. Emily's garden in the spring.

It had to be perfect.

He and his brother weren't just building a house here. They were creating a family with Emily—a life.

From the time Elijah Brooks and Levi Gantry laid the first cornerstone, Brookside had an unwritten tradition—a man provides a home for his wife. Back then, folks came together and built an entire town. These days, more often than not, an existing structure would be renovated for a newlywed triad to move into together.

Emily likely thought they'd make their home in one of the houses in town, as most folks did. Jake's work was there. Their parents. The shops. School. But for a good, long while now, Billy and his brother had something else in mind.

This place.

An equal distance from the ranch, her mother's Dutch barn, and town, the location was ideal. They'd build her a home with their own hands while bonding as brothers, and surely that would lay a solid foundation for their future. He and Jake had put a lot of thought into it.

Matthew Brooks and the town council granted their approval. They only had to meet with an architect to come up with a design, start construction, and keep their project a secret from Emily. Billy could already see the look on her face. Bringing her home here after the wedding was going to be the best surprise ever.

He kicked a rock into the creek. "Jake, get your ass over here. I just got an idea."

"What is it?" he asked, calling out from yards away.

"C'mere, will ya?" Billy waved him over as if that might hurry him along. "You won't be able to see what I'm sayin' from all the way over there."

A flash in front of his eyes, the vision came to him out of nowhere, striking him like a lightning bolt.

His sheepskin coat flapping as he went, Jake trudged through the snow. "Okay, I'm here."

"We need to move the stakes."

His brows pulling in, he cocked his head. "Why?"

"Because we're gonna move the house." Noting his brother's flat gaze, Billy went on before he could protest. "Just a little bit. See how the creek curves right here?"

"Yeah, and?"

"Instead of putting the house alongside it, let's build over it."

"Uhh…"

"Hear me out. Say we put a few bedrooms and the kitchen here on the downhill side. A big ole screened porch and an outdoor fireplace…" Billy took a leap across the six-foot-wide channel, landing on his ass in the snow. "…and our room can be over here on the far side. Maybe an office for you upstairs. Then we can have a living room with enormous windows on either side spanning across the creek. What do you think?"

"Keep going."

He stood and pointed in the opposite direction. "Plenty of room for a small barn over there for the horses. A workshop. Whatever we want."

"A little greenhouse for Emily so she can have her flowers all year long." Joining him, Jake smiled.

"You're seein' it, ain't ya?"

"I think I do." With a grin, his brother slung an arm over his shoulder. "You're a fuckin' genius, you know that?"

"Nah." Billy paused to chew on his lip. "I mean, we don't even know if it can be done."

"I'm no structural engineer, but I think it can." With a nod, his grin widened. "They build bridges, don't they?"

"Sure they do, but can we?"

Framing. Drywall. That stuff was easy. He'd worked on lots of projects for folks around town—even helped Mr. Mathers put up a new barn this past summer—but something like this was beyond their skill set.

"Heh. We're gonna need some help."

No shit.

A puff of white billowed from his lips as warm breath made contact with the chill December air. "Yeah, I reckon so."

The two of them stood in silence for a moment, listening to the murmur of the creek. The rustling of the pine. His shining gaze taking in the peaceful, snow-covered landscape, Jake parted his lips to speak, and softening his baritone voice, it took on a wistful timbre. "Emily's going to love it here."

No doubt, brother.

All three of them would.

"She's gonna freak when she sees it," Billy said, bouncing in his boots. With a lightness in his chest, he bumped shoulders with his brother. "Don't know how we're gonna keep her from findin' out, though. I ain't no good at lyin'."

"Me, neither," Jake said with a chuckle. "We'll just have to be creative with the truth, then, yeah?"

Truthful, almost to a fault, is what they were. It's how they'd been raised. Lying simply wasn't in them.

Billy looked up at the cloudless blue sky. "S'pose so."

"C'mon." Jake tugged on his arm. "Betcha Justin's got supper ready by now. You can tell him all about your ideas."

"Why would you want me to do that?"

"Because they're good, and he can put 'em on paper," Jake said, giving him a good-natured shove. "If the architect can see what you see, then maybe he won't think we're plumb fuckin' crazy."

Justin didn't say a word. As soon as Billy described the house, his father put down his fork and got up to snag his sketchpad and a charcoal pencil. A sought-after artist, his paintings hung in galleries from New York to San Francisco. Fingers flying over the paper, he drew, erased, and smudged until a most incredible rendering of the vision in his head appeared.

Stunned by the likeness, the crusty bread in Billy's hand fell onto his plate of chicken cacciatore. "How in the hell did you do that?"

The natural stonework, the placement of the timber wood trusses—every detail was exactly as he'd seen it.

His chest puffing out, Justin gave his head a little shimmy, and he chuckled. "I got it right then, I take it?"

"You sure enough did, Daddy J." Billy grinned, sopping up the gravy with his fallen piece of bread. "Unfuckinreal."

"William Gantry, you better watch that mouth of yours." With a lift of her brows and a tilt of her head, his mother tried to look stern. But Carrie couldn't quite pull it off. It was the upward twitch of her lips that gave her away.

Billy leaned across the table to kiss her cheek. "Sorry, Ma."

"I must say, the concept is brilliant." She released a smile then, her exquisite features softening. "You should go into home design instead of hanging around them smelly, old barns."

"But that's what I wanna do," he insisted, dark eyes locking with cornflower blue. "Told you, Mama, I'm gonna train horses with Tanner."

He had a way with them. Even Tanner said so. They had big plans to expand the equine side of things at the ranch, breeding the finest Friesians, Shires, and American Quarters in all of Wyoming.

Scratch that. In the entire U. S. of A!

"*You* are the son of a physician." His mother reminded him, tapping her pointer finger on the new Restoration Hardware dining table as if he'd somehow forgotten.

"And a painter." Justin pursed his lips with another shimmy of his head. "More polenta, dear?"

But Carrie ignored his offer. "Your brother threw away med school for..."

Maybe Jake didn't want to be a doctor, Mother. Ever think of that?

His brother did well serving Brookside. He had a seat on the town council, took on the historical preservation project, and often presented lectures at the school. Jake had a 4.0 GPA in college, for chrissakes. Graduated *summa cum laude* this past May with a major in history and a minor in political science from the University of Wyoming in Laramie. Of course, he helped at the ranch some, too—especially during calving season in spring and with the cattle roundups in fall, same as most every man in Brookside did.

"And you…" Carrie turned her attention back to him. "…you want to waste your talent mucking stalls?"

Justin's steel-blue eyes narrowed. Pressing his lips into a thin, tight line, he shot his husband a look.

"Carrie." Drawing his wife closer to his side, Victor kissed her brow. "All we've ever wanted is for our boys to be happy. Just look at them, honey, they are."

"I know, but…" She pawed at his chest, all but melting into him.

"No buts, sweetheart." He traced her lips with his finger to quiet her. "Billy and Jake are fine, exemplary young men. We've raised them well. Now, let them be."

Then, holding her face in his hands, Victor kissed his wife. When he released her, Carrie nodded. Blush staining her cheeks, she bit into her lip.

"I'm sorry, boys. I don't want you to think for even one minute that I'm not proud of you both, because I very much am." Then she gazed at her husband. "It's just that I always hoped at least one of them would follow in your footsteps, Vic."

"Medicine is a calling, Carrie, honey." His fingers swept through her long, blonde hair. "And not everyone is called to it."

"Well, I hope someone gets the calling soon, so you can retire, old man."

"I'm not old yet, woman." Sitting back in his chair with a chuckle, he winked. "Give it another twenty years."

Victor Gantry was forty-seven. Billy wouldn't call that 'old' exactly, but he understood what his mom was after. More time with him. She waited for his dad to finish with undergrad, and for Justin to come of age before they got married. Then there was med school. After that, his internship and residency kept him away. And all the while, she was at home with her brother and a baby. It's no wonder Billy didn't come along until six years later.

A doctor's life is not his own.

Patients come first.

Victor missed out on a lot.

Billy could count on one hand the number of times his dad made it through Christmas dinner or a birthday party without the phone ringing or someone knocking at the door.

"You'll always be young to me, my love." Justin blew Victor a kiss, then, looking back at Billy and Jake, he returned to the matter at hand. "Anywho, this house is going to be just marvelous."

Swallowing his chicken, Billy smiled so big his cheeks hurt. "I wish it was spring already. Can't wait to get started, ya know?"

"It'll come," Justin said with a gentle squeeze to his shoulder. "So don't go wishing your life away, son, because trust me, time moves quickly enough."

Not to him. Wishing and waiting was all Billy ever did. For graduation, the wedding, and everything that would come after. He was more than ready to leave his youth behind, and for his future to begin.

"You boys taking Emily to the bonfire tonight?" Carrie asked, spooning some polenta onto her plate.

I guess she wanted more, after all.

"We are." With a single nod, Jake poured some wine into a glass.

"Yeah, and Tanner's bringin' Arien."

"What about Kellan?"

What about him? Was he supposed to know what the broody fucker's plans were? Emily made no mention of him when she informed Arien she was going to the party and Tanner was taking her.

"Dunno. Ain't you talked to him?"

"I haven't." Jake emptied his glass in one swallow, then

shrugging his shoulders with a tired sigh, he said, "It's the last party of the year. He'll be there, I reckon."

And the last one he'd get to be with Emily. By the time they resumed, after winter and calving season were over, she'd be eighteen and off-limits until he came of age, too.

On second thought, maybe he shouldn't be wishing for spring to get here so badly.

Billy reached for the wine bottle and refilled his brother's glass.

Not giving a shit who saw him, he tipped it back.

A whole fucking year without her.

And it was going to be a long one.

Six

A week had gone by from the day he first saw her.

On the trail, a week felt like a year. Long days of hard riding, babies and cattle crying, hoofbeats pounding, and dust flying. He'd grown weary of it.

Beans and bacon at every meal. Johnnycakes, biscuits, and mush did little to ease the monotony. Sometimes, if they were lucky, and the hunt had been successful, they roasted buffalo, antelope, or prairie hen on a spit over the fire.

When they got to California, he never wanted to see beans on his plate again.

If they ever made it there, that is.

The first of September was tomorrow. That gave them two

months to cross the Rockies and the Sierras before the heavy snows began. And two months was being generous.

Walker said winter was coming early. He urged the travelers to make haste, sometimes pushing them twenty miles in a day over steep foothills. At such a grueling pace, most often they were forced to make camp after fifteen or ten.

And with every mile put behind them, Levi watched her.

He had yet to speak to her, though not for a lack of trying. Any time Levi came near, Lucy would scurry off and sneak a glance his way when she thought he wasn't looking.

But he was always looking.

Drawn to her in a way he couldn't explain, Levi couldn't help himself.

Wearing a chambray dress of pale blue, Lucy stood at the campfire with her sister. Their attention rapt, Victoria and Mary Alice studied her shoveling hot embers on top of a lidded cast-iron pot. The oven their mother tried to bring from back east, too heavy and cumbersome, had been long since abandoned. Preparing meals on the trail, especially without the conveniences the girls were accustomed to, had proven to be a laborious task.

"She makes it seem so easy." Her shoulders slumping, Mary Alice sighed. "Why, just yesterday, I burnt what would have been a perfectly good apple pie."

"It's trial and error, Mare, that's all." Pulling her close, Victoria consoled her twin.

Levi proffered a smile. "With practice, I'm sure you'll master it."

"I don't want to," she snapped. Her face reddening, his sister stomped her foot into the dirt. "I want a proper kitchen with a real stove."

"You will if you want to taste an apple pie again before we get to California," Victoria said.

"Won't get to, anyhow." Crossing her arms, her face took on a pout. "There's no more apples."

"Soon enough, fair sister." Drawing her into his embrace, Levi smoothed her tangled blonde locks. "I'll build us a big ole house with a mighty fine kitchen, and plant you a whole damn orchard."

"You promise?" Glancing up at him, her blue eyes brimmed with tears.

"Cross my heart, Mary Alice."

And Levi was a man of his word.

Looking around the desolate expanse of land surrounding them, he couldn't say why his father traded the lives they had for a new one out west. Maybe they hadn't been rich, but they were content. At least he'd thought so. Was it the lure of wide open spaces? Majestic mountains? Lush green landscapes?

Nothing but a dream.

Yeah, maybe so.

But at what cost? Would he have paid the price had he known? Their father. Their mother. Their brother. All of them gone, and for fucking what?

Didn't matter now. It was Levi's responsibility to care for his sisters and to make his father's dream come true.

Parched, he raised his canteen, draining the last dregs of murky river water, the taste so vile he couldn't force himself to swallow.

"Goodness' sake, Levi, you look like you're going to retch." Victoria giggled as he spat onto the dirt. "Go down and fetch yourself some fresh water. The river runs clear here. There was hardly any silt in the pail."

"Almost none at all." Mary Alice nodded her agreement. "Didn't have to waste any corn meal."

Most days, water gathered from the river was poured through the meal to filter out as much of the muck as they could, then boiled and allowed to cool. Still, they drank a lot of dirt. Out here, it was simply a given.

His gaze returning to Lucy, Levi wiped off his mouth with the back of his hand.

"And give yourself a good washing while you're at it," Victoria said, giving him a cake of soap. "You stink."

Noted.

"Stay right here, where Elijah can keep an eye on you. I won't be long."

With his hands in his pockets, Levi walked away from his sisters until the only sounds to be heard were the incessant winds and the burbling of the North Platte. Those same snow-capped mountains still loomed ahead. Never budging from the horizon, they appeared to be no closer than they had the week before.

A swift-flowing stream emptied into the brackish water of the river, the surrounding trees standing like shadowy sentinels against a dark sapphire sky. He unbuttoned his cotton shirt, its once light-blue color, now nothing more than a dingy gray, and grabbing it by the banded collar at his neck, pulled it over his head. The chill in the air prickled his skin. Though Levi was loath to do it, he toed off his boots and rid himself of the rest of his clothing, save his drawers. He could use a good scrubbing. Caked in dust and sweat, his scalp itched.

Colder than he expected, Levi let out a yelp as his bare feet touched the water. With the soap in his hand and the canteen around his neck, he waded to the center, dipping his head beneath the surface.

And it felt fucking good.

He cupped his hands to find the water of the clear running stream refreshing and sweet. It sluiced down his skin in jagged rivulets, carrying the stench, the filth, and his worries away with it. For the moment, at least.

After a time, with his fingertips shriveled to prunes, and his limbs numb, Levi rose from the water. He filled his canteen, and turning toward the grassy bank, the air disappeared from his lungs.

Bathed in moonlight, ribbons of ebony blowing about her

beautiful face, Lucy stood beside his pile of discarded clothing, a cloth-covered plate in her hands.

As if in a dream, because surely this must be, he moved toward the golden eyes that wouldn't meet his gaze. Levi knew what she was looking at. Even without daylight, he could see the flush darkening her cheekbones. His drawers, transparent and molded to his flesh, left little to the imagination.

That she saw him so stirred him. His cock twitched.

Water dripped from his beard to bead upon his chest. They stood toe to toe, and she said, "Victoria sent me this way to find you."

Did she, now?

Her golden gaze finally meeting his, she offered him the plate.

He lifted the cloth from the tin, and with a soaring heart, he smiled.

"Mrs. Clary gave me some eggs, so I made a potato pudding." Demurely, Lucy smiled back. "Thought you might like some."

Well, I'll be damned. She brought me pie.

Outside, icy winter air tickled his nose, but not in here. In here, the air sizzled. The heat of a hundred bodies—hell, likely more than that—filled the old, red barn. Drinking and dancing. Groping and kissing. Darn near everything except fucking in plain view for all to see.

And the smell. God, the smell. Whiskey and hay bales. The scent of Emily's hair. Jake breathed it in deep.

He wrapped his arm around her middle, and pulling her in close, pressed his lips to the top of her head. She angled her face to glance up at him. A wicked gleam in her pretty green eyes, how he longed to kiss her in that moment.

"That was fun." Emily giggled, still trying to catch her breath. "Did you like it?"

In a daring display of prowess, Arien brought Shiloh and his wild girl out on the dance floor to one-up Kellan. After putting on a show with Cassie to make his new stepsister jealous, which it did, judging by the amount of Fireball consumed, the dumb fuck made the mistake of challenging the girl.

And she damn sure showed him.

The three of them moved in sync like they'd been dancing together all their lives. Getting down low and winding it up slow. Hell have mercy on his dick because Jake didn't know his girl had moves like that. But goddammit, he should have.

"Everybody liked it." There wasn't a soul in place who didn't watch them.

Winding his hair around her finger, Emily raised a flask to her lips and swallowed. "I don't give a shit about them. Did *you* like it?"

"Yeah, baby." He spun her around to face him, his nose gliding alongside hers. "I liked it."

Too much, in fact.

His thumb tracing her spine, he saw Tanner lead Arien out of the barn while Kellan slammed down another shot.

"You're not to be messin' with Kellan no more, you hear me?" Jake chuckled, listening to Archer lay down the law to Cassie. "The man's got a girl of his own now."

"You sure about that?"

"Sure am," he said and plucked an unlit cigarette from her lips, snapping it in two. "Besides, I'll be eighteen in just a few months. I reckon you can wait for that long."

"But Griffy, what if I can't?"

"That's what you got these for, girly." Archer took her hand and, kissing her fingers, he sucked them into his mouth. "And I can watch."

Chrissakes.

Emily tipped her flask back, draining what remained of the Fireball. Jake took it from her. Again. "C'mon, I'll get you home."

"I can get myself home, thank you very much."

"You could, but I'm not gonna let you." He held out his hand, lifting his chin at his brother. "Gimme your keys. Billy?"

"Jake, I'm fine." Yet she dropped them into his palm.

That's a good girl.

Between the two of them, Emily and Arien had polished off eight ounces of the cinnamon-flavored whiskey. Maybe more, because he was pretty darn sure Emily connived a refill out of Deke Clary.

"I'm driving her home. Take Emily's car to the house." He winked, handing his brother the keys. "You can bring it back to her in the morning."

"Jake…"

"Listen to him, sweet cheeks. I love you." Billy kissed her, giving her breast a parting squeeze. "I'll be by bright and early tomorrow."

He didn't even get to start the truck.

Her hand on his thigh crept closer to the bulge in his jeans. Placing his hand on hers, Jake stopped her from going any farther. "Emily, behave."

"What if I don't want to?"

With a raise of his brow, he shot her a look. "C'mon, Em."

"I'm tired of all this waiting." Pouting, she laid her head on his shoulder.

Jake held her, his fingers sliding through the silky chestnut locks. "You know the rules."

"They're stupid."

"They aren't," he insisted, though at the moment he wanted to toss them out the window. "You're only seventeen."

"Jacob Gantry, sometimes I think you really don't want me." Emily scooted away from him.

"That so?"

Her arms crossed over her chest, she answered with a nod.

"And what makes you think this?"

Emily turned her head and said in all seriousness, "There's ways of touching without touching."

With a shake of his head, he chuckled. "That don't make a lick of sense."

"Does so." Her lips turned up, and looking at him, that gleam in her eyes returned. Emily raised the hem of her dress, fingers inching toward that triangle of lace between her legs. "And lookin' ain't touchin'."

"Emily, don't..."

"You want me to stop?"

"No." *Looking isn't breaking any rules.* "You're killin' me here, but keep going."

A slow, torturous death, yet one he was willing to suffer. This was his test, and so be it. Jake loved this girl, his wild one. It was as simple as that.

"Tell me what you want me to do, what you'd be doin' to me if you could."

I'd be inside you already...

He started the truck and turned the heat on. "Slide them panties off, baby. Show me that pretty pussy."

In the semi-darkness of the cab, his eyes drank her in. Smooth lips, a patch of dark curls at the cleft. The opening he'd be the first to take, glossy with her sweetness. She wet her lips, her tummy quivering with every breath.

"You're beautiful, Emily." Jake took her hand, kissing the back of it. "I want you so fucking bad."

"And I want you." She reached for his hair, but squeezing her hand, he stopped her before she could. He'd take her in his arms and kiss her. Fuck, he'd ruin her if she touched him like that, and Jake could not fail this test.

"Play with your nipples."

Glancing at him, she bit her lip.

"That's what I'd be doin.'" He closed his eyes, imagining it. "Suckin' on 'em. Bitin' 'em. Mmm, listening to your little cries."

When he opened them again, her plump breasts spilling out from their prison of lavender lace, Emily held her nipples between her fingers. Tracing the areolae with her thumbs, they puckered, accentuating her succulent rosy tips. "Like this?"

"Pinch 'em. Hard." *Damn.* He watched them swell. She rewarded him with a whimper. "Yeah, baby, just like that."

Dying to touch her, his dick strangled inside his jeans. Jake rubbed over the placket in an attempt to assuage the ache. It only made it worse.

Emily noticed. "I wanna see you."

And he wanted her to.

Looking isn't breaking any rules.

A painful relief, his dick slapped his belly. Hot and hard, his desire for her wept from the tip. He swirled it around the head with his thumb.

"I can't wait to taste you."

I can't wait either, my love, but I will.

"Let me watch you come." That he could have, at least. "I want to be lookin' in those pretty green eyes when you do."

"Do I get to watch you, then?" There was that gleam again, and her hands fell from her breasts.

"You want to see that?"

"I do."

My wild, wicked girl.

He stroked himself, tugging hard from base to tip, listening to the sounds. The rustling of her dress. Fingers rubbing wet flesh. Soft moans. Her cry as she came.

Jake's eyes never strayed from hers.

And through it all, he watched her.

Seven

A spring in her step, she scrambled to the bedroom window, searching for signs of snow. Seeing none, Emily smiled. Nothing but soaring pines and endless blue skies for miles and miles. With the weather on her side, today would be a productive day.

She skipped back to the bed, and plopping down upon it, shot off a text to her new best friend. The Eve of the Eve, there wasn't a moment to waste. Gifts were waiting to be wrapped. Cookies needed to be baked. Preparations had yet to be made.

Within seconds, Arien replied.

And her plan was a go.

Everything in her mother's house was done in warm shades

of ivory, cream, and white, from the rugs on the dark hardwood floors to the paint on the textured walls. Not a pop of color to be had anywhere. At least not until spring. Then Emily would color the outdoor spaces in brilliant blooms of orange and purple, pink and yellow, blue and red.

She looked forward to it every year. On Mother's Day, when the air was warmer and the danger of frost had passed, Emily served her mom a sumptuous breakfast she made, along with coffee, orange juice, and a bottle of champagne. Kimberly would sit on the porch drinking mimosas while she pushed plants into the dirt.

"That turned out so pretty, honey."

"Happiness comes in colors, Mama," Emily said. Pleased with herself, she smiled at the two large pots of flowers she'd planted flanking their front door.

Her mother shrugged, and raising the champagne to her lips, released a sigh.

This morning, she sat on the cream linen sofa, hunched over her laptop on the coffee table. Ledgers strewn about. Same as always. Kimberly had an office with a perfectly good desk at her disposal, yet she did her work at the kitchen table or here in the living room.

"Where you off to?" she asked, glancing up at her from the screen.

Emily bent down to kiss her mother's cheek. "Runnin' up to get Arien. We're goin' shopping."

"For what?"

"Christmas ain't the time to be askin'." She winked and walked over to the door. "Anything I can get for you while I'm out?"

"Don't think so." Her gaze traveled to the black-and-white photo on the wall. "Maybe dinner. I don't feel much like cookin'."

"I love you, Mama."

Sea glass eyes returned to her. "Love you more."

Lost in her thoughts, Arien gazed aimlessly out the window

as Emily drove away from the ranch. Was she happy here? Did she miss her old life back in Denver? A month since Uncle Matty's wedding, it seemed to her she was settling in just fine.

Instead of turning toward town, she punched the code into the gate.

Arien whipped her head in her direction. "I thought we were going shopping."

"We are." Emily couldn't contain her grin. "In Jackson."

"Starbucks," Arien squealed, bouncing in her seat.

"Figured you'd be itchin' for some by now," Emily said, the gate closing behind them. "Besides, I'm on a mission."

"Oh, yeah?" And her eyebrow quirked. "What's that?"

"Not sure, but I'll know it when I find it." Met with a blank stare, she explained, "I want to get my mom something special. No idea what, though."

"Ohhh." Understanding dawning on her, Arien nodded. "Couldn't find what you were looking for in town?"

"Didn't even try." With a shrug of her shoulder, Emily turned west toward the Tetons. "It's a small town, Arien, so it's hard to keep anything a secret here. Everybody knows what everyone is up to…"

"Including the gifts you purchase?"

"Now you're gettin' it." She glanced at her cousin and smiled. "I have to get Jake's birthday present, too."

"Oh, when's his birthday?"

"The thirty-first." *New Year's Eve. No midnight kiss for us, though, dammit.* "He'll be twenty-three."

"He's a year ahead of Kellan and Tanner, then."

"No, Jake and Kellan were in the same class—he made the deadline by a day. Born in November, Tanner missed it. He was one grade behind them."

"I did not know that." Her head tipping to the side, she released a breathy sigh. "Poor kid must've been so lonely at the ranch without his brother."

"My mom said that's when he started talkin' to the horses."

Tanner had a gift. Even the wildest bucking bronco would come and eat out of his hand with barely a whisper. To see it was darn near spooky.

"I don't know what to get him." Arien bit her lip and shrugged. "Kellan, neither."

"I guess you're on a mission too, then, ain't ya?" Playfully, Emily elbowed Arien in the ribs.

She giggled. "Guess so."

They strolled along East Broadway in Jackson's iconic town square. Gaslight Alley. Arien picked out Give'r leather work gloves for Kellan and Tanner. She even got them branded with their initials for a personal touch. Then, on impulse, she threw in matching chaps for them, too.

"Think they'll like it?" she asked breathlessly.

"I know they will."

"How do you know?" Arien went to hand the clerk her debit card.

"Don't use that one." Emily snatched it back. "Use the card Uncle Matty gave you."

"But that isn't my money."

She still had so much to learn. No matter their role in the community, every family in Brookside got an equal share of the town's combined profits from the ranch and other ventures to do with as they pleased. A portion was budgeted for the school, municipal improvements, and the like, with the rest set aside for the future.

And Arien was family now. A Brooksider.

Share the work, share the wealth.

"Trust me, it's yours." Winking at Arien, Emily gave the clerk the correct card. "And I know them boys are going to love what you got because it came from you."

"I hope you're right." Chewing on a fingernail, she looked at her with those doll-like eyes. Emily could see the uncertainty Arien was battling within the hazel-green irises.

"You're sweet on them, aren't you?"

"Sweet on them?" Arien scrunched up her face.

"You care for them."

"They're my brothers, boo," she said, pulling back slightly. *Stepbrothers.*

"Course, I do."

"That's not what I meant." Emily linked arms with her cousin. "Never mind. C'mon, there's an antique store I wanna get to."

After Emily found the perfect special something for her mom, and Jake, too, she opened the door of the shop, leaving the smell of a musty, old attic behind to be greeted by the glorious scents of cinnamon, balsam, and pine.

"Oh, look." Arien raised her package-laden arm and pointed. "They do those vintage photos here."

"Yeah, you dress up in Old West costumes and they take your picture. Wanna do it?"

She should want to. Photography was her thing, right? But then maybe Arien was more comfortable behind the camera rather than in front of it.

"Uh, I dunno."

"It's touristy, but it might be fun," Emily said, her lips turning up.

"What the hell." After a soft toss of her blonde waves, Arien went for the door. "Let's do it."

They were taken to a wardrobe room with row upon row of authentic-looking costumes. Saloon girl garb. Petticoats. Feathers. Satin. Lace. Emily pulled an ensemble from the rack and thrust it into Arien's hands. "You should wear this."

A corset with matching chaps of the softest white lace and a poncho of camel-colored wool to drape across her shoulders. Then she snagged a pair of suede fringe chaps for herself and hats for both of them.

"I don't think they dressed like *this* in the Old West." A stunning Arien gazed at their reflection in the mirror.

Okay, so the outfits she chose for them, an alluring mix of Western wear and scant lingerie, were likely intended for a boudoir shoot. They looked hella good, though, and wasn't that the point?

"Maybe not, but we're gonna." She adjusted her breasts in the sheer lace cups, plumping them, and grinned. "Gotta give them boys a little somethin' to look forward to."

"Jesus, Em." Arien tsked, and blushing, she turned away from their reflection.

Emily turned her back around. "What?"

"I don't need to give Kellan and Tanner anything."

Oh, but you want to.

"You give'm a good eyeful at home, I bet." Smirking, Emily slathered on some lip gloss. "I mean, your room's right there across the hall from 'em. You're so lucky."

"If seeing them walk around half-naked most of the time makes me lucky, then I guess so."

"I love you like a sister, Arien." And softly, she kissed her mouth, leaving a smudge of ruby stain upon her lips.

"Why'd you do that?"

Emily smoothed the gloss with her thumb and smiled. "Because I wanted to."

"I can take photos for you if you want," she said, smiling back. "Sexy ones. Better than what you'll get here. For you to give to Billy and Jake."

"Naked." Embracing her cousin, Emily giggled. "In nothin' but my cowboy hat and boots?"

"Straddling your horse's back." Arien was laughing, too.

Emily took a step back. "You do want them, don't you?"

She nodded, biting her lip.

"I knew it, Arien. You're one of us."

△

"I just love the smell of Starbucks."

They stood in line, waiting on Arien's second quad-shot latte of the day. Transferring her shopping bags from one arm to the other, Emily took in a deep breath. "Smells like coffee to me."

"Yes, but…" With a shake of her pretty blonde head, Arien let out a giggle. "…it's more than that. Can't explain it. You could put me in a dozen different coffee houses blindfolded, and I'd know which one was Starbucks just by the smell."

"Yeah?"

"Yeah."

"You're so darn cute," Emily said, handing her the latte. "Let's go."

"And just where are you goin'?"

Deep and velvety-smooth, she knew that voice. *Jake.* Her lips twitched.

Weighted with packages and sneaky smirks on their faces, Emily and Arien turned around to see their boys standing there.

"What're y'all doin' here?"

"Was about to ask you the same, Ems," Kellan said as he sidled up to Arien, eyeing the bags hanging on her arm. "What you got in there, baby cakes?"

"Nothing."

"Looks like you got somethin' to me." He leaned over her, trying to sneak a peek.

"Stop it." She nudged him away with her elbow. "If my hands were free, I'd smack you."

"He'd prob'ly like it." Chuckling, Billy rolled his eyes.

"You know I would," Kellan agreed with a waggle of his brows.

Then his dark smoldering gaze returned to his stepsister. "Here, let me carry 'em for ya."

"Thanks, but I got it."

"Got yourself one of them fancy coffees you love, pretty girl?" Tanner joined in, hugging a blushing Arien to his side.

"So, you didn't answer my question." Emily navigated them toward a table by the window. "What are y'all doing in Jackson?"

"Christmas ain't the time to be asking." Billy shared a look with his brother. "Right, Jake?"

"We had some things to take care of, is all." He tugged at the collar of his sweater as if it were choking him and shifted in his chair. "You girls finished with your shopping?"

"Yeah, I think so." Heaving a sigh of relief, Emily pulled the large envelope from her bag. "We got pictures taken, too. Wanna see?"

"No, no, no, no, no." Arien tried to stop her. "They're for—"

"Gimme those." Kellan snatched the envelope from her fingers and began rifling through the photographs.

"Christmas." Arien sat back with a shake of her head. "They're for Christmas."

Oops. Too late.

"Goddamn, baby cakes…"

Rendered speechless, Tanner let out a slow, deep whistle.

"Holyyy shit, I'm a lucky guy." With a grin so wide his dimples disappeared, Billy's silvery-gray eyes captured her own.

"And why's that?" Emily asked as if she didn't already know.

He leaned across the table and kissed her. "'Cause you're mine."

"And mine." Jake dipped his lips to her ear. "You're killin' me here, wild one."

"Good." She smiled.

Mission accomplished.

Eight

Chaser was miles away in a stable at the ranch. That was the one thing that sucked about living in the center of town, he couldn't keep his horse at home. The first thing Billy planned to do once they built their house on the creek was ride the chestnut gelding down to graze in his very own meadow. He'd already picked the perfect location for an adjacent paddock and barn.

Billy was nine the winter when Chaser found him. Checking fences with his brother, Kellan, and Tanner, the colt surprised him, nudging him on the shoulder with his nose. Tanner chuckled and said it was the strangest thing he'd ever seen—a wild Mustang making contact with a human like that. It was almost as if the horse had chosen him.

A coat of red mahogany, his mane and tail black, he appeared to be a yearling. Somehow separated from his herd, they haltered the lost little guy and brought him to the ranch. His nose pointed up toward the sun, he frolicked about the snowy paddock as if he were chasing it. Billy figured Sunchaser was a fitting name, but he called him Chaser for short.

Under Tanner's guidance, he worked with the horse every day. First, leading him at a walk and trot, teaching him to stop on command, and standing tied—basic groundwork. By the time Chaser turned two, he was easily put under saddle. Ready to ride, young Billy and his faithful companion took to the mountain. The perfect pairing. Together, he and Chaser were one entity.

And it was then that he knew training horses was *his* calling. *Sorry, Ma.*

Billy and Tanner had plans. Big plans. A vision for the future. He would study equine science in college after he finished high school, while he worked in the stables with Tanner, and Brooks Ranch would become known for not only raising the best beef cattle in the land but the finest horses, too.

"Hey there, Arien," Billy said with a tip of his hat upon seeing her in the barn tacking up Daisy. "Goin' for a ride?"

"Yeah, I'm gonna head over to Emily's." Brushing her hands off on her jeans, Arien looked up at him from the crossties. "She wants to take Ruby out for some exercise."

"You two be careful, ya hear? It's slippery with the ice and all. Nippy, too." He chuckled, but he meant it. Arien wasn't an experienced rider like Emily. "Tanner and Kellan know you're goin'?"

"Wasn't aware I needed their permission."

"You don't, but…" He hesitated. To say anything more would be interfering, not to mention it wasn't his place to do so.

"But what?"

"That's a darn nice saddle you got there." Billy lifted his chin at it, changing the subject. "A real beaut."

"Thanks." And her face lit up like a Christmas tree. "I just got it."

"Custom-made. The finest leather. Real sheepskin lining. Just look at that stitching," he said, his hand sliding down the rise of the seat. "Your brothers got it for ya, I bet."

"Yeah, for Christmas."

"Knew it." Billy winked. "Only the best for their girl."

"I'm not their—"

With a squeeze to her shoulder, he smiled at her. "Yeah, you are. They care about you, Arien."

"Because they got me nice things?" A single eyebrow lifting, she cocked her head.

"No, because they're making the effort to really know you. They want you to be happy here." Slipping his arm around Arien, Billy hugged her. "See, when you love someone, how they're feelin' matters to you."

"They don't love me," she scoffed with a flip of her blonde waves. "Not like that, anyway."

"No? Tanner tells me he and Kellan built you a coffee bar—brought your precious Starbucks home for you." He gently turned her, looking her in the eye. "Love ain't all flowery words like the storybooks, and it don't always look like it does in the movies."

"What is it, then?"

"Love is wonderful. It begins as an emotion and grows into a verb." Arien stared back at him, a blank expression on her pretty face. "It's being understood—the feeling that another person just gets you, ya know?"

She answered with a shake of her head.

"It don't mean you agree on all things, but you still feel accepted despite your differences. You feel…seen—safe and comfortable in their presence. And that makes you wanna do things for them that might be out of character for you."

Her brow knit in thought, and she smiled. "Like building a coffee bar?"

"Exactly like that." *You're gettin' it, girly.* "You feel drawn to wanting to know them and you want them to know you, too. You find yourself sharing both good and bad news with them before anybody else. You think about 'em differently and can't imagine what your life would be like if they weren't in it. Hell, you don't even want to."

"Is that how you feel about Emily?"

At the mention of his beloved's name, a tender smile rose. Billy nodded. "I've loved her for as long as I can remember, even before I knew that's what I was feelin', ya know?"

Arien only shrugged.

"When you don't have to ask yourself if you love someone, you know you do. Because love feels more like an answer than a question."

Her lip disappeared behind her teeth, then she asked, "Do you think it's harder for Jake to wait for something he's never had, or will it be harder for you to wait to get it back?"

Billy didn't need the reminder. Emily's birthday was just a few short months from now. *April.* There wasn't much time with her left.

"Don't rightly know." He swallowed, the saliva sticking in his throat, and helped Arien up onto Daisy's back. "You and Em have a good ride now. See ya tonight?"

"Of course. And Billy?" She leaned down and kissed him on the cheek. "Thanks."

Don't mention it.

Emily hoped Jake loved the birthday gift she gave him. Meticulously wrapped in shiny blue paper, she'd chosen it with great care. He loved old things, so when she spied the leather-bound journal in the antique shop, its brittle pages just waiting for words to be carefully written upon them, she snagged it with the thought she'd found him the perfect present. A vintage desk set with a dip pen, ink well, and a pot of India ink completed it.

But then Emily thought her mama would swoon over the authentic Tiffany lamp she got for her desk in the office she rarely used. Hidden away in a dusty corner of the antique shop, she nearly squealed out loud when she saw a fifty-dollar price tag on it and *TIFFANY STUDIOS NEW YORK* marked on the inside rim of the glass shade in all capital letters. The shopkeeper obviously didn't know what he had, and she sure as hell wasn't going to enlighten him.

Vivid colors of green and blue, red and gold, bounced off blanched white walls. Fingering the stained glass on Christmas morning, her mother simply said, "It's lovely, Emily. Thank you."

Lovely? No, it's fucking stunning, and I got it for a steal!

She wanted to shake her, scream at her, and wake her up from her boring, achromatic existence.

"Maybe that's just her preference, honey." Her future father-in-law shrugged.

"Do you paint without color?"

"Sometimes. Black and white is timeless, classic, and beautiful."

Justin's gaze followed hers. One look at Kimberly Brooks Keough told her differently. She stood off to the side, sipping on a glass of champagne alone, while she watched everyone else making merry with their significant others.

"Okay, maybe she's feeling a little blue," he conceded, his head tipping to the side. The twinkling luminescence of lights from the tree caught in his long pale hair. "The holidays can have that effect on some people."

"Since Uncle Matty got married, I've noticed she seems…I dunno…lonely?" That wasn't quite right. It was something else, but it was all she could come up with. "They leaned on each other a lot, and without having him and the boys to fuss over like she did, it's put her in this funk."

"Makes sense. Even after fourteen years, grief can rear its ugly head." Drawing her in, Justin curled his fingers around her waist. "Kim must miss Will and Tim very much."

"I know she does."

Nodding, he glanced across the room. "It looks like Billy and the birthday boy could use rescuing from their aunt."

"Miss Lilly?"

"Do they have another?" Gazing down at her, he chuckled. "Go on, honey. I think I'm going to chat with your mama. Cheer her up some."

"Yeah, good luck with that." Rolling her eyes, Emily exhaled with a snort.

"Are you doubting my fantastic charm and fabulous wit?"

Never.

"I've got this," he said and kissed her forehead. "They're waiting."

God, how she'd come to despise that word.

The hands on the clock on the wall crept closer and closer to twelve. Emily glanced over at Grams, and giving her a little wave, weaved her way through the crowded room to get to her boys. Seeing she was near, Jake reached for her, and she couldn't help but smile. He laced their fingers together and tucked her beneath his arm. Pushing a glass of champagne in her hand, his brother took up the other. Between them. Where she belonged.

Fingertips skating over her breast, Billy dropped a kiss to her bare shoulder. She bit her lip, nipples tightening beneath the silk of her dress. Jake's deep chuckle thrummed in her ear like a promise.

"The three of you together are a sight to behold." Her smile salacious, Miss Lilly smoothed Emily's hair. "I can't wait to make your gown. I have a vision."

"You do?"

"Mmhm." Warm lips lingered on her cheek. "Simple, yet exquisite."

Lilly Gantry could make magic with fabric, a needle, and thread. Like her grandmother before her, she made wedding gowns for all the Brookside brides. Oddly enough, she never married. A dark siren, sensual and alluring, with lustrous black hair and bewitching green eyes, Lilly instead took on a series of lovers throughout the years—both male and female, if the whispers Emily'd heard were to be believed.

"I already know it's going to be so beautiful."

All of her creations were.

"Just like you, sweet girl." Squeezing her shoulders, Lilly smiled and glanced at the clock. "It's almost time. Happy birthday, darling Jacob. I left you a gift in your room," she said, and then kissed him.

"Thank you, Auntie."

"Happy New Year, my boy." It was Billy's turn. "May the mountain continue to bless you with favor and good fortune." Her gaze flicked to Emily, then to Jake. "All of you."

And with that, she was gone.

"Why is it she's never married, you think?" Emily asked, her fingers sliding through Jake's soft hair.

"Asked her once." And he sheepishly grinned. "She said her life was her own and none of my business."

She pursed her lips. *Okie dokie, then.*

"C'mon, Jake." Billy handed his brother a glass and poured one for himself. "Let's drink to your birthday and a brand-new year."

"To our future."

They clinked glasses, and as the effervescent bubbles tickled her tongue, the countdown began.

Glancing around the room, Emily swallowed her champagne. Her mother stood, smiling at Justin. Lilly was nowhere to be seen. Victor filled Carrie's glass until it all but overflowed. Uncle Matty had one arm around Grams, the other holding onto his wife, while her cousins played Tug-of-war with Arien between them.

Three.

Two.

One.

"Happy New Year, Emily." His dark eyes shining, Jake pressed a kiss to her forehead and guided her to his brother's waiting arms.

Billy's lips took hers, soft and sweet. Tasting the champagne on his tongue, he deepened the kiss until everything else faded away. Jake held her from behind, warm breath fanning her nape, his fingers strummed her middle. Lightning erupted in her belly, the blood rushing to that empty place between her legs, making it so heavy she ached.

Jake's tongue traced the pulse beneath her ear. "*Michante.*"

Emily opened her eyes.

Her mother still stood there with Justin, looking on as Victor kissed his wife. Uncle Matty was kissing Jennifer, while Grams hid a chuckle behind her hand, watching Tanner and Kellan chase after their stepsister.

A smile coming to her lips, she closed them again. How lucky was she to call these people her family?

"Happy New Year, Em."

"Happy New Year, Billy." And she kissed him again for good measure. "I love you."

"I love you, too, baby."

She turned to the man behind her. "And I love you, Jake. I hope your birthday wish comes true."

"Already did." A smile in his eyes, he kissed her crown. "I've got you."

Nine

On the trail, grief was a luxury no one could afford. There wasn't a single soul amongst them who hadn't left behind someone, given up something, to make the difficult journey west. Levi often wondered if everything they'd endured, all they'd lost, would be worth it in the end.

Many of them would never see it.

The emigrants grew weaker and more haggard by the day.

Walker dropped back to ride beside him. "If we can keep 'em goin', at this pace we should reach the fort by week's end."

"Then what?" With a pent-up snicker, Levi clawed at his beard. He needed a shave. His skin itched.

"Get supplies. Rest a day. Maybe two." Then he said in all seriousness, "You got some decisions that need makin'."

Levi turned his head and just looked at him.

"You're runnin' out of time."

He knew it. Mid-September, the days were pleasant, but the nights had become increasingly colder—darn near close to freezing. Winter was coming. They were running out of time quick.

Levi stopped chewing on the nub of flesh inside the corner of his lip to ask, "You been there, Josiah?"

"Been where?"

"California."

The mountain man leaned back in the saddle, removed his hat, and raked gnarled fingers through his scraggly hair. "Yeah, I've been there."

"Is it all they say? Is it worth it?"

"Well, son." And he put the hat back on his head. "I s'pose that depends on what you're hopin' to find there."

Another clearing lay ahead.

They stopped to set up camp along the river. Levi leaned back against the wagon, staring up at the painted sky as the whiskey bathed his arid throat. He prayed to God for some guidance, but found none.

Outlined in the colors of the setting sun, Lucy stood at the fire. A shining beacon of light in the dark, his hope, and his salvation. When she looked at him, nothing seemed impossible.

"Papa says we'll be at Fort Bridger in a few days." Biting her lip, Lucy came over and handed him a plate of beans. "We'll be parting ways there. Saying our farewells."

For Walker, the post on the Blacks Fork of the Green River was the end of the line. He'd turn back while they moved on. It was likely he'd never see her again.

A pang of discomfort tore through him. "I don't want you to go."

"I don't want to leave you," she whispered, her golden eyes cast downward.

Gently, Levi lifted her chin, gazing into a kaleidoscope of liquid topaz, sienna, amber, and honey. His thumbs brushed her cheeks, and fingers sliding into her long, luxurious locks, he brought her lips to his.

Have mercy.

Warmth. Sweet, succulent warmth. His balls tightened in his britches. He took her mouth, cradling her head in his hands, and slipped his tongue inside. The moment he tasted her, he knew, somehow, he had to keep her.

"Stay with me."

"You can't mean that." Her voice cracking, Lucy peered up at him. "You don't know what you're saying."

Yes, I do. I know exactly what I'm saying.

"Stay. With. Me." His hands sliding down her arms, Levi pulled her close against him. "We can build a life together in California."

"I can't." Her bottom lip quivering, tears sprang from her pretty eyes.

"You can."

"You don't understand. I won't be accepted there with you… or anywhere. By anyone." Swiping beneath her eyes, she shook her head. "They call me half—"

"Hush your mouth. Don't you dare say it." His fingertips traced her lips. "You're beautiful, and I want nothing more than to call you *mine*."

He kissed her again, urgently this time. Laying his claim on her, Levi pushed his hardness into the softness hidden beneath her skirts. Not caring if Walker, her sister, or his came upon them, he vowed to kiss *"I can't"* right out of her. And God help the fool who dared to speak of Lucy as anything less than whole.

They came apart, and laying her head on his shoulder, she said, "My Shoshone name is *Chosro*. It means bluebird."

My bluebird.

"It's a lovely name." He smiled up at a darkening sky, smoothing her hair down her back.

"My mother gave it to me. She told me they were singing when I was born."

"How old are you, Lucy?" He hadn't thought to ask until now.

"Sixteen."

Good. Old enough.

To take to wife.

Then to his bed.

He'd speak to Josiah. Ask for her hand. They'd marry at Fort Bridger.

Jake cracked his window. February wind rushed in. It was cutting, but Billy had the heat cranked all the way up, making the air inside the truck dry and stuffy. He'd get a nosebleed, for chrissakes, and that was the last thing he needed.

"The fuck, bro?" His tone sharp, Billy glared. "It's goddamn freezin.'"

"You're roasting me from the inside out here—can't breathe."

"I'll lower the heat, okay?" He turned the knob, blowing out a noisy breath. "Just close that dang window."

"Deal." Jake sniffed. "My nose bleedin'?"

"No, but I'll make it bleed if you do that again," Billy said in jest, chuckling.

At the Tetons, Jake went south toward Jackson. A song that reminded him of Emily came on the radio. *Take my name…* He hummed along, tapping to the beat on the steering wheel with his thumbs.

Billy glanced over his way. "What you thinkin' about there?"

"Nothin.'"

"Explain that dopey grin on your face, then," he said with a playful nudge to his ribs.

Jake tipped his chin toward the radio. "Reminds me of when we asked Emily to be our wife."

She was sixteen.

He'd just graduated from UW.

Of course, they went to Miss Kim and her uncle, Matthew, to seek their blessing first. It didn't matter if the gesture was old-fashioned, or that by then, it was already a foregone conclusion that they'd marry. Their parents raised him and his brother to be gentlemen, and it was the right thing to do.

When Jake left for college, Emily was a gangly girl with wild hair and braces. Always hanging around his brother, he had a feeling she was meant to be theirs someday, but she and Billy were just kids at the time. In high school, the Clary sisters once sought his attention. Everleigh was the first girl he ever kissed, and her sister's pussy, the first one he ever touched. While he was away at Laramie, besides going to classes and studying, he did what most guys in college do—play hard and fuck harder. But as fun as it was, it never felt quite right.

When Jake came home for spring break his senior year, the braces were gone, and Emily wasn't a gangly kid anymore. Like a flower in her garden, she'd blossomed. She looked at him differently. Billy looked at her differently. He knew then that the feeling in his gut he'd pushed aside four years before was the right one. It was all falling into place. She *was* meant to be theirs.

Absently chewing on his lip, his brother smiled at the memory. "I was so relieved."

"Why? Were you scared she was gonna say no?"

"Hell, no." And he grinned. "I was scared those Clary sisters would get their hooks into you somehow, or worse, you'd meet some girl in Laramie."

"That was never gonna happen." With a shake of his head,

Jake chuckled, then glancing at his brother, he said, "Deep down, I think I always knew it would be us three. Just had to wait on the two of you, is all."

"Yeah?"

He offered a nod. "Yeah."

"I was makin' plans in my head to marry Emily on my own in case Everleigh and her sister got their way," he said with a chortle. "Those girls had it bad for you."

"So that's why they hitched up with Jamie Coulter so quick, huh?" He attended their wedding the summer before last. Between them, the sisters had three little ones now. "You were willing to take that chance, brother?"

While not unheard of, Matthew Brooks just did it, after all, a union other than a triad was rare. To do otherwise upset the tripartite nature of the world. One could lose favor, so few ever risked it.

Everything that comes in threes is perfect.

"For Em, yeah, I would have."

God, how Billy loved her. If only he'd paid closer attention when his brother and Emily were kids, Jake would have seen the depth of it. More than a feeling, he would have known, then, exactly what his future was. And he wouldn't have kissed Everleigh, or messed around with her sister, or fucked those girls in Laramie. Names and faces he couldn't even remember. He should have waited for her, as he was waiting now.

Billy was lucky. The only kiss, the only touch he'd known, was hers. Jake almost envied him for it.

He scored a parking spot only a block away from the architect's office. With ski season in full swing, Jackson was filled with tourists, and a space was difficult to come by. "Excited to see the plans, finally?"

"They're just prelims," he said, "but I am, yeah." His hat sat on his lap. Fingers gripping the brim, Billy's dark-rimmed eyes flicked over to him. "When do you think we'll be able to break ground and get started?"

"Late April, I'd guess." *May, the latest.* With any luck, the worst of winter had already passed. "Gives us a year to get it finished."

Reaching for the door handle, Billy nodded. "That'll keep me busy enough, I reckon."

"Us." Jake grabbed onto his brother's arm to stop him from opening it.

He paused before pasting a sorry-ass smile on his face. "Right."

"You okay?"

Billy couldn't hide it if he tried. Something troubled that brilliant mind of his.

"Yeah." Shoulders slumped, he sat back, staring down at the floorboards. "They're startin' to round up the cows. It's almost time."

So that's it.

Calving season.

And once it began, there'd be no time for anything else—Emily, included. It was all work, on very little sleep, until the last calf was born. That was just the way of it.

"Kellan said he shortened breeding from ninety days to sixty this time, so we'll be done in April," Jake offered. Calving came around nine months later and lasted just as long.

"I know," Billy muttered, his shrug half-hearted. "His dad wants to try out doin' two controlled breedings this year, so there's weaned calves to market both spring and fall."

With a growing herd of over thirty thousand, it only made sense. Besides, when it came to ranch business and making money for Brookside, Matthew Brooks was seldom wrong. Kellan, neither.

"It's a good move," he concluded, clasping his brother's shoulder. "Cattle prices hit their high in spring."

"Costs more to feed 'em through the winter too, but what do I know?"

"I'm sure Kellan and his father have taken all that into account."

Jake looked over at Billy, staring through the passenger window, his warm breath fogging up the cold glass. "I know what's weighin' on your mind."

"Do ya?" His head whipped around. "And what's that?"

"Emily." He knew because it weighed on him, too. "Bein' gone from her when it's the only place you wanna be."

"Won't deny it." Lips pursed to the side, his brother finally made it out the door.

Jake followed him. "I get it, Billy, believe me."

"Maybe." He put his hat on his head. "But it don't change nothin.'"

Ten

Sleet stung his face.

Billy swiped at it, and trudging through the muddy field, he searched for newborn calves in trouble or mamas in distress while urging them toward the barn. It was pleasant, in the fifties, only this afternoon, but a late-season storm bringing eight to ten inches of snow and temps below zero come morning meant the death of them if they stayed out here.

Thank fuck they had the cows sorted, with the ones due to calve the soonest pastured closest to the maternity barn. Billy pushed them inside, counting one hundred and fifty in the large group pen. Three had water bags bulging, two dropped newborns the minute they were out of the weather, and one had a pair of hooves peeking out her backside. No doubt another fifty would calve before his grueling shift was through.

He missed Emily.

It didn't matter Billy saw her just a few hours before. That felt like forever ago. She and Arien came by with supper for him, his brother, and the boys. A hale and hearty beef stew, fresh-baked biscuits straight from the oven, thermoses of strong black coffee, and a blueberry pie. Just seeing her warmed his insides.

"I had to come kiss this handsome face," she squealed, jumping into his arms. She didn't care that he was dirty and reeking of cow. Emily clung to him, peppering kisses all over his windburned cheeks, before scrambling off him to see his brother.

She squeezed Jake, holding him tight while his hands skimmed up and down her back. If they exchanged words, Billy didn't hear them, but then they were all too tired for talking.

Huddled together, they sat on hay bales, scarfing down their dinner. The girls sat with them, Emily between him and Jake, and Arien between Tanner and Kellan, wide-eyed with surprise they could consume that much food so quickly.

Her eyes flitting around the barn, Arien wrinkled up her nose. "The horse stalls smell better. It stinks in here."

Billy couldn't disagree. *Cowshit.* Not that horseshit smelled like roses. But along with the scent of sweet oats and hay, it hit different, he supposed. Maybe he was inclined to it, but like Arien, he was more at home with the horses.

"It's a calving barn, baby cakes." Kellan grabbed Arien's face, and kissing her, he chuckled. "What'd you expect?"

"Baby cows are so cute and—"

And?

But Tanner cut her off, taking her from his brother and planting a kiss of his own on her lips.

Truth be told, that wasn't the only source of the stench in

here. No amount of antiseptic that could wash away the stink of piss and shit, sour milk, and bloody afterbirth.

Arien's head shot up. "Wait, don't they have their babies outside?"

"Most of the time." Tanner's fingers caressed her cheek. "Sometimes, like when the weather's bad or if a mama is havin' a hard time, we have to bring 'em in."

"Yeah, and it looks like tonight is gonna be one of those nights." Kellan took a long swig from his thermos. "We've got a cold front comin' through."

"You can't fit all the mama cows and their babies in here."

"Don't have to, girly." He smirked with a shake of his head. "Only the ones that are close to calving."

"But how do you know which ones those are?"

"Easy." His fingertips traipsing down her thigh, they halted at her knee. Kellan squeezed. "We got a synchronized system here. See, gestation is roughly two hundred and eighty-three days."

Two hundred seventy-nine to two hundred and ninety-two, but semantics.

"We breed 'em in groups. The Angus bull gets turned out with the Angus heifers and has fun with them for a couple of weeks, then he spends a couple with the Angus cows. Then the Limousin gets his turn with his girls, then the Simmental, and down the line it goes. So, we know when each group is due to calve and who to keep a closer eye on."

"Oh." Her lips pursed, Arien accepted Kellan's explanation with a shrug. Then her pretty eyes glazed over and she cocked her head. "Wait a minute, what do you mean the heifers and *then* the cows? Aren't they the same thing?"

Exchanging a glance with his brother, Billy chortled. *City girls.*

Tanner's arm came around her shoulders, drawing Arien closer to his side. "Heifer means she's a first-time mama, pretty girl. A cow has calved before."

"The boys are bulls—until their balls get chopped off, anyway." Emily showed her, making a snipping motion with her fingers. "Then they're steers."

The look on Arien's face. *Priceless.* She gasped, turning to Kellan. "Why the fuck would you do that?"

"Not all the boys get to play." He winked at her, sporting his trademark smirk. "The best are for breedin' and the rest are for eatin'. Testosterone gives the meat a strong flavor—most folks don't like it, so…"

"I did *not* need to know that."

"And yet, you asked."

Most folks don't know what it takes to get that nice ribeye steak on their table. Hell, they don't want to know. The only thing they see is cuts of beef, prettily packaged for their consumption on plastic-wrapped Styrofoam trays at the grocery store.

Kellan followed in behind. Snapping him back to the matter at hand, he pointed at the cow with the hooves protruding from her backside. "How long she been like that?"

"Not sure."

He thrust his hand past the hooves, into the birth canal. "Calf's alive. Tongue's wigglin'. Let's give her another fifteen minutes. Might have to pull it."

"Yeah, all right."

"C'mon, get these girls into another pen," Kellan ordered, lifting his chin toward the three with bulging bags. "Then come back here and check on her. I gotta get these new ones up and sucking. They're cold."

Billy shooed the laboring mamas into individual calving pens. Cows prefer to be alone when calving, and the set-up gave them a sense of privacy while allowing him access should he need to intervene.

After settling them in, he returned to check on the progress of the heifer. Nothing had changed. The pair of hooves hadn't so much as budged. Noting the orange tag on her ear, Billy gave it a scratch. "C'mon, Miss 2079. I'm gonna help you get your baby out."

Supplies at the ready, he brought her to an open pen and secured her in the headlock gate. Patting her flank, he soothed her. "It's gonna be okay, Mama. Promise. I ain't lost a calf yet."

Now and then, a cow, especially a heifer, needed a little help. Exhausted Mamas. Dystocias. Breech births. Billy had just about seen it all.

Carefully, he wrapped the OB chain around the baby's hooves and attached the calf puller to it. "Ready when you are, Mama. Lemme see that baby."

With every contraction, the heifer heaved, and he pulled.

"Thatagirlll, push."

Billy looked up. In a fountain of bloody fluid, forearms and a muzzle with a wiggling pink tongue appeared.

"Let's get her done." Jubilant, he whooped. It was a tight squeeze, but the calf was presenting in the proper position. "Do it again."

At the next contraction, gripping the cold metal handles, Billy exerted steady pressure. Once the head was born, the rest of the calf needed to come out quickly or risk taking amniotic fluid into its lungs.

Mama lost the strength to make that final push. He let go of the puller, yanking the calf out by its forearms the rest of the way himself. Not moving, the baby just laid there.

"Oh, no you don't." Tearing away what remained of the membrane, Billy nudged the calf. "C'mon little buddy."

A rush of fluid exited the newborn's mouth, but otherwise, it remained still.

Vigorously, he rubbed the baby's back and moved its legs to stimulate him. Then, with time in slow motion, after what seemed like an eternity, the calf took a feeble breath.

Then another.

And another.

And another.

"Thank fuck." Billy got up off his haunches and went over to the heifer, who at last could rightfully be called a cow. He released her from the headlock. "Told ya, I ain't lost one yet. You got yourself a little bull."

"You done good, Billy." Kellan leaned over the pen, his arms dangling inside. "Now, get him suckin'. Two more heifers dropped calves while you were wrenchin' out this one."

But the little guy wouldn't suck and his mother wanted nothing to do with him.

Cows typically lick their calves clean, get them to stand, and offer them an udder. A newborn calf must feed within an hour of its birth. Sooner is even better. Its ability to absorb antibodies from colostrum, the mother's first milk, rapidly diminishes in the first day of life.

"What's the matter, 2079? Don't you like him?"

She replied with a throaty moo.

"C'mon now, you gotta feed your baby."

In the end, he did the mothering for her. Billy milked the precious colostrum from the dam's udder and fed it to her calf through an esophageal tube. Next, he dried the shivering baby off as best he could and placed him in a warmer.

"Don't you worry none, little fella. She'll come 'round." Looking down at his big brown eyes, he rubbed the newborn's head. "And I'll be by to see how you're doin' in a little bit."

Three hours and ten new calves later, with the storm raging outside, Billy sat on the straw-covered floor of the orphan pen with the sixty-pound bull's head on his lap, coaxing him to feed from a bottle. His mother still didn't want him. "I'm sorry, buddy."

"She knows."

He glanced up to see Kellan.

"His mama knows. Birth weight should be eighty pounds. Bull's too small to make it."

"So small I had to yank him out of her, right? He's gonna be just fine." Billy smiled down at the calf. "I'm gonna take him home to Em. She's always wanted a bottle baby to raise."

"He makes it through the night, you can have him." Kellan squeezed his shoulder. "When you're finished feedin' him, I need you."

By the time morning came, another forty-six calves were born. That made fifty-nine total, including Bodhi, during their time inside the barn. Yeah, he'd already picked out a name for the little guy. Billy didn't know what the word meant, but he liked it.

He opened the gate to Bodhi's pen, where he slept on a warm bed of straw. But as Billy came closer, he already knew. The calf was too still.

I ain't never lost one.

"C'mon, open your eyes for me, buddy," he whispered in vain, his fingers brushing over the baby's head. "I'm taking you to Em. She's gonna love you and she'll be such a good mama."

But Bodhi's eyes never opened.

"I wanted to be wrong this time." Kellen stood over him. "Sorry, Billy."

I ain't never lost one.

"Get cleaned up and go home. I'll see to the calf."

"His name is Bodhi."

Something warm and wet trickled from his eye. What the fuck? He wasn't crying over the death of a baby bull, was he?

I ain't never lost one.

"Go on, now, and take tonight off." Kellan crouched down on his haunches in front of him. "Spend some time with Emily. Wish her a happy birthday and love on her while you still can."

Eleven

Emily almost missed his call.

Cross-legged on the floor of her walk-in closet, the phone was buried in a sea of clothing she'd tossed out of drawers and torn from their hangers. It's not that Emily suddenly had this obsessive-compulsive desire to purge and reorganize or anything like that, but once the thought crossed her mind, she dove right in. Besides, she had nothing better to do.

Colder than a witch's tit, she wasn't about to take Ruby out for a ride.

Arien invited her up to the house, but watching her stuff mushrooms for her next vlog post held little appeal. She didn't even like them.

THE *Hardest Part* | 89

Shiloh's parents forced her and Cassie to go on a trip to Arizona together for some sisterly bonding before the wedding.

This time of year, her mom worked in town, from daybreak until midnight ensuring every tax return was flawless and filed by the April 15th deadline.

And her boys?

Up to their elbows in cowpoo, I bet.

Giggling at the image in her head, Emily followed the voice of Stevie Nicks belting out "Edge of Seventeen" and found her phone hidden beneath a pile of old t-shirts she no longer had any use for.

A photo of Billy on his horse lit up the screen. "Hey, babes. Whatcha doin'?"

"Just finished my shift," he said on a groan. "Is your mama home?"

"No."

"I'm comin' over."

It wasn't a request. His voice had an edge to it Emily couldn't quite place. "Okay, I can make you some breakfast."

"I don't want breakfast. I just want you."

After a sixteen-hour shift, and during a snowstorm to boot, Billy had to be cold, tired, and hungry. Except for stolen moments here and there, seeing each other while the cows were calving was a rarity, and surely, he missed her as much as she missed him…

There's more to it than that.

"What's the matter, Billy?"

"Nothin', sweet cheeks. See you soon."

"Nothin', my ass," Emily muttered, tossing her phone.

She had breakfast ready when the doorbell rang. A pan-seared T-bone, scrambled eggs, and fried potatoes waited for him at the kitchen table. Freshly showered, his damp hair smelling of shampoo, Billy didn't say a word. He took her cheeks in his cold, rough hands and warmed his lips with hers.

"Fuck, Em, I've missed you," he rasped into her mouth, taking in a gulp of air.

I've missed you, too.

"You just saw me yesterday."

"Not like this." Billy backed her into the living room, kissing her again as they went.

There was an urgency to it that startled her. All-consuming, his kiss sent heat coursing to that place between her legs, the nub within pulsing to the rapid beat of her heart.

"I made you some breakfast," she said, panting when he eventually released her.

He took her bottom lip between his teeth, sucking it into his mouth. "*You* are the only thing I want."

This man. He took her breath away when he said things like that, which he did all the damn time.

"You need to fill your belly and get some sleep. It'll be time to go back before you know it."

"Nope, I got tonight off." A wicked glint entered his eyes. "So, I ain't gonna waste the day sleepin."

"No?" Biting down on her lip, Emily couldn't contain her grin.

A faint smirk curved his mouth. "No."

"What do you wanna do, then?"

He turned from her, and stopping at the kitchen table, Billy picked up the steak from his plate, tore off a bite, and once he swallowed, he said, "Take me to your room, Em. I wanna see how many times I can make you come before you beg me to stop 'cause you can't take no more."

Ohhh.

"Yeah?"

"Oh, yeah." He wiped off his hands, his voice dark and smoky, then pulled her to his chest. "But I'm gonna make you come again, anyway."

"Promise?" Slick with need, that pulsing between her legs grew stronger.

His lips skating across her skin, warm breath fanned her neck. "Cross my heart, baby."

And Billy made good on his promise.

It might have been twenty below outside, but here inside her bedroom, it felt like ninety degrees. He knelt on the dark wood floor, fucking her with his fingers, jeans tangled at her knees, lapping up the juices from her thighs. God, she loved the way he fingered her. How he always seemed to know when to go harder, when to ease up, when to add another finger. Sometimes, two wasn't enough. Hell, there were times three wasn't either.

They were both naked by the time they made it to the bed. Writhing on cream linen sheets, Billy ate her pussy. She held his head to her cunt while he fucked her with his tongue and sucked on her clit. When she felt the first flutters, Emily widened the space between her legs, signaling him to fill her with his fingers as she came.

Fucking sublime.

What could feel better than his mouth on her cunt with his fingers inside her?

His cock. And Jake's.

It stood, brushing his navel, thick and hard, before her. Pearly drops wept from the little slit. Emily swiped her tongue across her lip and reached for him. "Gimme."

"You wanna suck me, baby?"

"So bad." She licked the fluid oozing from his head. "Make me choke on this big, fat dick and swallow every drop of cum."

She loved sucking his cock, too. The manly smell of him. The addicting taste of his salty semen. Some girls she knew didn't care to give blow jobs, and for the life of her, Emily couldn't understand why. She caressed his balls, raking over them with her nails, and rubbed the flesh behind them as her head bobbed on his dick. It was heady, a powerful feeling to be the one giving him pleasure.

He groaned and, pulling on her hair wrapped around his fist, he held a vibrator to her swollen clit.

"That feels too good." He sucked in air through his teeth. "I wanna fuck you so bad, Em."

She raised her head with a parting lick, wiggling her bottom to get the vibrator on the spot where she needed it. "I want that, too. One more year, my love."

"I don't wanna wait that long." Billy slid the vibrator from her clit, along her slit, to her ass. It tingled, the hole puckering. "Do you?"

Emily moved, getting face to face with him. "No, but that's the rules."

"This ain't breakin' the rules," he crooned, his finger rubbing around her hole. "It's almost your birthday, Em, and I won't even get to kiss you no more, then. Let me fuck you here."

Her pussy clenched at the thought. It wasn't breaking the rules, but it was bending them. Commonly talked about among the girls at school, they fucked that way often enough. Hell, she watched Griffin and Shiloh do it once, though they didn't know it. Seeing his cock in her ass and his fingers in her cunt got her so hot, Emily rubbed her clit right then and there.

Jake caught her at it, too.

"You like what you're seein' here, wild one?"

It's not like she could deny it. "I do."

"Good."

He must've been a little drunk because she could feel his fingers in her hair.

"That pleases you?"

"Very much."

Her head fell back on his shoulder. "Why?"

"Because one day, me and Billy are gonna fill up both your holes." His hand swept down her back, pausing at her ass. "Together."

She rubbed her clit harder and moaned.

"That's it, my wild girl."

Jake wanted Billy to fuck her ass, didn't he? It was likely he expected they'd already done it. It would be okay as long as Billy didn't penetrate her pussy with his dick, because that was definitely against the rules. Until the wedding, anyway, and then, being the elder brother, Jake would fuck her first.

How she longed for that day to come. Dreamt of it. Got herself off to the vision of having both their cocks inside her.

Emily wrapped her hand around his length. "Yes, baby, I'll let you."

"Tell me you *want* me to," he said, pushing his finger in. "I need to hear it."

"It's gonna hurt, isn't it?" Already, she felt the burn. "I don't care if it does. Fuck my ass, Billy. Please, I need to feel you inside me."

"We got all day and plenty of lube." He bent his head and licked her nipple. "We'll go slow, okay?"

"Okay."

Billy gazed down at her, smiling as he added lube to his finger. Slowly, he moved it in and out. Twisting. Gently stretching. "How's this feel, baby?"

"Weird, but a good weird, ya know?"

"Can't say that I do." He chuckled.

She smacked his ass. "Want me to do it to you, so you know?"

"Sure, if you wanna."

Not the answer Emily was expecting. She meant it as a joke. "You'd let me?"

"Baby, I love you." He placed a kiss on the tip of her nose, squirting some lube on her finger. "Go on. You can do whatever you want to me."

It was so beautiful, staring into each other's eyes, seeing into each other's souls as they pleasured one another. His ass, hot and tight, squeezed her finger. Liquid pooled between her thighs at the sounds he made.

"Damn, girl." Billy's eyes rolled back in his head. "Fuck."

"It feels good?"

"Too good." He groaned, pushing two fingers into her ass. "Keep that up, you're gonna milk the cum right outta me."

"So?"

He fingered her some more, then flipped her over. "I wanna come in you."

She smiled.

"Lube me up," he commanded, handing her the bottle.

Emily took her time, slathering it all over his shaft.

"Yeah, baby, make a mess with it."

"Too much?"

"Never." Billy winked and took the bottle from her, coating his finger with lube. He bathed the crack of her ass with it and pushed more into her hole.

"I'm dyin' here, Billy." Emily needed…something. "Put it in me."

The tip of his cock caressed her opening, prodding gently, and he pushed the head inside.

It fucking hurts.

"Relax. Don't fight it, baby" He leaned over, kissing his way up her spine. "Play with your pussy. Can you do that?"

"Uh-huh," she squeaked with a nod. "Gimme the bullet."

"You're doin' so good."

She held the vibrator to her clit, but it didn't distract her. "It burns."

"Want me to stop?"

"No, baby, please don't." As foreign as it felt to have his big dick wedged in her little hole, Emily found she liked the feeling. "Fuck."

"You takin' care of your clitty, baby?"

"Yesss." *Fuck, yes.*

Billy pushed himself in farther. "How many fingers you fuckin' your pussy with?"

"Two."

"Put in another one." And his hand came down on her ass. "I want you full."

"Fuck. Me."

"God, I'm all the way inside you, Em. It hurts some. I know." His hands holding onto her hips, he thrust in and out of her. "You feel so damn good and I love you so damn much...fuck."

And with the vibrator lost somewhere among the sheets, she pinched her clit hard, a spectrum of colors bursting behind her eyelids.

It was dark when Emily woke, entwined with Billy, naked, on the bed. She watched him sleep, stroking his skin, twirling his hair around her fingers. He blinked his gray eyes open, and she smiled.

"What time is it?"

"Almost ten."

"Shit, I didn't mean to fall asleep." Billy sat up, scratching his head. "I should go before Miss Kim gets home."

"It's okay." She reached for his hand, giggling. "We should probably get dressed, though."

"Thank you." He kissed her fingers.

"What on earth for?"

"Being you. Lovin' me like ya do." Letting go of her hand, he got up from the bed. "I know how lucky I am."

I'm lucky, too, then.

"I just wanted you to know that." Billy got dressed and sat back down beside her. "Now, give me a kiss goodnight and make it a good one."

"You're leaving?"

"I sure don't wanna, but it's best I do."

She reached behind his neck, making him bend into her kiss. "I love you, William Gantry."

"I love you, Emily Keough." And he pressed his lips to her forehead. "Goodnight."

Twelve

L evi didn't miss the look on his sisters' faces. They'd long been looking forward to their arrival at Fort Bridger. Nothing but two crude, rough-hewn log houses, maybe forty feet in length, joined by a pen for horses. The post was a disappointment. Not nearly as well outfitted as Fort John had been, Laramie was almost luxurious in comparison, but at least they had a blacksmith here.

While the twins bore identical features, their temperaments couldn't have been more opposite. Victoria, the elder by five minutes, as she often reminded them, always saw the cup as half full. Mary Alice would say it's half empty. She's the one he'd have to make see reason.

With Lucy and Fallon at his side, Walker preceded them into

the trading post. Following suit, Levi held onto his sisters and led them inside. "Purchase what we need. I'm going to inquire about procuring some new oxen. The horses need shoeing, too."

"I sincerely doubt this place has anything we need." Her hand resting on a burlap grain sack, Mary Alice surveyed the wares on display and slowly shook her head.

"You're a bit late, Missy. Weather'll be turnin' soon, so most travelers have already passed through." Skin weathered, his cheekbones high and prominent, a rugged-looking man leaned over from behind a rudimentary counter. "Pickings might be slim, but we got provisions for ya. Cornmeal, beans, bacon, and the like. Where y'all headed?"

"California."

The man responded with a quick burst of laughter until a warning glance from Walker silenced him.

Her chin held high, Mary Alice put the man in his place. "Do I amuse you, Mister, uh...?"

"Name's Bridger. Jim Bridger," he said, contrite, with a tip of his hat. "And no, ma'am, not at all."

"I have a list, Mr. Bridger," Victoria cut in, sliding it over to him on the counter. "I'd be much obliged if you could get these items ready for me."

"I'll do my best, Miss."

Walker pulled him off to the side, leaving his daughters and Levi's sisters to browse the goods on hand. "This is where you've got to set your course, son."

"I'm aware of that, Josiah."

"You know what yer gonna do?"

Ain't got a fucking clue. Glancing down at the dirt floor, he rubbed the back of his neck.

"A little advice?" A gnarled hand came down to rest upon his shoulder. "Gather your people after supper, pass around a bottle of whiskey, and talk to 'em. You'll figure it out."

"They're not gonna listen to me."

"Some will, some won't. There's strength in numbers, but not every man follows the same path. You get me?"

And nodding, Levi sighed. "Yeah."

"I can help you talk to 'em if you like."

"I would, and there's another matter I want to discuss with you."

The left corner of his mouth subtly rose as he propped a hip against the wall. "I'm listenin'."

"In private."

Perhaps Levi hadn't yet chosen his path, but wherever it led, Lucy was going with him. Because that's the only thing he was sure of. When they left Fort Bridger, she'd be leaving as his wife.

"All right, then." Turning toward the counter, he chuckled. "Jim, we're camped just outside. We'll be back in the mornin' to settle up. C'mon, girls."

Walker held the door open for his daughters. Levi and his sisters left behind them. Trapper's lodgings, shabbily constructed of poles dabbed with mud, along with several teepees, dotted the surrounding landscape. The mountain man nodded over his shoulder. "They'll have a good supply of skins, coats, and moccasins to trade."

"Trade for what?"

"Coffee. Flour. Sugar." Walker stopped dead in his tracks. "A horse. A cow. A woman. You'll give 'em whatever they want if you wanna survive the winter."

Levi let Victoria and Mary Alice walk ahead of him and lowered his voice. "A woman? That's absurd."

"Don't you worry none. There ain't a Shoshone or Bannock here itchin' to get their hands on yer girls. To them, a good horse holds more value," he said with a shrug. "But a trapper's life can be a lonely one. I'm sure plenty of 'em would be glad to trade for a wife."

"Over my dead body."

"And that's what you'll be, young man. Your sisters, too." The mountain man poked Levi's chest as he spoke, driving his point home. "All of you are gonna end up dead unless you get that head outta yer ass and listen to what I'm tellin' ya."

"I'm listening."

"When the girls are busy fixin' supper, I'll come find you. We can talk more, then."

Surely Josiah wasn't serious, was he? What in the hell could lie ahead that would force a man to resort to such a desperate, savage act? Levi couldn't imagine trading his sister for a buffalo hide. He wouldn't be able to live with himself if he did.

The twins stood before the fire, tending to a pot of stew. Though the cost of goods at the post was exorbitant, they splurged on beef, potatoes, and fresh vegetables to have a generous supper. Cash, they had, but the traders outside the fort had little use for it.

Levi scanned the camp for Lucy, and not seeing her, went around to the back of the wagon, taking stock of what was left of their meager possessions.

"Walk with me."

It wasn't until they reached the soapstone bank of the river that the mountain man finally spoke. He sat on a log, a bottle of whiskey in his hand, looking out at the flowing water to the rolling sage-covered vista beyond. "My wife was Shoshone. Her people call this river *Seeds-kee-dee-agie*. The Prairie Hen River. It's too late for you to turn back, and you ain't gonna make it over those mountains in time. That leaves you with two choices."

"What are they?"

"Bridger might take y'all in for the winter. You could set off again come spring. Would come at a hefty price, and one I don't think yer willin' to pay." He slugged down some whiskey, then exhaled with a sigh. "That's not what I see for you, though."

Almost afraid to hear the answer, Levi asked, "And the other?"

"Do you believe in visions?"

His head cocked, he took the bottle from the old man's hand.

"Dreams, Levi."

"Can't say that I do." And he drank, the fiery liquid burning a hole in his gullet.

"Follow the *Seeds-kee-dee-agie* north." Josiah squeezed his knee, and then he stood. "That's where you'll find it."

"Find what?"

He smiled. "Home."

Maizie's bakery was his first stop this morning. He'd ordered the cake weeks ago, lemon and a touch of elderflower cordial, frosted in a Swiss meringue buttercream, lavished with candy pearls and sweet flower petals in all the spring colors she loved.

Eighteen. It's not a big number, but it is an important one.

And Jake wanted everything to be perfect.

Armed with a bouquet of blooms and her favorite breakfast of scrambled eggs, maple sausage, and blueberry pancakes from the town diner, he knocked on the painted wood door.

Her hair in a loose pile on top of her head, dressed in grubby old sweatpants and a t-shirt three sizes too big, Emily's eyes opened wide when she saw him. "Jake?"

"I didn't wake you, did I?"

"Would you look at me?" She glanced down at her attire. "I'm a mess."

Oh, I'm lookin', and you're a beautiful sight.

"It's your birthday, sleepyhead." With his hands full, he couldn't sweep her into his arms like he wanted to and kissed the silky-soft skin of her cheek instead. "You wanna waste away the day in bed?"

Brow raised, the corners of her lips twitched.

"What are you doin' here this early, Jacob Gantry?" She finally grinned, and relieving him of the flowers, Emily took a sniff. "They're so pretty."

"I couldn't go to work without seein' my girl first to wish her a happy birthday, now could I?"

"You did that at midnight."

True. He could've been here in person when the clock struck twelve—any other man waiting as long as he had likely would have. But Jake wanted to give his brother one last evening alone with her. The coming year was going to be a difficult one for him.

"FaceTime don't count." He followed Emily into the sun-filled kitchen, setting down the bags from the diner. "And I wanted to have breakfast with you."

"You brought me Harry's?"

"Sure did."

"Blueberry pancakes?"

"It's your favorite, ain't it?"

"Oh, look," she squealed, opening the to-go container. "They're shaped like hearts."

Emily got up on her tiptoes. Soft lips sweeping across his jaw, he put his arms around her. It felt so good to hold her close that he never wanted to let go. Then he remembered, he didn't have to anymore.

His hands sliding up her back, Jake held Emily against him. He reached her nape, and fingers slipping into her hair, he pulled out the clip. As fragrant wildflower waves tumbled down in disarray, his lips brushed over hers. How he'd hungered for their delicate sweetness. How he'd longed to feel their pillowy softness touch his own.

Gazing into enchanting green eyes with her beautiful face in his hands, the organ in his chest beat a thunderous tattoo. Her lips parted. Jake brought her mouth to his. And the moment he kissed her only affirmed what he already knew.

He loved this woman.

One kiss. That's all it took. Fingers sinking into the back of his neck, Emily gripped him tighter and slung her legs around his waist. Jake sat her on top of the island, and, pressing in even closer, his cock lurched in his jeans. Sweet essence from her tongue infused him, imprinting her in every cell of his body. He breathed her in, her breath giving him life as if he'd only been a shell of himself until now.

This girl. This amazing, beautiful, wondrous soul was the reason Everleigh Clary and her sister never had a chance, why his college years left him empty, and aching, and wanting. Hit with the fact that Emily made him whole in a way he couldn't have comprehended before had him reeling.

It's only a kiss.

Still, Jake could keenly imagine how completely lost in her he'd be once he touched every square inch of skin. Tasted her. Made love to her.

Jesus, he was fucked.

This is what put Levi on his path.

Why Matthew Brooks risked it all.

It's what turned Tanner into a heartsick puppy and Kellan a feral dog.

Absolute love.

Just the thought of losing it could drive a man mad.

"I love you, Emily." With her face nuzzled against his neck, Jake's fingers sifted through her hair. "Happy birthday."

The hardest part of his test was over now.

But for Billy, it was just beginning.

Thirteen

H oly hell, this man could kiss.

Her knees growing weak, Emily locked her legs around Jake's waist and held on with her fucking life. It didn't matter it was her lips he was kissing, his tongue exploring her mouth, she could feel that kiss everywhere—from the hairs on her head to the tingle in her pink-painted toes. With those fireflies stirring in her belly, her nipples throbbed and her pussy ached.

Only hours ago, she cried for his brother.

Billy came by before supper.

He stood on her porch. Wisps of hair blew around his face, sunlight catching in the dark chocolate strands, while he curled the fingers of one hand around the pinky of the other and twisted on repeat.

"I was hoping I'd get to see you." *Before it's too late.* Her arms twining around his neck, Emily nestled into him and inhaled the soothing familiarity of his scent.

His muscles tensing, Billy squeezed her, but then released her far too quickly for her liking. "Ain't nothin' could keep me away. You know that."

"Still…" Emily tried to force a smile, rubbing her fingers over the place in his chest where his heart lay beating. "Come on in, and I'll fix you some supper."

"Can't stay, baby," he said, his lips pressed against her forehead. "Have to get over to the ranch for my shift, but I wanted to see you first and give you somethin'."

"What is it?"

With the barest hint of a smile, Billy tipped his chin at the old, wooden rocking chair beside him. A bright pink box sat upon it, tied with ribbons in a rainbow of colors. "You can open it after I go."

"Stay."

"I can't." He gazed into her eyes, tucking a lock of hair behind her ear. "But the calving'll be over soon. There's gonna be a bonfire next weekend to celebrate."

"It's so fucked up."

"What?" he asked, taking a step back.

I'll be eighteen in a matter of hours, and then I can't kiss you, or touch you, or anything…

"Last week we got a foot of snow, today it's all but gone, and next week they're throwing a damn party."

His mouth quivered and he began wringing his pinky again. "That means we can get started on your flowers soon."

She placed her hand on his to save his poor finger. "Yeah?"

"Yeah." And with her palm in his, Billy squeezed it. "Nothin's gonna change, Em."

Then why did everything feel as if it already had?

"C'mon, give me a kiss now." Billy smiled at her, but it didn't reach his eyes. They were gray, like Jake's, except for a dark ring that circled the irises. Had she ever told him how beautiful they were?

He dipped his head, and threading his fingers into her hair, gently held her cheeks. Their lips met, his tongue touching hers, and Emily's tears began to flow. Her hands roamed to every part of him she could reach, memorizing the feel of his hard, sculpted body beneath her fingertips.

Fuck these stupid rules. It isn't fair.

Who made them up, anyway?

All too soon, it was over. Still, her lips remained on his. They tasted salty, and whether the tears were hers or his, she couldn't say.

"I gotta go, babe."

Nooo.

Emily couldn't bear even the thought and held him tighter.

"Please, don't make this any harder."

One minute before midnight, Billy texted her.

Just remember I love you, baby. I'll be kissing you in my dreams.

Jake's text came a moment later.

She read it and cried herself to sleep.

But Emily wasn't sleeping now. She was wide awake. And this was not a dream. With her ass planted on the granite-topped island, her legs squeezing his like a vise, Jake was here in her kitchen, kissing her.

She'd dreamt of it all of her life. Loving him and Billy. Being loved by them. So, why did she suddenly feel out of sorts, as if enjoying the kisses of one brother made her disloyal somehow to the other?

With her heart splintered into two jagged pieces, she wondered if her mom had ever felt like this. Grams? Arien? Of all of them, her step-cousin would best understand.

After a breakfast of kisses and heart-shaped blueberry

pancakes, Jake left for work and Emily left for her uncle's house to pay Arien a much-needed visit.

She walked right in and ran straight up the stairs to the room across the hall from Kellan's. Arien looked up from her laptop, and a smile lighting her pretty face, she patted the space on the bed beside her. "Happy birthday, Ems. You're early. Grams isn't even here yet, and she's helping me do the cooking."

Sunday dinner at the ranch.

"That's okay." Emily grabbed her cousin's hand, kissed it, then held it at her side.

"Tanner and Kellan are still out mucking around with the cows, or whatever it is they do," she said with a giggle. "And I haven't seen Billy or Jake yet today, if that's what you're wondering."

"That's not it." Exhaling with a sigh, Emily stared out the window. "I saw Jake this morning."

"Eek," Arien squealed, clapping like she'd won tickets to see a Taylor Swift concert or something. "He kissed you, didn't he? Was it wonderful?"

Her gaze went from the paddock outside the window to her cousin.

"That's a silly question, huh? Course, it was."

"Mmhm, it couldn't have been more perfect, but..." Emily paused to swallow. Was it awful of her to even say it?

"But?"

"I feel...I dunno...guilty?" She drew her knees up, hoping to relieve the tightness in her chest, and returned her gaze to the window. "It's like I'm betraying Billy. Trading one brother for the other."

"It's no such thing, Ems." Arien got in her face, forcing Emily to look at her. "You're a triad."

"You ever feel like that?"

"Torn in two? Yeah, all the time." Her lip disappeared behind her teeth as she slowly nodded. "But not between Kellan and Tanner. It's my heart and my head that's the problem. Because what feels right to me, the rest of the world sees as wrong. Maybe if I wasn't an outsider, I wouldn't feel like such a whore, and with my brothers to boot."

"Stepbrothers." *Enough with that shit.* Emily heaved a sigh. "Chrissakes, you didn't even know 'em six months ago, and you're *not* a whore, so don't you dare think like that."

"She's right." Kellan poked his head inside the door.

Tanner came in right behind him. "You're just ours, little sister."

"How long have y'all been out there eavesdroppin'?"

Kellan winked at her, strolling across the room like he owned it, and claimed the other spot next to Arien on the bed. "I know it sucks, Ems. It can feel like forever, but y'all are favored. You *will* get through this test, and that's all this is."

He stopped talking long enough to kiss his stepsister, his hand snaking beneath her shirt to fondle her breast. "It's your time to know Jake."

"I do know him."

"Not like you know Billy," he countered, and stretching his arm out behind Arien, Kellan poked her on the shoulder. "And I ain't talkin' about his dick here, neither."

"Jesus, Kellan." Arien smacked him.

"Hush now, baby cakes. It's all right." He took Arien's hand, and holding it to his chest, leaned forward toward Emily. "You deserve to know all of him. He deserves to know all of you, too. Look inside every part of that man of yours—mind, body, and soul. What are his dreams? His fears? His strengths? What's his weakness? See, you and Billy have already done all that. Jake loves you, Ems, and he's been waitin' for you a helluva long time. He'll tell you everything there is to know if you listen."

Wow!

All this coming from a man who typically spoke in grunts and one-syllable words, Emily took what he said to heart. "Since when did you become Yoda?"

"Heh." Kellan shrugged, his cheeks turning pink.

"I love y'all," she said, climbing over Arien to kiss him. "I should get goin' before Grams gets here and make myself pretty for my birthday dinner—act all surprised and shit."

"Yeah, ya brat, you should. C'mon, I'll walk you out to the car." He got up to go with her, Tanner taking his place by Arien on the bed. Kellan paused, tracing his finger up the sole of her foot, then said, his voice husky, "And don't you go nowhere."

"You happy, Kel?" Emily asked once they were outside.

"Arien's here. I'm happy." His head bobbed, blond hair falling in his eyes, but as much as he tried to, Kellan couldn't contain his grin. "You know I love ya, right?"

"I love you, too, even though you can be a real motherfucker sometimes."

"Auntie Kim needs to wash that mouth of yours." He chuckled, opening up her Mustang. "Look, I know it's hard, but nothin' worth havin' comes easy."

"Loving them *is* easy." She got in. "It's the stupid rules that are hard."

"I know." He held onto the roof, hanging his head inside the window. "And more so for Billy than anyone. So, when Jake is kissin' on you, make sure Billy knows how much you love him, that you yearn for him too, and not just with your words."

"I can't touch him. They're all I've got."

He backed out of the car and winked. "There's ways of touchin' without touchin'."

"So I hear." Emily giggled, then chewed on her lip. "Can I say something?"

"Could I stop you?"

"Doubt it." Shielding her eyes from the glare of the sun, she angled her head to look up at him. "I see you, Kellan Brooks, and I know you're not an asshole. You're just scared. Arien loves you, so maybe take your own advice. You can trust that she won't hurt you. Let her in."

"I'm tryin'."

"I know." Emily turned on the ignition. "Nothin' worth havin' comes easy, right?"

"Right." He sent her off with a knock on the Mustang's hood. "Happy birthday, Ems."

The gentle breeze blowing through the trees almost felt too warm. It lifted the ends of her hair, its sweet floral scent perfuming the air as he kissed her. Jake grasped the back of Emily's thighs, and urging her legs to straddle his waist, he carried her around the corner of the barn. He didn't need an audience. Hidden from the fire's light and prying eyes, here in the shadows, he held her against the decaying clapboard, burning to know the feel of her skin beneath his fingers.

A low, sweet sound, the coo of a dove, flowed from Emily's lips. She pulled on his hair, tethering herself to him, as her legs slipped from his hips. Jake wedged his knee between her thighs to catch her. Damp silk on worn denim.

He kissed his way along her jaw and down her neck, licking the salt from her pulse as he eased the straps from her shoulders. Soft, pliant flesh, embellished by lace, molded to fit in his palm. Jake squeezed, and pushing the offending fabric away, caressed her nipple with his thumb.

With a breathy gasp upon his cheek, she squeaked.

Her fingers gripping the hair at his nape, Emily pressed her weight against his leg that held her. His lips on her skin, he smiled, and dipping his head, Jake took that nipple in his mouth. One hand splayed on her back, the other at her breast, he suckled. He licked, and laved, and sucked, and nipped, while soft coos became whimpers and she rocked herself on his knee, seeking friction.

"You okay, Billy?" It was Arien's voice, wafting outside, through slats of thin, worn wood.

Fuck.

His brother. Her cousins. Their friends. They were all in there, mere inches separating them, on the other side of the wall.

Still, no one knew they were out here.

Kneading the fleshy pillow of her breast, Jake sucked on her nipple harder.

"Yeah, babes. This too shall pass, right?"

She moaned. Or perhaps groaned. Was there anguish in the sound he heard?

Maybe not.

Because Emily kept on rocking and panting, her fingers holding onto his hair. He hadn't learned her body yet, the noises she made, or all her tells.

Oh, but I'm going to, dammit.

And he'd learn it well.

Jake would come to know her better than she knew herself.

"One year…"

He focused on Emily, encouraging her to come while tuning out the voices. Her arousal seeped through his jeans. His saliva saturated the lace, her nipple swollen beneath his tongue.

"Jake." His name spilling from her throat, she sagged, weightless, against his chest.

He held her head on his shoulder, and listening to her breathe, placed a soft kiss on her lips.

"A man who can't be with the woman he loves is missing a piece of his soul, Arien. I feel like I'm dyin'."

Her breath catching, Emily stiffened in his arms. "Billy?"

Somewhere in the distance, lightning rolled across the sky. Woodsmoke mingled with the smell of a coming storm.

Jake just held her tighter.

And she raised her head, a tear sliding down her cheek.

Fourteen

There's something to be said for the smell of freshly cut wood, its oils, and sap releasing their aromatic particles into the air. Earthy and warm, the scent reminded him of Christmas or a ride through an evergreen forest. If Billy didn't love working with the horses so much, he supposed he could be quite content building houses.

He put down his nail gun and sat in what would one day be their living room. They'd made darn good progress in the five weeks since the foundation was poured. The engineers constructed the bridge. Last weekend, he and Jake finished the subfloor. With any luck, they'd have exterior walls going up today, and that stack of lumber would start looking like a house.

Billy leaned back on his elbows and listened to the soothing gurgle of the creek. The orange glow of the rising sun kissed the mountain, evoking feelings of warmth and optimism, and inspiring dreams of possibilities yet to come.

New beginnings.

Like a movie playing in his mind, he could see it. Emily dancing in the kitchen, their children at her feet. Jake transcribing old letters in a chair by the fire. Chaser frolicking in the pasture. A dog. A garden. His family. His home. The promise of a new day filled with wonder and joy.

I best get off my ass, then. Time's a wastin'.

The last weekend of May, Brookside's cookout was taking place this afternoon. Billy looked forward to it every year. He and Jake promised Emily they'd meet her there at twelve, and that left them less than six hours to get some work done today.

Billy picked himself up from the floor. Measuring sixteen-inch intervals on lengths of Douglas fir, he made marks for the studs, while Jake cut them. Then, together, they fastened the studs to the plates with framing nails.

With his elbows resting on his knees, his brother sat on his haunches opposite him. "Should we put the sheathing on now, before we raise the wall?"

"We could. It'll be a helluva lot easier to attach here on the ground." He glanced over at the pallet of plywood sheets. Each one weighed a good seventy pounds. "But then it's gonna be a helluva lot harder to lift the wall into place."

"I reckon between the two of us, we've got the muscle to do it." Clearly, Jake overestimated their capabilities. "And if it's too heavy, I'm sure Tanner and Kellan will give us a hand."

With a half-hearted snicker, he said, more to himself than his brother, "We're gonna need Archer, too."

"Think we can get four walls done this morning?"

"Sure do." Because with each wall that went up and every stone set in place, Billy was one step closer to seeing his vision come to fruition, and not just the house, but Emily as their wife.

"Let's knock 'em out, then, brother."

And they did. Working alongside his brother, every nail he drove, and each piece of wood he cut, gave him a sense of purpose.

▲

Billy often wondered how the ones who came before them had built such an incredible place, especially now that he was building a home of his own. Long before power tools, electricity, and big box stores came along, the only resources the Brookside settlers had were those the mountain provided them. With timber and rock painstakingly hewn by hand, they created this idyllic Eden he was fortunate enough to call home.

From the highway, an unmarked five-mile drive led to their half-million acres, and a coded gate. Once inside it, a right-hand turn went farther up the mountain to the ranch and left went into town. With green space at its center, shops lined either side of the square. Behind the old bunkhouse, which now housed the school, a clear, running stream bordered the far end.

Freshly showered after this morning's labor, Billy walked over to the square with his brother. With many of the structures built in the 19th century, he marveled at the town with a renewed appreciation. They reached the crowded green, and he hurried his steps when he saw her.

Chestnut hair framing her beautiful face, Emily sat waiting on a blanket in a pretty white dress, Arien, her mom, and the rest of the Brooks family surrounding her. She glanced up; her smile radiant, the moment she spotted him and Jake amongst the townsfolk. God, he loved her. Every fond memory he had was tied to this girl, from taking her for a ride on the handlebars of his new ten-speed bike to sharing their first kiss over a glass of Grams' lemonade. Just fifteen, he remembered being nervous, wondering if there was food stuck in his teeth, his breath stank like barbecue, or that he'd mess it up somehow.

But I didn't.

Two years had flown by since then, and hopefully, so would the next. Billy would push through it because a lifetime of kissing Emily was worth it.

"There's my handsome cowboy." She took his hand, and pulling him down to sit beside her, Emily kissed his cheek. "I missed you."

He saw her only yesterday, but he'd take it—the sentiment and the kiss.

"How's my girl?"

"Fine, now." She held onto his hand and took his brother's with the other. "Both of my boys are here."

Long hair curtaining his face, Jake dipped his head to kiss her. On the lips. Billy turned his head, and holding her hand in his lap, aimed his gaze at anything but them. Matthew Brooks doted on his very pregnant wife, rubbing her feet. She reclined in a lawn chair, her hand resting atop her enormous belly. Tanner snoozed on Arien's lap, his hat covering most of his face, while she combed the hair out of Kellan's eyes with her fingers. Her back to them all, Miss Kim rifled through a cooler, but Grams had her eyes right on him.

With her head tilted to the side, and her smile knowing, Melinda Brooks gazed upon him kindly. Emily's grandmother, and his teacher in first grade, she'd known him his entire life. "Did you have a nice birthday, Billy?"

"Yes, ma'am, I did." He blew out seventeen candles on his cake just two days before. "Thank you for the shirt and the cookies you sent with Em. Your chocolate chip cookies are my favorite."

"Of course, dear." And she winked. "I'll make sure I give Emily the recipe."

Billy looked at her then.

Beaming at him, Emily held onto his arm and laid her head

on his shoulder. "I love you, Billy. I'll bake 'em for you every day if you want."

I don't want no damn cookies, just you.

He let his fingers slip through her wavy locks. "I love you, too."

The mouth-watering smell of barbecue wafting from the smokers and grills parked in front of the square had Billy's stomach talking to him. In a friendly competition, Harry Coulter, who ran the diner, and Charlie Tyndall, their ranch foreman, and whose great-grandfather emigrated on the trail west from Texas, attempted to outdo each other every year. One of them claimed bragging rights, but it was the rest of them who reaped the real reward. Best damn barbecue on the planet, bar none.

Everyone here contributed to the shindig in one way or another. The meat came from the ranch, some folks brought desserts or made sides, and others organized fireworks and activities for the kids. Share the work and share the wealth. They shared the fun, too. That was the Brookside way of doing things.

"I'm dang near starvin'," Tanner grumbled, raising his head from Arien's lap. "Is it chowtime yet?"

"You're always starving." Arien took his hat and put it on her head.

His face breaking into a grin, he waggled his brows. "You know what that means, don't ya, little sister?"

"Cut the shit, Tanner." Kellan flicked the hat off Arien's head.

Her butter-blonde curls shaking, Grams hid a chuckle behind her hand. "I see folks lining up, honey."

"About damn time. C'mon, Billy, let's go get us some of that barbecue." Tanner picked up his hat, and shooting his brother a look, put it back on his head. "Don't get up now. We'll bring plates back for y'all."

By the time they got over there, the line was a mile long, figuratively speaking. It went all the way to Aunt Lilly's dress shop, though.

"Billy-boy, where's that head of yours at?" From behind, Tanner nudged him. "Line's movin'."

"Sorry, my mind went somewhere else, I guess." After moving ahead, Billy turned around. "Hey, I was wonderin'…think you and Kel can help us raise some walls tomorrow?"

"Happy to."

"Great, thanks." Just as he'd predicted, he and Jake hadn't been able to budge them at all. "I'm gonna ask Griffin, too."

"Heh, good luck with that, my dude." Tanner hitched his thumb out toward the green, where it appeared Archer was playing referee to the spitfire Lewis sisters. "Betcha between graduation and the wedding, Shiloh and Cassie got the poor guy runnin' round in circles."

"Serves him right." Griffin knew what he was in for with those two. Oil and vinegar, they were. Still, he loved them a heck of a lot, and with their wedding less than a couple of weeks away, his wait was almost over. "Lucky bastard."

"And you ain't?"

"I am." Billy blew out a breath and moved up in the line. "Just don't feel like it much right now."

"Hey." Tanner turned him around. "Chrissakes, stop it, will ya? At least you know there's gonna be a weddin'."

On Wednesday, after I turn eighteen. The May 29th date was set in stone.

"Three hundred and sixty-seven days from today."

Yeah, he was counting them.

"See? Lucky." Then he leaned in close to his ear. "Folks keep askin' when I'm gonna announce mine."

"Go on and do it, then."

They'd reached the front of the line.

"Hey there, Mrs. Coulter. Don't you look extra pretty today?" And he laid one of his smiles on her. Tanner was such a charmer. That must be why all the ladies loved him. "Can you put ten plates together for me—a little of everything?"

"Go on with you now." Harry's wife held her hands to her cheeks, trying to hold back the blush. She failed. "Wait over there by the beer keg. I'll bring it to ya."

"Mr. Coulter's such a lucky man. Thank you, kindly." He kissed her hand, then turned back to him and said, "Can't announce nothin' 'til we know what Arien's fixin' to do, and we don't."

"She hasn't talked about goin' back to Denver in a while." When Arien first got here, it was all she ever talked about.

"A letter from UC came for her a few weeks back."

Oh. Shit.

"She told me herself she hasn't decided yet."

"Kel know that?"

"No, and I ain't tellin' him, neither." He lifted his chin toward where Kellan and Arien sat together on the lawn. "Just look at 'em, will ya? They've gotten so close lately. Makes my heart happy to see it. If my brother found out, she was still thinkin' about leavin', he'd shut her out again, and I can't let that happen."

"Arien loves y'all, Tanner."

"We love her."

Billy could hear the anguish in his voice and clasped his shoulder. "Your father saw it, and he's never been wrong, so don't worry none. Yer dream girl ain't goin' nowhere."

"Oh, I know she ain't." Tanner took a step back, and cocking his head, an odd expression came over his face. He almost looked angry. "Because I won't let that happen, either."

Mrs. Coulter came with the food, and in an instant, it was gone. "I fixed y'all a *lot* of everything. I know how much you boys can eat. There's an extra slice of chocolate cake in there for your stepmama, too."

"Thank you, ma'am." Billy tipped his chin, carefully placing bags of food and plates on Tanner's arm. "Got it, bro?"

"Yeah."

Billy wasn't sure how, but they made it back to their spot on the green without spilling or dropping a thing, and with blankets and lawn chairs to weave through, that was no easy feat. As a rule, cowboys are not dainty. He and Tanner had just finished passing out the food when he looked up to see his dad deep in conversation with Matthew Brooks. His mom and Justin, his arm around her as if he was holding her up, stood off to the side.

Concerned, he rushed over to her, Jake and Emily coming along behind him. "Ma, are you all right?"

"I'm fine, sweetie." Carrie leaned in to kiss his cheek, her brother holding her steady. "It's just a headache."

"You should go home and lie down, Mama." Jake stepped in and held her on the other side.

"She's going. She's been dizzy, too." Justin said with a toss of his silvery-blond mane. "A darkened room, some aspirin, and a cool glass of tea will have her feeling better in no time."

She reached up to smooth Jake's hair. "I had to see my boys first."

"Sorry, we can't stay." His father came over and pulled him into a hug. "Your mama's not feeling well."

"Is she gonna be okay?" Billy couldn't recall his mother ever being sick. Not once. Not even a cold.

Victor patted his shoulder. "Nothing to worry about. She'll be just fine, son."

He hugged his brother and Emily, and then they were gone.

"Something ain't right, Jake."

"What do you mean?"

"With Mom." Fuck's sake, was he the only one who saw it? "Have you ever known her to be sick?"

"She's not sick, Billy." Jake slung an arm around his neck. "You heard her. She has a headache."

"It could be a migraine." Emily took his hand and held it in both of hers. "They can make you dizzy. Grams gets them sometimes."

Maybe.

He was overreacting, wasn't he?

Billy kissed her cheek. "Yeah, I'm sure you're right."

Fifteen

Today was going to be a wonderful and beautiful day.

She just knew it.

Emily slipped into her new pretty dress of soft, flowy cotton. Short and sassy, with criss-cross straps, tiered ruffles, a tie-back waist, and a bustier bodice, the delicate floral was ideal to wear to the Archer wedding. She studied her reflection in the mirror. *Jake and Billy'll like it, too.*

High school was behind her. A week ago, she got a new baby cousin, and now, two of her very best friends were about to get married. Life was sure moving fast.

Except for her.

It would be another year before it was her turn to walk to the stones, and as far as Emily was concerned, that's when the best part of her life would begin. Not that she didn't have other things to look forward to, or occupy her time with until then. She did. Besides planning a wedding of her own, she had Ruby to ride, Arien to hang around with, and classes to take in the fall—to be a teacher someday, like Grams.

Exhaling with a sigh, she sat upon the tufted velvet stool, put on the cream-colored boots she wore to graduation, and pulled the sock curler from her hair. She'd seen a tutorial for the heatless method online some months ago, and after seeing how fabulous the results were, had been using it ever since. Who cared if she looked ridiculous when she went to bed, right? Her boys were as obsessed with her hair as she was with theirs. One of them, if not both, always had their fingers in it, so it was well worth the effort.

"Emily, honey, are you ready yet?" Her mother's sweet voice echoed down the hall. "We don't wanna be late."

"Yeah, Mama." Hurriedly, she ran a brush through her hair and dabbed some gloss on her lips. "I'm comin'."

Most Brookside weddings were held outdoors at a parents' home unless they live in the center of town. In that case, the joyous occasion took place on the green or in a picturesque field along the mountain's stream. No one ever missed a wedding here, or any other event, for that matter. The true definition of an extended family, in good times and in bad, this community always came together, so plenty of space was required.

Since their fathers were both attorneys with an office in Dubois, and also sat on the town council, Shiloh and Cassandra Lewis lived in a big, beautiful house a couple of streets over from the school. And while their mother kept a lovely garden, the backyard wasn't nearly large enough to accommodate the twelve hundred people who'd be coming. Fortunately for them, on the outskirts of Brookside, Griffin's parents' home could.

Magical. It's the only word she could come up with to describe it. The mountainscape provided a majestic backdrop. Rows of white chairs on either side of a lantern-lit aisle led to the triangle of stones, a woodpile at its center. Translucent draping. Flowers of ecru, cream, and white. Shiloh and her sister may have fought each other tooth and nail over every last detail, but the end result was positively stunning.

"*Michante*, you can make a man forget he needs to breathe." Jake swept her hair to the side, his lips brushing the skin beneath her ear. "You look beautiful."

"You sure do." Billy took her hand and kissed her fingers.

Her chest was close to bursting. Warmth spread through her. These brothers adored her so. Emily glanced at Arien, taking her seat with Tanner and Kellan, praying she'd realize just how amazing their love could be.

Everything that comes in threes is perfect, sweet cousin. You'll see.

With a kiss to Billy's cheek, she held onto his hand, and taking Jake's with the other, they slid into their row of white chairs, following Victor and Carrie Gantry, her mom, and Justin Sawyer.

In a dress of the palest mint, the ends of her honeyed brown hair floating in the breeze, Kimberly quietly sat in between Jake and Justin. A widow at the tender age of twenty-four, she'd never re-married, though Emily imagined that would prove difficult around here. Still, her mama was far too young, and much too beautiful, to spend the rest of her life in that house all alone.

She twirled the emerald-cut diamond around her finger, waiting for the ceremony to begin. Noticing, Billy placed his hand on hers to quell her fidgeting. His silvery-gray eyes shimmered in the light of the setting sun, and he winked at her, the corner of his perfect lips lifting, as if he knew exactly what she was thinking.

Our day is coming, my love.

Jake felt it, too, the anticipation of everything yet to be. His arm came around her shoulders, and fingering the strap of her pretty new dress, he pressed a kiss to her temple.

Griffin stood at the stones.

Together with their parents, Shiloh and Cassie came down the aisle to meet him there. Sheer tulle and lace. The ethereal, breathtaking gowns they wore only enhanced their beauty.

Turning to Arien, Emily sighed. "Miss Lilly creates the most beautiful dresses."

She couldn't wait to see herself wearing her own.

The trinity ceremony is a sight to behold. Their hands cut, joined, and bound together, the three of them became one. And as they lit the fire in the center of the stones, Emily watched its flames soar into a darkening amethyst sky.

"That's it, they're hitched," she heard Kellan say behind her. "C'mon, I need a beer."

What you need, cousin, is a swift kick in the ass.

Ever since the bonfire party, when Kellan found out his stepsister hadn't entirely given up on her dream of going back to Denver, he'd been pricklier than usual. Unable to cope with the thought of her leaving him, he stormed off and never came back. Jake had to drive Tanner and Arien home.

After dinner, champagne, and a slice of Maizie's vanilla buttercream cake, Emily danced in the arms of the two men who loved her. Pressed to her back, Billy's head lay on her shoulder, the cock in his pants teasing at the wisp of silk beneath her dress. She lifted her gaze to Jake. His lips quirked up, and grabbing his brother by the belt loops, he pulled her to him even closer.

Fuck, I'm in so much trouble.

One at her front, the other from behind, the brothers held her tight between them.

Pulling on the end of his braid, Emily brought Jake's lips down to hers, and with Billy's face nuzzled against her neck, she kissed him.

The music all but faded away.

Her feet stopped moving.

She tasted the whiskey on Jacob's tongue while Billy tasted salt from her skin. And when their kiss ended, Emily raised her head and smiled, because it felt right, and perfect, and beautiful.

"Looks like they made up." Billy softly chuckled.

Their eyes only on each other, Kellan and Arien swayed together on the dance floor.

"Yeah, I knew they would." And giggling, she kissed him on the cheek. "I could've told him she wasn't goin' anywhere. She threw her award letter in the trash."

"Why didn't you?" Jake asked.

"You told me not to interfere," Emily said with a shrug, her finger poking at his chest. "Besides, why spoil all the fun? I kinda like watchin' it all play out."

Then, Tanner came out to the floor, but it wasn't because he wanted a dance. One minute, the three of them were talking, and the next, they went running toward Kellan's truck.

What the hell?

But before Emily could get the words out of her mouth, her mother came rushing at them on the dance floor. "We have to get over to the ranch. Now." Choking on the air she was breathing, she turned to Jake. "Your father's already left."

"What's going on, Mama?"

Her beautiful face crumpled. "Something terrible's happened."

"You're scaring me, now."

"It's Jennifer…" And she sobbed.

No, no, no, no, no. Please, don't say it.

"She's dead."

Emily couldn't explain it.

Because Christ, what are the fucking odds?

Three women were dead within days of giving birth to her uncle's sons.

Amanda and Heather died from natural causes, they said. A weak heart or some such shit. She didn't buy it. Not anymore. Jennifer's death was no coincidence.

"How the fuck could this happen, Jake?"

"I don't know." His hand dropped from the steering wheel to her knee, and he squeezed it.

The closer they got to the house, the more it felt like she was going to vomit.

How did Jennifer die? Did she stumble down the stairs and break her neck? Fall asleep in the bathtub and drown? Her mother hadn't said. And, fuck, what about the baby? Only a week old, she hadn't mentioned poor Benjamin at all.

"Hurry, Jake." Champagne churning in her stomach, Emily held a hand up to her mouth. "I think I'm gonna be sick."

"Slow breaths, Em." Billy rubbed her tummy. "We're almost there."

A nightmare.

That's what this was.

A horrible B flick she didn't want any part of.

Emily got out of the truck to see Arien running toward the trees, Kellan chasing after her, and Tanner holding up a sobbing Grams, the baby in her arms.

He's okay.

With a sigh of relief, she wiped the tears from her face.

Justin and her mother pulled in right behind them. They ran past her, going straight inside the house.

Cautiously, she went up the porch steps, and that's when she heard it. The sound of suffering. Agony. A deafening, plaintive wail coming from the strongest man, and the only father she'd ever known. "Uncle Matty?"

Grams ceased her sobbing long enough to look at her, then turning to Jake, she said, "She's on the sofa. At first, we thought she was just sleeping. Your father is giving him something."

Jennifer did look like she was asleep. Kind of.

Tanner's voice boomed through the door. "He's got her."

It all moved quickly after that.

Kellan carried Arien to his room, dressed her in his t-shirt, and laid her on his bed.

He held her, wiping her tears as his own rolled down his face. Emily had never known her cousin to shed one.

God, Arien, I'm so fucking sorry, but I hope you can see how much this man loves you. Tanner. How much we all love you.

Victor pulled a syringe from his pocket. Within minutes, she was out.

The coroner's van came and went.

And their world as they knew it went with it.

At two weeks old, Benjamin attended his mama's funeral. A mama he'd never have the chance to know. His sister was a mother to him now.

Every day, Emily, Grams, and Kim went to the house to help however they could. Fending off visits from well-meaning neighbors. Making sure they got food in their bellies. Laundry and dishes. But it was Arien who cared for the baby.

"Leave her to it, Tanner."

"That's all she does, Auntie. If it weren't for Benjie, she'd never get out of bed."

"Arien just needs time. Trust me, everything's gonna be okay."

But Emily wasn't so sure.

Her uncle walked around like a zombie, though hiding away upstairs or in his office, they hardly saw him at all.

The coroner ruled her cause of death undetermined. No one could say how Jennifer died.

"It's a curse," Matthew said.

Maybe it was.

Maybe the mountain was angry.

Maybe he lost favor for marrying Jennifer as everyone else had feared.

Nope, I don't think so.

Someone must've done something bad to Jennifer, someone evil, and that meant whoever hurt her, hurt Amanda and Heather, too.

Emily just couldn't imagine who that someone might be.

She looked over at Arien, her once vibrant eyes now vacant, rocking the baby in a chair. With a lot of love, somehow, they'd all see her through.

One day, you'll be happy again, sweetie, I promise.

It was supposed to be a most wonderful, beautiful day.

And it was.

Until someone turned everything to shit.

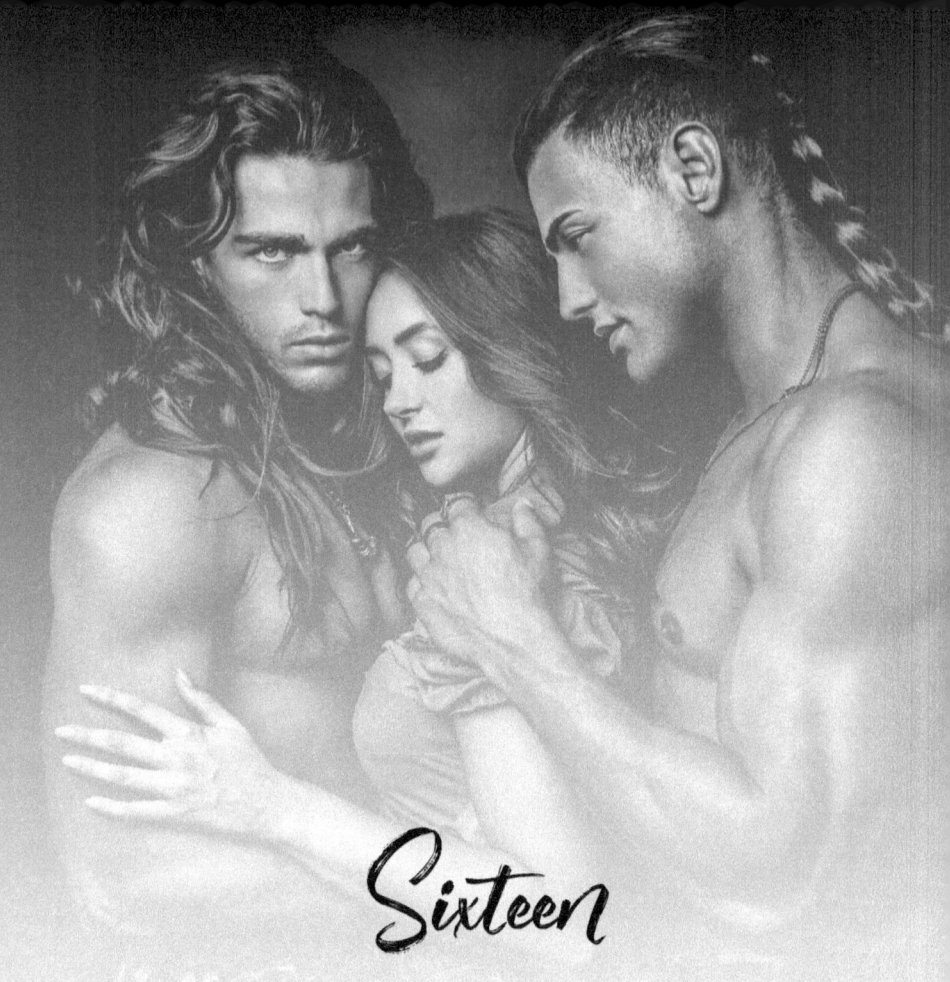

Sixteen

Levi sat on that log long after Walker left him. He sipped his whiskey, watching the sun descend upon the snow-capped peaks. Wind swept through the valley, a chill settling deep inside his bones. *Follow the river.* The old man was right, goddammit. And with his path laid out in front of him, he stood. He only prayed it was the right one.

"Where in tarnation have you been, Levi Gantry?" With her hands on her hips, Mary Alice let out a loud sigh. "We've been holding supper for you."

"Sorry, I was talking with Josiah. Lost track of time."

She glanced across the camp to where Walker sat eating with

his daughters, then lowered her gaze to the bottle in his fingers, and with a lift of her brow, gave him a pointed look.

"The stew sure smells good," he said to appease her. "Where's Eli?"

"I'll go and fetch him." Victoria jumped up from a rickety wood stool at the mention of his name.

"Do that."

At supper, Elizabeth sat on Victoria's lap, a bowl of stew cradled in hers. Eli gazed at the elder twin, flush darkening his cheekbones, while he sopped up gravy with a chunk of fresh-baked bread they'd gotten at the fort. If Levi didn't know better, which he did, he'd swear the man was smitten with his sister. "This is a mighty fine supper, Victoria. Mighty fine."

"But I didn't—"

"Would you imagine that? I managed to fix a meal without burning it." Her tone haughty, Mary Alice set Elijah straight and thumbed her nose at Levi. "And without a proper stove, too."

"Practice," he said with a wink, ignoring her petulance. "Didn't I tell you?"

She folded her arms across her chest with a harrumph.

Levi turned his attention to Eli. "After supper, I need you to help me round up all the families. Me and Walker need to talk to 'em."

"Why?"

"We're at a crossroads here, good brother." *Literally and figuratively.* Levi set his bowl down, pursing his lips to the side. "This is where every man has to decide whether to continue on to California, Oregon, or spend winter here and pick up again come spring."

"We are going to California," Mary Alice insisted, kicking her foot at the ground. "Papa said so."

"Well, father isn't here anymore, is he?"

"I will *not* stay here, Levi. Do you hear me?"

"And I will not risk losing *you*," he shouted, holding onto her shoulders. Levi looked into her innocent, doll-like eyes and calmed his voice. "Or your sister. We've lost far too much already."

Their mother. Their Father. Caleb. Elijah's parents and his sister, too.

"What are you saying, brother?"

"It's too late, Victoria." He gazed at her, the child on her lap, as if he'd failed them somehow, his hands falling away from her twin. "We'll never make it through the mountains."

"So, we're staying?" Elijah asked.

"No."

"Where are we going, then?" Her lip trembling, Mary Alice placed her hand in his.

He squeezed it. "Home."

Only Levi couldn't tell them exactly where that was yet. Following the Prairie Hen north was the only workable option. With winter looming, he couldn't risk taking them into the Rockies, and the trading post was no place for young Elizabeth and his sisters. They understood that. Elijah did, too.

The man he called brother came to his side. "You reckon we'll be able to convince the others?"

"Not even gonna try," Levi said, pushing the hair out of his face. "All we can do is tell 'em what their choices are. Whichever road they choose is up to them."

He just nodded.

"One more thing." And he hooked his arm around Elijah's neck. "Lucy is coming with us. I'm going to ask Josiah for her hand."

Mary Alice gasped.

Looking at her twin, Victoria grinned. "Told you so."

"Is that all right with you, little sister?"

"Well, I suppose so." She pretended to mull it over for a

moment, then a smile came over her face and she giggled. "Lucy is a far better cook than I'll ever be."

The head of every family in their party gathered around the campfire. Elijah opened a bottle of whiskey and passed it to Archer. Levi handed a second bottle to Lewis while he and Walker told it to them straight.

"I say we keep goin'," George Dalton said. "We got another month, maybe two, before the snow comes."

"Heh." Walker took the bottle from Lewis, and after downing a swig, he wiped off his mouth on the back of his hand. "That's what the Donner folks said, too, and y'all know what happened to them, don't ya?"

"Can't say that I do."

"A damn tragedy, George, that's what." With a shake of his head, he passed the bottle to Dalton. "Just last year, they got caught in an early storm up in the Sierra Nevada. Thirty-nine souls perished, and the ones who didn't? Well, rumor has it they had to eat the flesh of the dead to stay alive."

"Don't believe it." He waved Josiah off and raised the whiskey to his lips. "I still say we keep goin'."

"If that's what you wanna do, ain't no one gonna stop you." With a half-hearted shrug, Walker looked away, his gaze flitting from one man to another. "Y'all are gonna have to decide for yourselves. Sleep on it. Tomorrow you can rest, but unless you plan to make arrangements with Bridger to shelter here, you'd be wise to get movin' by the following morning."

Dalton turned from the fire with a nod, taking the bottle of whiskey with him.

Then, one by one, the others got up and followed.

Levi cast his glance to Lucy, who sat over by the wagons with Fallon, Elizabeth, and his sisters, and, taking in a lungful of courage, he tapped on Walker's shoulder. "There's something I need to ask you."

"Go on, then. Ask."

"I find myself in love with your daughter, sir."

"I know." Cracking a grin, he picked up the bottle Archer had left and tipped it into his mouth.

"I want to take her with me." Levi took the whiskey from his hand and set it down. "So, I'd like your permission to ask her to be my wife."

"Yup, seen it comin'." Walker bent his neck back, and gazing skyward, he closed his eyes. "You have my blessing, young man, but know, you have to take her sister, too."

It never occurred to him that Lucy and Fallon wouldn't want to be separated. Perhaps it should have. But was their father prepared to say his farewells to them both? Because it was likely that once they left this place, they'd never set eyes on each other again, and the mountain man would be all alone.

"But what about you, Josiah?"

"Never mind me." His golden eyes glowing in the firelight, he sat back on an elbow and held the bottle poised at his lips. "I'm an old man, Levi. Raised 'em as best I could. I'll be able to rest easy knowin' my girls will be cared for, settled, and loved. This ain't no kinda life for 'em."

That he understood. It's what Levi wanted for his sisters, wasn't it? He only hoped that when the time came to let them go, he'd prove to be as selfless.

"Of course." He patted Josiah's shoulder, offering some comfort. "Fallon is welcome to come with us, if that's what she wishes."

"She does." And he drank. "My daughters will favor you with many sons."

Daughters?

"Sir?"

"You heard me right. Did you mistake my meaning?" Laughter bellowing from his throat, Walker put the bottle in his hand. "Judgin' by that look on your face, I reckon you did. See, if you want my Lucy as your wife, then you'll be weddin' my Fallon, too."

Every person who's ever been, whether living or dead, is connected to everyone else. The ripple effect of their existence, their contribution on this earth, great or small, indelibly marks it. Jennifer Brogan Brooks might not have been among them for very long, but her absence was keenly felt. Forever woven into the rich tapestry of their story. Life in Brookside would never be quite the same, but it would go on, all of them fortunate to have known her.

The circumstances of her tragic demise remained a mystery. She was only thirty-six, yet the coroner ruled that since there were no indications of foul play, her death was because of an unknown natural cause. In the two months since Jennifer's passing, folks hadn't stopped talking about Matthew's curse and the similarities in the deaths of his three wives. And who could blame them?

Because Jake wondered, too. He had his theories, but kept them to himself. What good would it do to voice them? The only thing that mattered now was being there for Arien, Matthew, and his sons, helping them out at the ranch, and giving them whatever they needed to heal.

In summers past, on any other pleasant Sunday morning, Jake, his brother, Tanner, and Kellan would saddle up the horses and ride out to the lake to go fishing. Bring home the trout they caught for supper. He missed those days. They didn't have a care in the world back then.

"Billy, wake up." So what if it was six a.m.? He crossed his brother's room and plopped down on his bed.

He rolled over. "Fuck off, Jake. I'm sleepin'."

"C'mon, bro." He pulled on Billy's shoulder. "I got an idea."

"Chrissakes, what is it?" And he sat up, rubbing his eyes.

"I was just thinkin' about when we used to take off for the day and go fishin'."

Billy's eyebrows squished together, and rubbing his temple, he tilted his head to the side.

What? Did ya think I woke you up to reminisce?

Hardly.

"Let's go get Emily. Take her to the lake." His brow raised, Jake nodded, tugging on the ends of Billy's hair. "What do ya say?"

"Can't."

"Why not?"

"Smitty's meetin' us over at the house today, remember?" Billy leaned back against the headboard, tucking a pillow behind his head. "He's helpin' out with the electrical."

Shit.

"I forgot, dammit." And he'd been the one who scheduled it, too.

Like his father and grandfather before him, Tyler Smith gave up cowboying for his trade. For the past one hundred and twenty-five years, once they could harness the energy of the mountain's running stream, it was his family who gained the skills that powered Brookside's homes. Hell, master electricians, the Smiths probably wired half of the houses from Jackson to Dubois. Ranching was in Tyler's blood, though. Same as his. Every year, they jumped back in the saddle to round up the cattle for market in the fall.

"We both don't need to be there." Stretching his arms out over his head, Billy closed his eyes and smiled. "Take Em to the lake. She'd love that."

"She would."

"With everything goin' on at the ranch, she could do with a day away."

Her devotion to those she loved was unmatched. Emily was there, sunup to sundown, doing anything she could to ease her uncle's sorrow or see her cousins smile.

How lucky was he to be loved by her?

Pretty darn lucky.

"You sure?"

"Yeah," he said, and with the sleepy smile never leaving his face, Billy turned onto his side. "Now, go."

"She's gonna ask where you are, bro." And the same as he'd done since they were kids, with a parting noogie, Jake stood. "What am I supposed to tell her?"

"Tell her I'm workin' on building our future."

Indeed.

But Jake couldn't exactly say that, now could he?

And just the same, he couldn't lie.

The dapple gray and sorrel gelding walked side by side, their gait unhurried, along the bank of the clear-running stream. With a forceful chuff, Blaze cleared the dust from his nose. Named for the wide, white marking that ran down the middle of his face, while not very original, it fit him. Jake patted the horse's smooth mane, taking his gaze from the beauty beside him to a small copse of trees up ahead.

It was the perfect spot. While picking up a picnic lunch at Harry's, he decided the lake wouldn't do. Anyone could come upon them there, and Jake wanted Emily to himself. Here, at a bend in the stream, they could hide away from the world, on a blanket in a shelter of pine.

He pointed to it. "We can stop there."

"Okay." Shielding her eyes from the sun, she smiled over at him. "Why didn't Billy come with you?"

What did I tell you, bro?

Prepared, the answer rolled off his tongue. "He wanted to, but he promised Tyler he'd do some wiring with him today."

"Oh." She didn't question it. *Thank fuck.* "Have you heard from Kellan or Tanner yet?"

"No." Jake glanced at her. With green eyes sparkling and her grin wide, Emily looked positively giddy. Bursting at the seams, it was apparent to him she was having a hard time holding something in. "Should I have?"

"Eek! They're gettin' hitched, baby," she exclaimed, bouncing in her seat.

"No shit?" Not that he was surprised.

"No shit." Emily dismounted, leaving Ruby to graze by the trees. "They're announcing the news at supper tonight, so act like you didn't know, but Arien called and told me this morning."

"When?"

"They don't have a date yet, but soon."

"Every good thing in the world is born of something not."

Levi's words rang true. The sun always shines after a storm. Tragedy gives way to happiness. Matthew's vision realized, they truly were meant to be. Did it take her mother's death for Arien to see it? Maybe. But then, without the bad, it's difficult to appreciate the good.

"Arien said it was all thanks to you—for talkin' sense into her." Emily stepped into the circle of his arms, her pretty greens gazing up at him. "What in the world did you say?"

"Didn't say nothin'." He let his fingers slide through her hair. "We can all see it. They love her. She loves them. I just asked her why she was fighting it."

What's in your head can fuck you up, but your heart can't lie.

Leaning into him, Emily palmed his cheek. "I guess she couldn't find a reason to fight no more."

"There never was."

"Now, we can all find our way back to happy." And with a pat on his chest, she turned from him and spread the blanket on the grass.

"I am happy."

He had her.

"Kiss me, cowboy."

And he did.

Holding her close, Jake slammed his mouth on hers. He breathed in primrose, beebalm, and the fresh scent of pine, sliding his hands inside her denim shorts. His fingers on smooth, bare skin, he pushed her softness into the hardness in his jeans.

Rubbing the sweat on his neck with her lips, Emily whimpered. "Yes. Jesus, touch me."

He took off her shirt, then his own. Her breaths quickening, he watched her chest rise and fall. Big, rosy nipples protruding against transparent lace, he lowered the cups and freed them.

Teasing her a little, his thumbs skimmed around the areolae. He loved how the contractile flesh puckered at his touch, how the goosebumps sheeted her skin. But those dusky-rose nipples beckoned for his attention. Barely there circles, flicks, and pinches, and rubs. He toyed with them, listening to her sounds, watching them swell. His mouth watering for her, Jake sucked a swollen bud into his mouth.

As if she had milk, he fed from her, his cock throbbing at just the thought. Someday, she'd give birth to their babies, and with her breasts round and full, he and Billy would lie in their bed beside her, suckling on her nipples, their fingers fucking her warm, wet cunt. God, how he longed for it. All of it.

Sharing Emily with his brother.

Breeding her together.

Seeing her grow big and round with their child.

Drinking her milk from her breasts.

He hoped they had a dozen babies, though he'd be just as happy with one. She and Billy were the two people he loved most in this world. He'd do anything asked of him, risk life or limb, for either of them.

"Fuck, Jake, I'm dyin'. Please, baby, I need your hands all over me."

I need that, too.

"We're alone here, *michante*." Sliding her shorts and panties down her legs, Jake lowered himself to his knees. "And we've got all day."

I wanna worship this pussy.

"I don't care if the whole damn town is watchin' us."

He looked up at her. Her pupils were as big as saucers. "I think you'd like it if they were."

"I just might."

He'd gladly give her that if she wanted it. Jake knew Emily enjoyed watching. Maybe she was into being watched, too.

"My wild, dirty girl." He kissed the bare lips of her pussy, his tongue sweeping over her clit as he parted her thighs. "Spread."

That's my girl.

Sweet essence dripped from the place his dick ached to stretch open. With his hand in his pants, Jake stroked himself, slurping the juice from her hole. She held onto his hair, squirming against his tongue that circled her clit.

"Wider." He slid two fingers inside her. "Yeah, baby, just like that."

"Don't go easy, Jake," she said on trembling thighs.

"You tell me when it's too much."

Because I've got to ruin this pretty little pussy, baby. Stretch it wide and fuck you hard.

It was his duty to prepare her body to take them inside her someday. Emily wasn't the only one who dreamt of them fucking her together. He and his brother dreamt of it, too. They spoke of it often. Many a night, they jerked themselves off, imagining what it would feel like with their dicks side by side in her pussy, especially now that Billy couldn't touch her.

"Never." Emily rode his fingers and, bearing down, she took him in deeper. "It'll never be too much."

And it'll never be enough.

Not until his brother was free to love her with him.

He fucked her hard for them both, telling her how they couldn't wait to stuff their cocks together into her tight little hole. How he watched his brother beat his dick, blowing like a freight train, every time they talked about it.

"Oh, Jesus. Fuck."

Jake watched the cum spray out of her. Holding her lips open, he slapped her clit over and over again. And she kept on coming.

He pushed his fingers back inside her. "Again?"

"Yes, please." She widened her stance. "And this time, fuck me even harder."

This. Girl.

He and his brother were so incredibly favored. No one on this earth could love them better than their wild and beautiful Emily. And no one would love her better than them.

A few weeks later, he and his brother watched Emily in Miss Lilly's lavender dress as she preceded Arien down the aisle to meet Kellan and Tanner at the stones. Jake glanced at Billy. He gave his hand a squeeze. Neither one of them had to say it. In their mind's eye, they saw her as a vision wearing white.

Seventeen

Happy to be out of school, Billy got in his truck and headed up to the ranch. The upperclassmen were excused from classes during calving season in spring and for the cattle roundups in fall. They had extra homework to make up for it, though. He'd do everything from home if they'd let him. Without Emily, Griffin, and Shiloh around, the place just wasn't the same.

The horses were his sanctuary.

Building the house kept him sane.

They were making decent progress. Now that the plumbing, electrical, and ductwork were in, he and Jake had to get going on the insulation. The drywall was set to be delivered next week.

His back to him, Tanner stood at the crossties with Airdrie.

The Friesian mare, happy to see him, whinnied a greeting as soon as he came inside. Horses are always communicating. From ear positions to tail swishes, every movement and sound told him what a horse was feeling.

"That you, Billy?"

"Expectin' someone else?"

"Never know around here." Tanner let out a chuff, methodically rubbing the currycomb in a circular motion. "Hand me that brush, would ya?"

"How you doin', Airdrie?" Heavy with foal, Billy ran his hand along her flank.

"Our girl's just fine." He gave the horse a pat on the rump, then looked his way. "How're you doin'?"

"I'm all right."

"You sure about that?" Tanner slowly tipped his head to the side as if studying him. "You're lookin' a little bit…mopey."

"Yeah, whatever." Billy tossed him a dandy brush and changed the subject. "The boys still headin' back in today?"

"That's what Kellan said." And with a bob of his chin, Tanner returned to his grooming. "We best get ready for 'em."

Two dozen horses were coming in. Billy went right to it, preparing to untack and care for them. Sweat dripping off his brow, he filled hay bins and water troughs in the pasture where he and Tanner would turn them out to rest and recover once they checked them over. Chasing cows down a mountain for three nights and days, he knew there'd be cuts, abrasions, and wounds to treat. Hooves that needed trimming. He assembled the supplies, ready for that, too.

The only thing left to do now was wait. Fuck, how he'd come to hate the word.

Billy needed to be doing something. Anything. Everything was fine as long as his hands were busy and his mind had a task to focus on. The more laborious, the better, too, so at the end of the day, he could pass out in his bed and dream a dreamless sleep. His days and nights ticked by faster. The waiting was easier that way.

He left the tack room, twisting his sweat-drenched hair back into a tie, to see Shiloh, Cassie, Arien, and Emily breeze in through the open barn doors. A breath of fresh air with an infectious smile, her green eyes lit up the moment she saw him. She broke away from the girls, her arms outstretched, moving toward him in all eagerness.

"Hey, pretty girl." Hooking an arm around his wife, Tanner kissed her. "What're y'all doin' here?"

"Griffin texted Shiloh. They're close and she wanted to be here to meet him."

"And you're missin', Kel, ain't ya?" He winked with a sly, lop-sided grin. Surely, he'd kept her occupied while his brother was away, but now that they were married, Arien wasn't shy about show-ing the world how fiercely she loved them both. Knowing her and Kellan as he did, Billy had no doubt they'd disappear into the house together as soon as he got off his horse.

"Course, I am." Smiling up at Tanner, Arien palmed his cheek. "But it gave me an excuse to come see you, too."

"You don't need no excuse."

"I know."

Tanner lifted Arien off her feet and, wrapping her legs around his waist, he kissed her as if no one else was here with them to witness it.

Shiloh burst into a fit of giggles.

Cassie rolled her eyes.

Emily reached him then. "Billy."

Leaning against the tack room door, he swept her into his embrace and pressed her tightly to his chest. Her warm, soft body molded onto his had to be the most wonderful feeling in the world. She just smelled so damn good—so good he wanted to eat her. Except he couldn't. So he closed his eyes, reveling in all the sen-sations bombarding him, and smoothed the hair down her back.

"Hey, sweet cheeks," he whispered and kissed her crown. "How's my girl?"

Before Emily could answer him, he heard Cassie croon. "Awe, would you look at him? He reminds me of a little lost puppy in a pet store window."

"Does she always have to be such a bitch?" Arien asked, her legs sliding off Tanner's hips.

Shiloh pursed her lips, rubbing the baby bump that wasn't noticeable yet. "She does."

"Just an observation. Wasn't meanin' to be." With her lips curving into a smirk, Cassie lit a cigarette. "And for your information, Griffin didn't text Shiloh. It was *me*."

She exhaled a plume of smoke, sauntering her way out of the barn.

"Didn't Griffin tell you not to smoke near me?" Waving a hand in front of her face, Shiloh coughed and gagged. "It ain't good for the baby."

Cassie flipped her sister the bird and kept on walking.

"She did that on purpose."

"Are the two of you ever gonna get over your bullshit?" Billy wanted to know. Hell, they all did. Most sisters were close, or at the very least amiable, but not these two. They bickered all the time, and honestly, it had grown tiresome.

Looking at him, Shiloh only shrugged. "Even when we were little, Cassie was never very good at sharing."

Right. He knew better.

His brow raised, Billy gave her a look that told her so.

Shiloh crossed her arms over her chest. "What happened with Reed wasn't my fault."

"Seriously, I don't know how Griffin puts up with it." He put on his hat, and taking Emily by the hand, he shook his head and led her toward the door.

"He loves me," Shiloh said.

"And your sister," Billy reminded her. "Seems like you keep forgettin' that part."

"Who's Reed?"

"Reed Archer." Emily spun around and walked backward for a step. He's Griffin's brother."

"Griffin has a brother? Why didn't I know that?"

You were sittin' not a dozen feet away from him, girly.

He showed up for his brother's wedding, surprisingly, but considering everything that transpired that night, it was likely Arien couldn't recall meeting him. Then again, maybe she never got the chance to.

"What happened?"

"Not now," Tanner muttered low. "Okay, pretty girl?"

"Gotcha."

He heard them first. The continuous, low rumble of "moo" created a constant hum in the background of hooves hitting the ground, snorts, bellows, and the sound of the boys guiding the herd home. Cattle are better when handled calmly. The ranch's cattle are all used to being handled horseback, and they're used to the boys being quiet around them, but sometimes a cow has a mind of its own.

Like his father and grandfather before him, Griffin Archer knew a thing or two about herding cattle. He'd been sitting saddle from the time he could walk. More than his physical capacity, it was his indomitable will that was his strength. Kellan didn't make him his lead rider for nothing. The guy didn't know the meaning of the word, quit. It simply wasn't in his vocabulary.

A critter broke away from the herd and took off, going back in the direction they had come from. In the blink of an eye, Griffin went chasing after him. The steer ran fast. He rode faster. His arm raised overhead, he twirled the rope, moving only his wrist. Billy counted in his head, *one, two, three, four,* waiting for him to throw the rope. The lariat soared through the air, capturing his target.

Arien looked awestruck, watching him. "Damn, he should be in the rodeo or something."

"Nah, that ain't real cowboyin'. It's just showin' off." Flipping her hair back, Cassie held her chin high. "What you're seein' out there? Now, that's the real thing."

Archer turned his horse around and trotted their way. Cassie hopped over the fence and ran toward him. He swooped her up into the saddle, peppering kisses all over her face. She didn't appear to care that he was covered in dirt and grime, or stank of cattle and sweat. With her arms clasped around his neck, and her smile a mile wide, Billy had never seen her look happier.

"Miss me, baby cakes?" His lips quirked up into a devious grin. Kellan dismounted and handing the reins to Tanner, he kissed his wife like he hadn't seen her for three years, never mind three days.

But then sometimes, a day can feel like a year. Billy knew that all too well.

With his hands gripping her ass, Kellan smashed Arien against the bulge in his jeans. Whimpering, she climbed him like a tree.

"Yeah, I'm thinkin' you did," he rasped with a loud smack to her bottom.

"Asshole."

"You know it." And he kissed her again.

"Go on, you two. I got work to do here." Looking on, Tanner shook his head and chuckled.

No resentment.

No jealousy.

Billy saw nothing but absolute love for his brother and the wife they shared shining in his eyes. He squeezed Emily tighter. "You know what that means."

"Yeah," she said on a sigh. "I do."

"I'm so happy I got to see you." Gazing into the green eyes that loved him, he tucked a wayward strand of hair behind her ear.

He didn't want to let her go, but for him and Tanner, the day was just beginning. Griffin was getting off his horse. Billy should take the stallion off his hands. Instead, holding onto Emily, he watched him get down on his haunches and kiss Shiloh's tummy.

Cassie's face crumpled, but Griffin didn't see it.

"Think they're ever gonna be okay?"

Billy held her to him tightly one more time.

Lighting another cigarette, Cassie walked away.

Don't look like it.

"I sure hope so."

Eighteen

The absence of moonlight cloaked the room in murky darkness. There were no shadows. Emily could barely make out her white dresser or the blush-covered chair in the corner. She gazed toward her window. It looked even darker outside.

Must've stopped snowing.

It was coming down hard when Jake brought her home last night.

Drawing the covers up to her chin, Emily burrowed into the silky softness, and closing her eyes, she willed the dream to return.

But sleep evaded her.

She tried counting sheep and making a boring to-do list in

her head, but neither worked. Her brain went into overdrive, and random thoughts crept in, sabotaging her efforts.

Christmas is just two weeks away. I still have to go shopping.

Finals start tomorrow. Did I study enough?

Have to plan a baby shower for Shiloh. Gah, and one for Arien, now, too.

"And my wedding." Rolling over, Emily sighed.

Okay, so what if she hadn't tackled her Christmas list yet? As soon as as finals were over, she and Arien could go to Jackson and knock it out in a day. She didn't have to worry about studying. The education she'd gotten in Brookside was so advanced, her college classes were a joke. Shiloh wasn't due until March. In the middle of Thanksgiving dinner, Kellan announced Arien was going to have a baby in July.

Plenty of time.

Not really.

Classes would start up again in January, and her wedding was in May.

For as much as her mom and Carrie Gantry had accomplished in that regard, there was so much left for Emily to do. Her dress. The cake. And where were they going to live once they were married? Jake and Billy hadn't so much as hinted, and guarding their secret well, neither had anyone else.

With all of that on her mind, it's no wonder she couldn't sleep.

And she needed to, dammit.

Because at night, in Emily's dreams, the wait was over.

Jake and Billy were there with her.

Sometimes she dreamt the silliest things, like the three of them putting together furniture from Ikea, when there wasn't a store anywhere in Wyoming. She recalled Arien talking about it that Sunday when she made Swedish meatballs for supper. Every time she and her mom went shopping there, they'd have them in the upstairs cafe.

That might explain it.

Another time, Emily had a dream they were planting a garden. Jake dug holes in the dirt while Billy handed her pots of white blooms. *As if.* She wouldn't even dream of doing that, except she did. Wasn't there a castle in England with beautiful white gardens they'd read about in school once?

Yup, Sissinghurst Castle.

But not all of her dreams were nonsense, some were actually quite delicious. The ones where Billy and Jake kissed her, lying on a blanket beneath the stars. Waking up between them in a big brass bed, their hard, muscled bodies pressed against hers.

Emily shivered, her hand sliding under her shirt to squeeze her breast.

Thump.

Thump.

Thump.

It sounded like someone banging on the front door, but who would be here at this ungodly hour? Surely, it was a loose shutter or something. *The wind.* She ignored it.

But it came again, loud and insistent.

"Fuck's sake." She threw off the covers. "Hold your damn horses. I'm comin.'"

Her mother got to the door right behind her.

Emily opened it, and the cold winter air, along with snow from the lintel, blasted her in the face. "Jesus."

Barefoot, wearing only a camisole and panties, Arien cradled her baby brother to her chest.

"Fucking hell." And she pushed the door all the way open. "Get in here before you both freeze to death."

They walked her to the sofa, Kim grabbing a throw off the back of it. She wrapped it around Arien, and sitting her down, she gently took the bundled infant from her arms. "You all right, Benjie?"

He gazed up at his aunt with big blue eyes and a gummy grin, proudly displaying his two bottom teeth.

"Thank goodness," she said, breathing a sigh of relief. "Arien, honey, what happened?"

But she sat just there, staring straight ahead, shaking, her teeth chattering so hard she couldn't speak.

"I'm going to call Matty, start a fire, and make some tea to get something warm in her." Her gaze never leaving Arien, Kim tapped on her phone. "You go get her some clothes."

"He was supposed to fly out to Denver this mornin', remember?"

"Shit, that's right. I'll call the boys then," she said and started all over again. "And Victor."

"Victor?" Glancing up at her mother, Emily cocked her head. "Why?"

"Arien and the baby need a good looking over, that's why."

Oh.

"La…la…" Her eyes wide, Arien pointed a shaky finger at the door. "Lock it."

"What on earth? She's terrified." Kim moved over to the door and locked it. No one ever locked their doors here. "Everything's gonna be okay, sweetheart. You're safe."

"Nooo." She shook her head. "I think he wants to kill us."

The fuck? Who?

The sky had just lightened from charcoal to a heavy purplish-gray when Jake and his father arrived. Emily had Arien dressed in an oversized sweatshirt and leggings, a pair of warm, fuzzy socks on her ice-cold feet. She fitfully dozed on the sofa, Benjamin asleep in a makeshift cot beside her. With a fire roaring in the hearth, Kim set out coffee for them all.

"I spoke to Kellan. He and Tanner should be here any minute," her mom said, pouring a cup for Victor. "They're stopping at the house to grab some diapers and bottles for the baby. At least she had the wherewithal to bundle him in a blanket. He seems to be all right. It's Arien I'm worried about."

"Has she said anything else?" he asked, glancing at Arien.

"No."

And after what she'd already said, they were almost too afraid to press for more.

"We thought we should let her rest until y'all got here." Emily traced the veins on the back of Jake's hand that rested in her palm. "Then she'll only have to tell the story once."

"I don't want her traumatized even more, especially in her condition. She was shaken up pretty badly." Kim exhaled, her teeth raking over her bottom lip. "Those boys are gonna tear this town apart lookin' for whoever did this."

The notion that someone in Brookside had to be the culprit seemed preposterous. "It could be an outsider, couldn't it?"

"Doubt it." Exchanging a glance with his father, Jake gave her hand a squeeze.

Her mom sipped on her coffee, her gaze flicking between father and son. "What are you thinkin', Vic?"

"Same thing you are."

Huh? Someone wanna clue me in here?

The door flew open. Ready to barrel in, she'd never seen such a look on either of her cousin's faces before, especially Tanner, her gentle bear. Hands clenched. Nostrils flaring. Emily could see the veins straining against his skin. It was rage, pure and simple.

Then his eyes locked on Arien, and letting out a huge breath, he muttered, "Thank fuck."

"They're okay?" Kellan dropped a bag at the door, and looking at Victor, made his way into the room.

"I believe so."

"Kellan?" Upon hearing his voice, Arien raised her head.

"I'm right here, baby cakes."

"Me, too, pretty girl."

They went to her. Kellan took one side and Tanner the other. Arien palmed their cheeks as if the simple touch somehow soothed her. She relaxed against them; the tension disappearing from her body, calmer just being in their presence.

"Can you tell us what happened, sweetheart?" Leaning in, his elbows on his knees, Victor steepled his fingers under his chin. "Whatever you can remember?"

"I remember all of it."

Tanner took her hand and kissed it. She looked up at him. "Dad brought Benjamin to me and said you'd be coming in soon, so I didn't think much of anything at first."

Emily glanced at Jake and laced her fingers with his. Uncle Matty was still on an airplane. He didn't know about any of this yet. She could only imagine his reaction when he found out.

"But the noises I heard didn't sound right."

"What do you mean?" Kellan asked.

"The dogs always come in with you." She smiled up at him, her fingers rubbing at the whiskers on his face. "I can hear you shush them to be quiet, but you end up making more noise than they do."

Sharing a glance, her cousins chuckled.

"My gut told me it wasn't either one of you." Arien reached for their hands and wet her lips. "So, I got up to look."

"And?" Tanner prompted.

"It wasn't you," she said, her voice trembling.

Victor crouched down in front of her. "Did you see who it was?"

"No, it was dark, and he wore a hood. I never saw his face."

Tanner's brows drew together, then his eyes widened and his jaw went slack. He looked over at his brother, but Kellan didn't appear to notice.

"I was hiding in a doorway at the end of the hall. He came up the stairs and went right for Benjie's room." And with the dam now broken, Arien sobbed. "I didn't think. I just picked up the baby, snuck out the back, and ran."

"Sh, sh, sh." Kellan wiped the tears from her face. "Seems to me you were thinkin' just fine. You're both okay, and that's what matters."

"That's it." Tanner slammed his fist into his thigh. "We're gettin' you a car."

"I told you, I don't need one."

"What if I hadn't left my keys on the dresser, or if none of the trucks were there at the house?" He grabbed her by the shoulders, making her see reason. "With Benjie and a baby comin', you *do* need one."

"Oh, God, what if Daddy had brought me the baby monitor instead of Benjamin?" Arien squeezed her eyes closed, clapping a hand across her mouth.

The man would've found him in his crib and he'd probably be…

Wait. Baby monitor?

Emily's gaze shot up to Jake, and as if he'd read her mind, he looked over at his father.

Victor glanced at her mom, then with a nod he turned back to Jake and said, "We need to check the house."

Nineteen

The fort never slept.

All night long, Levi gazed up at a starless sky, listening to the cacophony of drunken, raucous laughter, whores plying their trade, brawls, hooves on dirt, and gunshots. He breathed in the dung, the blood, the mud, and the piss. It seeped into the soil of this godforsaken place, forever becoming a part of it.

How long had it been since they set off on this never-ending journey? Four months? He'd grown so fucking weary of it. And as weary as he was, sleep should've claimed him the moment he closed his eyes, despite the sounds, the stink, and the cold, hard earth he'd lain upon.

He could tell himself he remained awake to ensure no harm

came to his sisters, and while indeed that was true, Levi gazed across the camp at the object of his utmost desire and the overwhelming source of his restlessness.

"If you want my Lucy as your wife, then you'll be weddin' my Fallon, too."

Walker couldn't have meant it. Why, the notion alone was preposterous. *Like them crazy Mormons.* Booted out of Ohio, Illinois, and Missouri, they'd heard the polygamist followers of Joseph Smith were staking their claim farther west in the Utah Territory desert, and there they'd build their Zion. He'd seen them along the trail. Men, young and old, with twenty wives a piece, proselytizing their faith.

It wasn't his.

She raised her head. Wisps of sable blowing with the wind, her golden eyes locked on his. Men milled about the camp. Shoshone and Bannock, trappers, traders, godless and god-fearing men alike, walked past Lucy as if she wasn't there. But powerless under her gaze, Levi went to her.

"You spoke to my father." It wasn't a question.

"I did, but…" He wasn't sure what to say or how to go about it.

"I love you, Levi, and this is what I want." She grabbed onto the collar of his shirt, bringing his forehead down to hers. "A life with you and my sister."

"Why?"

"It is the way of my mother's people," she simply said.

Taking a step back, Levi pulled away. "Do you understand what you're asking of me?"

"Do you love me?"

"You know I do."

Her lips quirked up. "Then what else is there for me to understand?"

"You want me to lie with her, to bed her, and put children in her belly?" His words louder than he intended, Levi brought her to the fencepost, raking his fingers through his hair.

She cupped his face, tenderly stroking his beard. "Yes, and the love we have will be even stronger for it."

"How?" And with his hand on Lucy's, he stilled hers.

"The earth says so. The spirit says so." She kissed his lips. "My father has seen it come to pass."

His brows drawing together, he cocked his head.

"It's the nature of the universe. Heavens, waters, and earth. Mind, body, and spirit. Even your Christian faith teaches the Father, the Son, and the Holy Ghost." Pawing his chest, Lucy smiled up at him. "Everything that comes in threes is perfect."

Jesus.

"I'm not like them."

"Like who?"

Brigham Young and his Nauvoo Legion, or whatever the fuck it is they call themselves.

"Those Mormons."

"Good, because it will only ever be us three." She leaned in, gently biting her lip, and laid her head on his shoulder. "You, and Fallon, and I."

"Oh, so that's how it works?"

"Yes, silly." His question was rhetorical. She answered it, anyway. "Brothers share a wife. Sisters share a husband. Cousins, sometimes. It's how impenetrable community is built."

"We'd be shunned, Lucy. Ostracized. The very thing you fear." Levi had to make her see reason, to cast aside this foolishness. They ways of her mother's people would never be accepted in this world.

"Would we be, though?" She combed his hair with her fingers, gazing up at him with hope-filled eyes. "In a new, unspoiled land, a place where we can all live a life of our own choosing?"

Isn't that what they'd left the East and everything they'd ever known behind them for?

"Wild and free."

"As the earth intended." And she smiled.

But Levi knew better. "It doesn't work that way."

"It can and it does, I promise you."

He held her chin, tracing the outline of her lips with his thumb. "Lucy…"

"Talk with my sister." She turned her head to kiss his fingers. "Then, you'll see."

How could he say no?

He waited for her at the river.

She came to him like an offering.

"*Behne.*" Hello.

"Fallon." While rubbing his jaw, Levi tipped his chin. "You're agreeing to this?"

"Yes." Her smile tremulous, she looked up at him with eyes of warm chocolate suede. Shimmering with flecks of cinnamon and honey, he could see every broken promise, every wish left behind, untold and unheard, within the soulful orbs.

Fearing he'd get so lost in them he'd never find his way out, Levi lowered his gaze to see her breasts heaving beneath the thin, worn cotton of her gown.

Christ.

"How old are you?" he asked. Anything to keep himself from touching her.

"Eighteen."

Then she reached for him, and it all went to hell. Fallon bent his head at the neck, and bringing his lips to meet hers, she kissed him. *God's blood.* Unexpectedly, his cock sprang to life in his breeches. Giving in to his baser nature, Levi reached inside her bodice and, fondling her breast, his thumb flicked over her nipple. She whimpered, making no attempt to remove his hand from her person. And considering that her acquiescence, he freed them from the confines of their cotton prison to reverently gaze upon them.

"Do you have a Shoshone name, Fallon?"

"*Kimana.*"

Beautiful, like you.

"What does it mean?"

"Butterfly."

Then she lowered his head to her breast.

He took her nipple into his mouth.

Mine.

The morning sky appeared heavy and gray, as if the clouds were still deciding whether or not to open up on them. Jake listened to the crunch of snow beneath the Lariat's tires, and glancing at his dad in the passenger seat, he curled his arm around Emily. If he was right, and he was pretty darn sure he was, dark days were looming ahead.

His father felt it, too.

It was written all over his face.

Just as Levi and Elijah had been, from the time they were small, Victor Gantry and Matthew Brooks were the best of friends—tight, like brothers. When Amanda Jacoby passed away within days of Kellan's birth, everyone just thought it tragic, and undoubtedly, it was, but then her sister, Heather, suffered the same fate three months later, soon after Tanner was born. Double tragedy? Coincidence? Neither the grieving widower nor his father thought so.

The midwife couldn't explain it, and the old doc, long since dead now, figured the girls had the same weak heart or some such bullshit. Victor was in med school at the time, but he wasn't buying it. Left with two babies to raise on his own, Matthew didn't either.

And to make the strange occurrences even stranger, instead of supporting his grandsons and their father, John Jacoby ran around telling anyone who would listen that Matthew was responsible for their deaths.

Folks came up with their own conclusions.

Matthew Brooks wasn't the one to blame.

Now, over two decades later, with Jennifer's death under the same circumstances, it was a certainty.

Jake knew who was responsible. His father, Matthew, and Emily's mom knew, too. Proving it would be an altogether different, and perhaps impossible, story, but they had to at least try. Three women were already dead. The psycho was targeting a baby now, and Brooksiders saw to their own.

Emily pointed out the windshield. "Isn't that Justin's car?"

"It is. I asked him to meet us here." Stretching out his arm behind Emily, his father nudged his shoulder. "Pull in behind him, Jake."

Blowing in his hands to warm them, Justin paced the length of his ruby-red Porsche Macan that he bought just because it was fun, and because it was big enough to carry large pieces of artwork in.

"It's fucking cold out here," he said before pecking his father on the lips. "How's the girl?"

"A little shaken, but she's fine." As if the peck weren't enough, Victor kissed Justin once more. Even after twenty-five years of marriage, they couldn't keep their hands off one another. "Now, show me."

"Nobody has gone up this driveway." Justin led the way and crouched down in front of the snow-covered drive. "See that? Two sets of tire tracks—identical treads, mind you—come down and turn in the direction of Kim's."

"Makes sense," Emily said, huddled underneath Jake's arm. "The boys have matching TRXs."

He held her close against him, doing his best to keep her warm. "Arien drove one. She took Tanner's truck. Kellan drove the other."

"This third set must be Matthew's from when he left for the airport," his father said.

Emily glanced around, as if looking for an answer. "But if no-body drove up, then how did he get in?"

Some other way.

"Should we call the sheriff or somebody?"

"We can handle this, Emily." Jake squeezed her shoulders to reassure her. "Let's go up to the house."

Justin surveyed the scene, taking pictures on his phone like he was the lead detective on *CSI*. Under any other circumstances, it might've been funny. "We're lookin' for footprints. Be careful where you walk."

None were found at the front door.

The side door from the kitchen out to the barns was a mess.

And Arien's bare footprints went from the deck down to the drive.

"Well, yeehaw," Justin whooped. "Will you look at this?"

A set of large footprints—a man's size twelve, unless he was mistaken—came out of the trees to the French door in the living room and went back out again.

"My guess is whoever these belong to came in from the stream," Victor said as Justin followed the trail toward the woods, taking photos along the way.

Jake turned to follow his uncle. "I'll go check."

"We will, son. I want to look inside the house first." And his father reined him in. "Emily, do you know if that baby monitor records?"

"I'm not sure, but I think so."

He prayed it did. It was their best shot, and likely their only shot, to get the evidence they were looking for.

"Looks like the asshole had the decency to wipe his feet. There's not a smudge of a footprint or a melted puddle of snow anywhere," Justin muttered, coming in behind them.

Up the stairs and to the right, they made their way over to Matthew's wing of the house, of which there were four. The house had stood here for generations, added on to and renovated throughout the years. There were twenty bedrooms here once, but families were much larger way back when. It was a necessity for survival.

As if he were in there sleeping, they crept into Benjamin's room. A woodland forest was painted on the walls. A plush bear rug covered the floor. Stuffed toy rabbits, foxes, and deer waited in a playhouse teepee. An empty rocking chair sat in the corner. Jake glanced at the adjoining door that connected the nursery to Matthew's suite. It hit him then. *Jennifer did all this.* For a son, she hardly had the chance to hold.

Emily went to the dresser. "It does record."

"Play it." And Jake held his breath.

Huddled together, the four of them watched a figure, dressed all in black and wearing a hood, enter the room, and then, finding the crib empty, he left through the connecting door.

"Who the fuck is that?" Her hands trembling, terror laced Emily's voice.

Justin pursed his lips. "I have a hunch."

Jake looked at his father.

His father looked at him.

They said his name together, "John Jacoby."

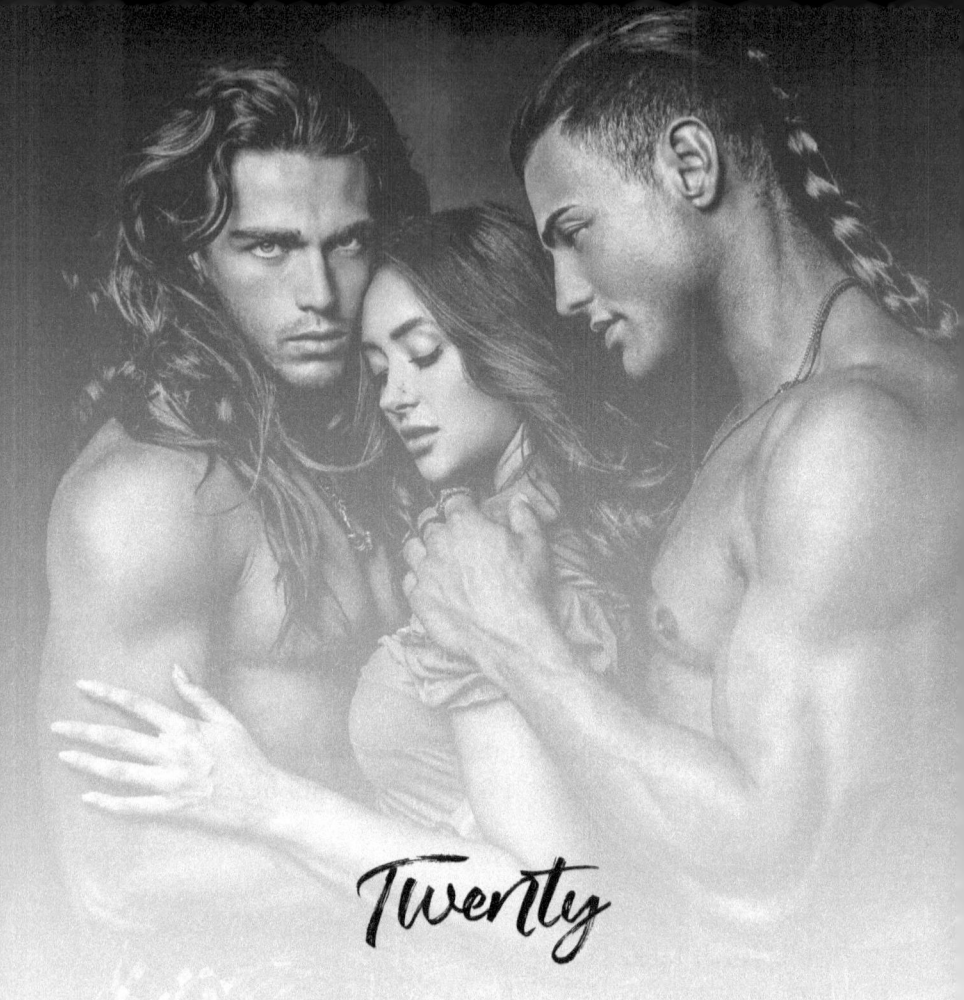

Twenty

January is fucking cold in Wyoming.

Grateful the power got connected, and they had heat, Billy and his brother nailed down hardwood flooring in their living room over the creek. Everything was coming together just as he had envisioned it. After this, they had the cabinetry, counters, and fixtures to install, but that was easy enough. Then, come spring, once all the snow had melted, they only needed to do the exterior grading and some landscaping.

Between Emily, school, the horses, and the John Jacoby situation, what little time Billy had to spare was spent here. Now, seeing how far he and Jake had come, with the help of family and friends, he was certain the house would be finished in time for the wedding.

At least, after tomorrow, no one would have to think about John Jacoby anymore.

Crazy shit.

He always thought the old man was a little off, but Billy never figured the guy was capable of murder, and his own daughter at that, until they went to his house and confronted him with the proof his father had found.

They stared evil in the face that day.

Billy was still trying to make sense of it all. Tanner's mother, the elder sister, offs Kellan's mother, injecting her with a fatal dose of insulin because she was jealous, then tells her father what she did, so he offs her—why? How could a father do that? The man was twisted. His daughter, too. John Jacoby's hatred for Matthew Brooks drove him to do the same to Jennifer. Benjamin would have been next.

So, yeah, it was good that no one had to worry about him anymore.

He was going in front of the town council in the morning.

And Billy was going to be there.

The day dawned just as cold as the day before, but the sun shone. Not a cloud to be had in the bright winter sky. He buttoned up his shirt, tucking it into his best blue jeans, and pulled his hair back in a queue. It was likely the whole town would be there, except for Emily, that is. She was taking Arien and Benjie to Jackson for the day. Pregnant with twins, Kellan and Tanner didn't want her witnessing any of this shit.

Jake tapped on his doorframe. "Ready, bro?"

Billy put on his hat. "Yup."

Victor and Justin waited in the kitchen. Impeccably dressed, as they always were, they sipped on coffee, scrolling through their phones. He went to pour himself a cup. "Where's Ma?"

"She woke up with a headache this morning." Glancing over

at him, his father put the phone down. "Gave her some Tylenol so she can sleep it off."

"It's time," Justin said, tapping on the face of his Movado.

Billy gulped down his coffee in one swallow. "Yeah, okay."

The short walk to the town hall was a silent one, but then what was there to say? A man's fate would be determined today. And it had been a long time coming.

Like sardines in a tin, folks packed themselves into the hall. Billy stood off to the side with Griffin, Tyler, Deke, and the others who lined the wall, waiting to fulfill their duty. The proceeding itself was brief. Two men brought Jacoby to stand before the members of the council, his brother among them. He'd never been so proud to see Jake up on that raised dais.

The Lewis attorneys presented the evidence. The syringes, empty insulin vials, photos of footprints, and the recording of a figure in Benjamin's room. His father testified to what he'd found, and to Jacoby's eventual confession.

When asked if he had anything to say, Jacoby only said this, "It isn't me you should fear." Then he half-turned, and pointing a gnarled finger at Matthew Brooks, he cackled like a madman. "This is the end of my story."

And the hall fell silent.

After a moment, the chairman stood, and looking at the men on the wall, he nodded. "Take him."

Surrounded by the older women, Maizie quietly wept as they led Jacoby away. Billy and the others followed, the townsfolk filing out right behind them.

There'd be no hanging. No lethal injection, firing squad, or electric chair. Brookside has its own way of doing things.

With no food, no water, and wearing only the clothes on his back, they brought Jacoby far beyond the treeline, to the top of the snow-covered, craggy peak. And there, whether from starvation, the elements, or a wild animal, the mountain would decide how and when he'd meet his fate.

Matthew Brooks, his sons, and the townsfolk watched their trek from the lake far below.

Jacoby stood there, a maniacal grin on his face, and waved.

Then he did the craziest thing. He turned around, and spreading his arms wide, fell back off the icy ledge.

"Holy fuckin' shit." Griffin scrambled toward the edge, and lying on his stomach, looked down into the rocky gorge below. "I don't see him."

"C'mon." Jake gave him a hand up. "Ain't nothin' to see here."

"Yeah, let's go," Deke said, hooking his arm around Griffin's neck. "He'll turn up downstream somewhere."

But he never did.

Weeks later, Billy saw him in a dream. *A goddamn nightmare.* Battered and bloody, his broken limbs disfigured, Jacoby hobbled up to him and laughed in his face. "You should fear me, boy. It's not my story that's over, it's *yours.*"

It was so vivid and real that he woke up breathing all heavy and clutching his chest.

Some dreams have meaning, so he went to Justin about it. "Jacoby's end was a hard thing to witness, I imagine. It's bound to mess with your head a bit."

"Yeah, I guess so." Billy shrugged, stabbing a fork into his steak and eggs. "They never found his body, you know."

"That's what's really fuckin' with you, ain't it?" He sat back with a sigh. "I'm not surprised it wasn't found."

"Where'd it go, then?"

"It's amusing how y'all think two hundred pounds of flesh and bone can tumble ten thousand feet down a mountain and land at the bottom all in one piece. I doubt he even made it that far."

He swallowed. "Gee, Daddy J, thanks for the visual."

"That dream of yours has no meaning, son. It's your mind

DYAN LAYNE

playin' tricks on you, that's all." Justin's hand came down on top of his and he squeezed. "The man took the easy way out, which is a helluva lot more than he deserved."

Yeah, maybe.

The dream still gnawed at him, though. Maybe he should feel sorry for the old loon, but he didn't.

It was that time of year again. The heifers would start dropping calves any day now. After he and Jake spent the entire day working on the house while they still could, Billy was looking forward to having dinner, and afterward, game night with the family. The five of them being home together on a Saturday evening was a rare occurrence these days, and with their schedules, who knew when they'd have the chance again.

As much as he couldn't wait to share a life with Emily and his brother, and start a family of their own, Billy was going to miss everything he'd had here. Justin waking him up for school, his dad helping him with homework, and his mother's constant, loving presence. Movie nights. Birthday parties. Hanging ornaments on the tree. His childhood flashed by in front of him and he smiled.

He'd never get to be that kid again.

Life changes, but isn't that how it's supposed to go?

Soon, he'd pass down the love and all they'd taught him to children of his own.

But for tonight, he just wanted to hang out and share a laugh or two with his brother and their parents like they used to. Listen to them chatter about nothing over supper. Watch his father gloat after winning another round of Trivial Pursuit. *Don't he always?* Billy was going to soak up every last fucking moment of it.

"Somethin' sure smells good in here, Daddy J," he said as he walked past the stove and took the seat next to Jake at the island. "What's for dinner?"

"Beef Burgundy. Mushrooms, carrots, pearl onions. I used the entire bottle of Pinot Noir for the sauce." He turned around and grinned. "Delicious. Oh, and my creamy mashed potatoes you love so much, too."

Jake chuckled. "Not gonna ask about dessert."

"Tiramisu dip with ladyfingers." Justin bopped him on the head with a dish towel. "So we can satisfy our sweet tooth while we play Yahtzee."

"You mean Trivial Pursuit, don't you, baby?" Squeezing his ass, Victor laid a smooch on Justin's cheek.

"I do not." He rolled his eyes, laughing at the same time. "It's no fun for the rest of us when you always win."

"He's right." Carrie playfully swatted Victor's behind and pulled silverware out of a drawer. "Parcheesi gets my vote."

"You can only have up to four players," Jake reminded her. "What about Monopoly?"

Hell to the no. I fuckin' hate Monopoly.

"Aggravation! It's just like Parcheesi, 'cept you can have up to six."

His brother threw him a look, wrinkling up his nose at the suggestion.

"It's what Mama wants, ain't it?"

"That's right, honey." She kissed the top of his head and ruffled his hair. "Table's all set. Let's eat before your daddy's phone goes off and he gets called away again."

"Carrie..."

Billy shifted in his seat to see his mother in his father's arms as he gazed into her eyes, tenderly stroking her hair.

"...you know that isn't fair."

"Yes, it is. I can't remember the last time we got through dinner without an interruption." She patted his chest. "It is what it is. I'm not complaining."

"And this is why I didn't go to med school," Jake said, leaning into his ear. "Emily deserves to have us both present, ya know?"

He knew.

"And I don't wanna miss a thing."

As luck would have it, his father's phone didn't go off once.

Billy piled a second helping of mashed potatoes onto his plate. Justin wasn't lying. Creamy and buttery, he did love them. Without even having to ask, his mother passed him the burgundy sauce. "How's the house coming along, honey?"

"Great." He smiled at her. "We put the kitchen counters in today. Ain't that right, Jake?"

"We'll get the bathrooms done tomorrow."

"I'm gonna have to come see it." And her blue eyes seemed to glaze over. "We…ha…go…shop…ture."

The fuck?

"Ma?" Billy shook her shoulder. "Dad, something's wrong."

"What is it?" He rushed across the table to her side. "Carrie?"

"She was talkin' just fine and then all of a sudden one side of her face froze up."

"Get the car." Victor held his wife against his chest. "Now."

***

The closest hospital was in Jackson, fifty miles away. On snowy mountain roads, the trip usually took an hour, but Jake got them there in thirty minutes, their dad holding their mom in the back seat, while he and Justin followed in his Porsche.

By the time he parked, and they dashed inside, Jake stood alone in the waiting room.

Hours that took forever ticked by, and still, they waited.

They drank shitty coffee in paper cups from a vending machine.

They scrolled aimlessly through their phones.

They paced, then sat, only to get up and pace again.

"I can't take this fuckin' waiting no more." Billy yanked at his hair, turning away from looking out the window. "When's Dad gonna come out and tell us somethin'?"

"When there's something to tell us, son." Justin patted his back to calm him. "You know what they say, no news is good news. Your mama's gonna be just fine."

"You don't know that."

"I don't, but I can choose to believe it."

With a nod, Jake pocketed his phone. "Emily wants to come up, but I told her to sit tight until we know what's goin' on."

"There'd just be four of us wearing out the floors, then, right?" he bit out.

"Everything's gonna be okay, bro."

Billy wanted to believe them. Truly, he did. But with every minute that went by, he could only imagine the worst.

Then, the double doors opened, and his father finally came out. He looked so tired, as if he'd aged ten years since supper, but Billy couldn't tell by the look on his face if he was coming to give them good news or not.

"She's had a stroke."

Billy glanced at Justin and his brother. It felt like his heart stopped beating in his chest.

His dad got on his haunches in front of him. "Her speech is impaired, and she's weak on her non-dominant side, but the good news is we got her here in time. They were able to start her on tPA."

"What's that?"

"It stands for tissue plasminogen activator, a powerful clot-busting medication. If we can restore normal blood flow to her brain, we can stop the damage, maybe even reverse it." Victor took his hand in both of his. "Your mama's going to be all right."

"You sure?"

"They're getting ready to take her upstairs." His lip ticked up, and he nodded. "She wants to see you."

They followed him through the double doors into a world of

pungent smells, beeping monitors, and green cotton scrubs. She was in the back, behind curtain-covered glass. IVs in her arms. Wires taped to her head and her chest.

"Hey, Mama." She looked so tiny, and so fragile, lying there. Gingerly, Billy wrapped his arms around her. "I love you."

"Ungh." Her left arm remained still, but her right hand patted his back.

"You scared the shit outta me."

She smacked him for swearing, and pulling away, he laughed.

Yeah, she's all right.

Jake and her brother each took a turn to lean in and kiss her. Justin sat by her side, combing his fingers through her hair, and she motioned to their father. He handed her a pad of paper and a pen.

I'm going to learn to talk again.

By the time you get married.

I promise.

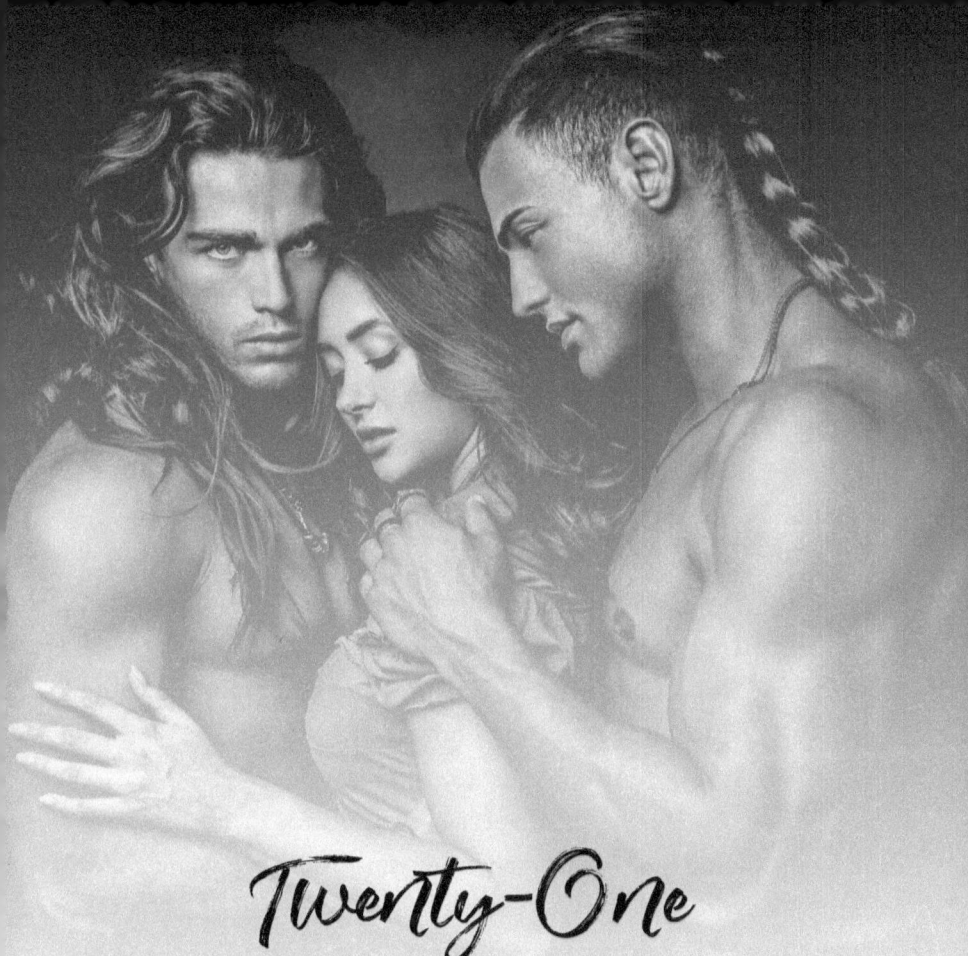

Twenty-One

She loathed the month of February. It was the worst goddamn month of the year. Tax season. Calving season. Come to think of it, March wasn't so great either, but it warmed up some at least.

Emily threw a frozen dinner in the microwave, leaned on the counter, and sighed. Her mom was at her office in town, where she'd stay until fuck knows when. Arien was happy at home, making vlog posts and getting fat, and Shiloh, due to have her baby any day now, was busy…nesting.

Yeah, that's what she said.

When the boys weren't up at the ranch pulling calves or mucking in cowpoo, they were at home, doting on Carrie. Not that Emily begrudged them for it. She didn't. At all. They loved their mama;

if anything, it proved what good men they were. Of course, she already knew that. Besides, wouldn't she do the same for hers?

It's just that it was February—no, scratch that—almost March, and she missed seeing their faces a whole heck of a lot.

The microwave signaled her dinner was done. Emily tossed it onto the island, burning her finger in the process, and sat down to eat it.

She poked at what the package said was Salisbury steak. It resembled a hockey puck covered in… "Shit. It looks like shit."

"Probably tastes like it, too."

Startled, she screamed, and throwing her fork up in the air, she turned around. "Jake? Jesus, Jake, you scared me."

"I'm sorry. Didn't mean to." But he was laughing. Then he handed her a white paper bag. "I brought you dinner."

"Harry's?"

"Wednesday's meatloaf special," he said with a wink, his arms coming around her. "Mashed potatoes, mushroom gravy, and a slice of cherry pie."

"I got your cherry pie right here, cowboy." Emily licked her lips, and sliding her hands inside the back pockets of his jeans, she pulled him close against her.

Warm breath fanned her face, his lips skating across her skin. "Yes, you do."

And gazing into eyes of liquid metal, those perfect lips found hers. Effortlessly, his tongue slipped inside as fingers pressed into her spine, holding their bodies together. One kiss and the winter blues went out the window. They might come back again tomorrow, but even if it was just for tonight, she'd take it.

She nuzzled into his neck, taking comfort in his warmth, the familiar scent of his skin. "You're stayin' to have supper with me, aren't you?"

"I wish I could, but I have to get up to the ranch. I'm already late." With his fingers trailing through her hair, he kissed her crown. "I wanted to come see you, even if it was just for a minute."

"I miss you." She expected as much, but hoped they'd have a little longer.

"And I miss the hell outta you." Jake squeezed her tight, emphasizing his words. "This isn't gonna be forever. My mom's gettin' better every day, and calving will be over soon."

Feels like forever.

"Not for another month."

"Emily..."

Her nerves fired all at once. She clasped her hands around his neck and kissed him with every ounce of longing she had in her. And when she was done, Jake would leave here with swollen lips and a hard-on in his pants to think of her by.

He pulled away. "I'm sorry."

"I know. You've gotta go."

"I do," he said, his lips skimming over her forehead. "I'll try to stop by on my way home in the morning. Okay?"

"Okay."

"I love you." And he kissed her once more.

"I love you, too."

She watched him go, tossing the shit-covered hockey puck into the trash.

Harry's meatloaf, while delicious, was little consolation. Her vision blurring, Emily stared at the slice of cherry pie. Any other day she would've devoured it, but with the funk she was in, she had no appetite.

"Might as well just go to bed." She huffed out a breath. "Great, and now I'm talkin' to myself."

The scrapbook Billy gave her for her birthday sat on her bedside table. Every memory they shared was in it—from playing in a sandbox as toddlers to the last bonfire party they went to before she turned eighteen.

Her fingertips rubbed over the leather cover. She opened it to the last page. A picture of her with Arien and Shiloh on the dance floor next to a shot of her sitting on a hay bale with her arms around Billy and Jake.

"That's my future right there." Emily smiled through the tears sliding down her face.

She realized then why he gave it to her. Not only to remember the past, but to remind her of what lie ahead. *A crazy, beautiful, wonderful life.* And with that thought, she wiped the tears from her eyes, turned off the light, and went to sleep.

Jake never came by.

Emily lingered in the kitchen, long after her mom left for town, but after two cups of coffee and a bowl of instant oatmeal, she headed out to the barn. He'd know where to find her. Besides, she couldn't leave Ruby hungry and waiting.

"Mornin', sweet girl," she cooed, giving the horse an apple from her hand. "You know I'd never forget about you."

Uncle Matty gave her the dapple gray mare on her tenth birthday. Tanner trained her himself, knowing who she was going to. A darker gray when Emily got her as a two-year-old, her coat changed drastically as the dapples appeared. Eventually, as Ruby got older, she'd likely turn all white.

"And you'll still be gorgeous, won't you?"

She made quick work of cleaning the stall and laid down a fresh layer of bedding. After giving her water and filling the feeder with a mix of hay and grain, Emily led her toward the door. "How about a little fresh air, huh? It's cold, but you can run in the snow for a bit, then I'll give you a good brushing."

"Jake told me you were sad." Billy stood with his hip propped against the wall. How long had he been standing there, watching her?

"I'm not sad, exactly." With a pat on the rump, she sent Ruby out into the paddock. "I just…"

"I know. I miss you, too." He pushed himself off the wall and came toward her. "So fuckin' much. You have no idea."

"I think I do."

"Trust me, you don't." Billy shook his head. He picked up a strand of her hair, rubbing it between his fingers. "Baby, I'm dyin'."

"Oh, Billy." She took his hand, and kissing it, Emily held it to her face.

Calloused fingers stroked her cheek. "With my mom and everything…"

"Jake told me she's getting better."

"She is." With a subtle nod, his forehead dropped to hers. "Justin takes her to Jackson for therapy every day. She's determined to speak like she did before in time for our weddin'."

"Then she will."

"She just might. Stubborn woman." He chuckled, his fingertips still on her face. "Don't matter to me none. She's still here. And to think I almost lost her."

"But you didn't."

He looked lost, and so very tired, the worry and fear etched in the lines of his eyes. Lines that shouldn't be there yet. When had he slept last? Everyone was taking care of his mother, but who was looking out for him?

"Can't I just hold you, Billy?"

"Prob'ly not a good idea." His lips pursed, he stared down at his boots. "Bein' we're alone and all, we're playin' with fire here."

"Yeah, in a smelly, cold barn." She cupped his cheek. "Don't be silly, now. C'mere."

He stepped into the circle of her arms. Holding his head to her shoulder, she traced soft circles on his back. Emily could feel his cock grow hard beneath his jeans, but she ignored it.

"See, baby?" She kissed his brow. "It's okay."

"It's not," he rasped, his nose buried in the hollow of her throat. "You don't know how close I am to sayin' fuck the damn rules."

"Aren't rules made to be broken?"

"Not this one."

But his lips were on her skin. He dragged them up the side of her neck, catching her earlobe between his teeth. And all good reason left her, then. A tremor shooting through her at the contact, tingles popped between her thighs, and she whimpered.

"Fuck it."

Maybe it was instinct. Maybe he didn't mean to do it, but in a swift move along her jaw, those teeth took her bottom lip into his hungry, wet mouth. And like an animal who'd been deprived of his food, he kissed her.

Messy and primitive and raw. Choking on tongues. Biting on lips. Hands groping at whatever they could reach. They found an oasis in each other.

He rucked up her shirt and pulled down the cups of her bra. "Gimme those tits."

Then his mouth was on her nipple, sucking and nipping the sentient flesh. God, how she'd missed this with him.

"Has Jake been takin' good care of you, baby?"

"Yes." Now, she could imagine what it was going to be like to have them both together.

"I can't wait to watch him fuck you."

Billy unzipped her jeans.

"Stretch that little hole wide open for me."

His fingers went inside her. She was dripping.

"Yeah, baby, I'm gonna shove my dick right in there beside his and fuck you with him."

And she gushed into his hand.

"That's what you dream about, ain't it?"

Please.

"Yes." She grabbed onto his wrist. "Finger-fuck me, now. Hard. I need to come."

He pushed her into the tack room and, pulling her pants down to her knees, Jake bent her over a chair. "How many fingers, baby? Jake get you up to four yet?"

"Sometimes." Her thighs were shaking.

"Mmm." He put in one, then two, then three. "Just wait 'til you take all five."

"Fuck."

"Like the thought of that, too, do ya?"

"Yes." She heard his buckle unlatch.

He rubbed the hot fluid dripping out of her up the crack of her ass. "Me too, baby. If you can take my fist, then you can take us both inside you."

"Are you gonna fist me now?" God, she wanted him to.

"Fuck, Em." He fucked her cunt with his fingers, kissing his way up her spine. "You don't know how bad I want to see my hand disappear inside you. It's gonna happen, I promise, and when it does, we'll all be together on our bed. Jake suckin' on your titties. Rubbin' your clit."

Jesus.

"We'll always know what you need." The head of his dick poked at her asshole. "Play with your nipples, baby."

"You don't have lube."

"I could get enough right here from you." Billy's fingers were in her pussy. He wasn't wrong. "But don't worry, I ain't fuckin' your ass here."

He slid his dick between her cheeks, pumping his hips while he fucked her with his fingers. "I just love you so much."

"And I love you."

Sweat dripped from his hair onto her back, and he thrust faster and faster. His dick and his fingers were in perfect sync.

Hot semen spurted onto her skin.

Then he went still. He stayed like that for a moment, then catching his breath, Billy turned her around.

"I'm so sorry." He scrubbed his face with his hands. "Fuck, what have I done?"

Twenty-Two

He'd become too well acquainted with this log by the river. Levi sat on it, staring out at the vista before him as he had with Walker the day before. He could smell the beans and bacon cooking. It did little to motivate him. Even though today was for rest, he had to get going. There was still so much to do.

Get the horses shod.

See about the oxen and winter supplies.

Repack the wagon to make space for the provisions they'd purchased.

And for my wives.

Yes, plural.

He couldn't have one without the other, and Levi wanted them both, so the world be damned, he was taking them.

How he would explain his decision to Elijah and his sisters, Levi did not know. Of course, he wanted their approval, not that he thought he'd get it, but they were his family. He didn't care what anyone else might think. In time, he hoped they'd at least come to respect it.

Another hour rolled by when Elijah sat down on the log beside him. He was quiet for several moments before he cleared his throat. "Walker told us."

"Told you what?"

"That there's going to be a wedding." His gaze shifted away from the water. "For Lucy, Fallon, and you."

Damn you, Walker.

"It's all right, brother." Elijah cupped his shoulder. "He figured you'd have a helluva time comin' up with the words, so he spared you. Had a sit-down with me and your sisters. Explained the ways of his late wife's people."

"You must think I'm mad."

"Back home I probably would have, but that's not our home anymore." With a half-shrug, he rubbed his lips together. "Oddly enough, the things he said made sense. Our lives here will be different. Harder in some ways, but simple in many others, so no, I don't think that. Besides, if the Mormons can have twenty, why can't you have two?"

Elijah's lips slowly curved into a smile, and they shared a chuckle.

"And my sisters?"

"Shocked, as you might expect, but not abhorrently so." And he patted him on the back. "Given some time, I'm certain they'll come around. They like Lucy and Fallon, but more than that, they dearly love *you*."

Levi turned his gaze back to the river. "I hope you're right."

"Lucky bastard." He could hear the smirk in Eli's voice. "Two women warming your bed at night. However will you manage?"

"Honestly?" Levi turned to look at him. "I don't know."

"C'mon." Eli rose, pulling him up from the log. "We have to go and wish Dalton farewell."

"Farewell?"

He nodded. "He and some of the others are setting off this morning."

Levi counted twelve wagons. *That's half of us.* Lined up, their oxen hitched, the bedraggled travelers took up positions alongside them. He surveyed the scene, his hands on his hips, and with a shake of his head, walked over to the first in the line.

"George?" His back to him, the man lashed a barrel of water to the wagon's side. "Dalton?"

"Levi."

"Are you sure about this, George?"

"I am." Nodding, he wiped the sweat from his hands on his britches. "No offense to you, Gantry, but I've thought on it. I'm taking my family to California."

He glanced at his wife, their young child strapped to her back. The man was a couple of years older than Levi, at most.

"But—"

"I know you don't think we can make it, but I believe in my gut that we will." His hands slipped inside his pockets. "Winter *is* coming, though. You're right about that. So, I'm not about to waste another day sittin' here."

"And the others?" Had Dalton convinced them all to follow him into what could very well be their deaths?

"St. John and the rest of 'em decided for themselves." He glanced at the wagons down the line. "It was a simple choice to make. See, you don't even know where you're going and nobody wants to stay here until spring. It's not safe for the womenfolk."

There was nothing left for Levi to say. "This is farewell, then."

"It is." George grasped his hand, his shake strong. "Good luck to you, my friend. I've been privileged to travel this far with you, and I hope your journey takes you to whatever riches you seek."

A place to call home.

That's all he wanted.

"I wish you well, Dalton." Levi let go of the man's hand and hugged him. "Godspeed. Perhaps someday our paths shall cross again."

He stood there and watched them depart, knowing in his heart it was the last time he'd ever see his friend.

"Don't be so glum." Walker slung an arm around his neck and pulled him away. "Didn't I tell you every man has his own path to follow?"

"You think he'll make it?" He was looking for some assurance that they could.

"Can't say," the mountain man said, and spat tobacco into the dirt. "Come along, now. There's some folks I want you and Eli to meet."

He brought them to a wagon. It looked the same, but was outfitted differently than the others he'd seen during their travels. Besides a water barrel, a small chicken coop was affixed to its side. A panel in the back was folded down with a swinging leg that formed a table. A stout man with ginger hair, his arms folded across his chest, propped himself beside it.

"Hank, get over here." Josiah waved the man toward them. "Meet Levi Gantry and Elijah Brooks. Them here are the young men I was tellin' you about."

He traded a wary glance with Eli.

"Boys, this is Hank Coulter."

"You can call me, Cookie. Most do." The man extended his hand, shaking each of theirs with a firm grip. "Pleasure."

"Hank was a cook for the Army, but he's done with that life, ain't ya?" Like he was an old friend, Walker drew him to his side.

"He's ready to settle down. Stay in one place. So, he's agreed to go with you."

What?

As stunned by this as he was, Elijah raised his brow. Levi could count the number of creases on his forehead.

"My wagon's empty. Provision it with what I say and I can guarantee no one'll starve," the man assured them. "We'll have plenty to see us through."

"Take some of the burden off the girls, too," Walker said, throwing in his two cents.

"How many wagons in your party?"

"Twelve now."

"Fifty people?" Hank, Cookie, or whatever he called himself, rubbed the red stubble along his jaw.

That sounded about right. "Yeah, give or take."

"That'll work." And his hand came down on the table. "I can take care of 'em all."

"So, what do you say?" His head cocked, Walker looked at them expectantly.

Flabbergasted, Levi didn't know what the hell to say.

Eli, on the other hand, had no such issue. "We'll have to discuss it with Archer and the others, but I'm guessing it'll be all right."

"You hear that, Hank? Yer leavin' in the mornin'." Josiah slapped him on the back and motioned to a group of men sitting by the fire. "Tyndall?"

Three men rose.

"Oliver Tyndall, free man from Texas. Cooper Hawkes started off in Kentucky. They know cattle, and they know horses. Yer gonna need 'em."

One man was dark-skinned, the other light. Both wore boots, chaps, and wide-brimmed hats. They tipped their chins.

"And this is Taghee Smith. He's from the Bannock tribe. He knows the land. Very resourceful. Yer gonna need him, too."

Levi turned to Elijah. He only shrugged. "Why?"

"All in good time, son." He patted his shoulder. "Now, y'all need to get everybody ready."

Then he turned around to leave them with these men they didn't know.

"One more thing." And with a bob of his head, Walker grinned. "Found you a preacher. You'll be wed come supper."

A mild morning for this early in March, surprisingly, the temperature was above freezing. Usually, that didn't happen until late April or May. Both of them working the same shift, Jake and his brother quietly slipped from the house before dawn. He'd been subdued these past few weeks, certain he'd lose favor, that the earth would punish him somehow for his 'mistake'.

Billy came to him that very morning to tell him what he'd done, that he'd failed his test, as did Emily, shortly thereafter. He understood. Jake couldn't blame either of them, and to be honest, it surprised him they hadn't given in to each other sooner. They weren't the first, and they surely wouldn't be the last, to have done so.

His brother's concern, though, was a valid one.

He had broken the rule.

Still, Jake didn't believe he'd be punished for it or lose favor.

I hope not, at least.

Not looking forward to another long day mucking through snow and shit, he pulled in and parked behind Kellan's truck. "A couple more weeks, this'll all be over, and we can get back to work on the house."

"Yeah." And he tapped away on his phone. "Griffin ain't comin' in today. He's a daddy. Shiloh had the baby last night—well, early this mornin.'"

"Tell him congratulations from me." Glancing at his brother, Jake smiled. "What'd they have?"

"A boy. Named him Jaxson."

"Jaxson Archer. That's a good name," he said, and dropping his phone onto the console, he reached into the backseat. "I wonder how Cassie's takin' it."

"Don't know, and I ain't askin'."

The way his brother said it had them both laughing.

"Ready?" Jake tossed Billy his work bag.

"As I'll ever be."

He opened the door. "We best get to it, then."

Calving is repetitive work. A lot of it is observation, looking after the cows and heifers to see if any need intervention. After delivery, it's making sure the calf is warm, can stand, and is nursing. Once that's going well, and the calf's gotten a bellyful of colostrum from its mother, it's time to process the baby critter—tag, inoculate, dip the navel, castrate the bulls, get a weight, and write it all down.

Jake was doing just that. Processing. Tanner and Billy were on the opposite side of the snowy pasture, pulling a calf. A flash of red in his periphery made him look toward the gate. Arien swung it open, and holding her pregnant belly, went over to Kellan. They spoke for a moment, then she turned around and headed back inside.

Thinking little of it, he returned to his task until Kellan tapped on his shoulder. "Justin called. He needs you and Billy to come home."

"Did he say why?"

"No, just that he's been tryin' to reach you two on your phones." He pursed his lips, rubbing at the back of his neck. "And he said to hurry."

He drove like lightning. Neither he nor his brother spoke on the ride back to the house. Billy tore up the steps the moment he put the truck in park. Jake could hear him shouting from the sidewalk, "Ma? Dad?"

But no one was there.

"What the fuck, Jake?"

"I'm texting them."

Then Billy handed him a note, written in their father's barely legible scrawl.

We couldn't wait.

Come to the hospital.

And come quickly.

Twenty-Three

He felt like he might be sick.

Acid churned in his gut. Emotion gathering in his throat made it difficult for him to breathe.

His brother was trying to keep his shit together, but Jake looked about as ghastly as Billy felt.

What the fuck was happening?

And what was Dad thinking about leaving a note like that?

It was too much information and nowhere near enough.

"Text them again."

"I just did." Billy glanced at his phone. "No one's answering."

It had to be Mom. He and Jake knew that. But what could it be? Did she take a fall? Have another stroke? Or worse, was she...

Anything but that. Please, don't let it be that.

Dark clouds and the Tetons loomed ahead. And Billy couldn't help but wonder if everything that was happening was all his fault.

Jake turned south on 89, and the angry skies opened, unleashing a torrential downpour. Water cascaded down the glass in sheets. The wipers couldn't keep up with it.

"Fuck, come on." Forced to slow down, his brother slammed his fist into the steering wheel.

They had to hurry, but the closer they got, the more he didn't want to get there.

The rain had slowed to an annoying drizzle when they reached Jackson. It was just enough to need the wipers on to clear it, but not enough to keep them from squeaking on the glass. Jake pulled into the parking lot next to Justin's Porsche and, shaking on the inside, Billy tried to take a deep breath.

"It's gonna be okay." Jake rested his hand on his.

"You don't know that."

And he squeezed it. "Yes, I do."

"What if…" Billy couldn't even say it.

"Whatever it is, we'll get through it together." Then he let his hand go. "It's gonna be okay."

The automatic doors opened. Justin paced in the waiting room as he had only a month before. With his hands clasped behind his neck, he stared down at his shoes wearing tracks in the puke-green carpet.

Jake got to him first. "Is it Mom? How is she?"

"I don't know." His fingers plowed through his hair and he hitched his thumb toward the double doors. "Victor carried her in there and I haven't seen either of them since."

"What happened?" he asked.

"She said she had a terrible headache and asked me to get her some aspirin. When I came back with it, she was asleep."

Justin's head shook, a faraway look in his eyes. "But I couldn't get her to wake up."

What does that mean? Billy glanced at Jake for an answer, not finding one.

"I was only gone for a minute." Justin sighed and sat in a chair. "I called your Dad. Then you. He said we couldn't wait. I'm sorry."

"Do you think it's another stroke?" Jake took a seat beside him.

"Maybe." He lifted a shoulder, staring at the floor again. "I don't know. I'm a painter, not a doctor."

Chrissakes, you gotta know something.

Billy got down on his haunches in front of him. "Did Dad say anything?"

"No, he just held her, whispering to her, running his fingers through her hair, all the way here."

"What do we do?" he asked his brother.

"We wait."

Every minute seemed like an hour. An hour felt like an eternity. They didn't bother with shitty vending machine coffee. Nobody spoke. No one looked at their phone.

"You know what they say, no news is good news. Your mama's gonna be just fine."

Billy held onto that thought. It repeated in his head over and over again.

Mid-afternoon, the sun peeked out of the clouds and the double doors finally opened.

His eyes red and glassy, Victor sat in a chair across from them. "They're taking your mom upstairs now."

"Can we see her?"

His elbows on his knees, his father leaned forward. "Yes, but we need to talk first."

Billy tried to swallow past the lump forming in his throat. "Did she have a stroke?"

Jake asked, "Is she okay?"

"Your mom had a cerebral hemorrhage," he said, using his doctor's voice. Maybe it was the only way he knew how. "Her blood pressure caused an artery in her brain to weaken and bulge like an inflated balloon—it's called an aneurysm, and it ruptured."

"Can they fix it?" But he already knew the answer. His father's golden eyes brimmed with tears.

He took his hand. "No, son, they can't."

Beside him, Justin wept.

"What do we do, then?"

Victor closed his eyes, and the tears spilled down his face. "Say goodbye."

The Lakota don't have a word for goodbye. Instead, they say 'toksa ake' which means I'll see you again. And they were the words that Billy whispered when they lowered her into the ground.

Long after the grave was filled with dirt and the flowers were laid on top, the four of them stood there in silence, too numbed by grief to move.

Victor gazed up at the three-headed peak, a slow smile spreading across his face. "Do you hear that?"

"Hear what, my love?"

"The mountain." His father held onto Justin's arm. "Carrie used to say if you listen closely, you can hear it hum."

"We need to go now, Vic. Everyone is waiting in the hall." Patting the hand on his arm, Justin turned him away from the grave. "Come on. We can come back tomorrow."

Toksa ake, Mama. Forgive me. I love you.

The luncheon after the funeral was a blur. Like a fuzzy dream.

Billy ate the food, but couldn't taste it. Emily sat with him and Jake, squeezing his hand. He squeezed hers back, but he couldn't feel it.

He wanted to cry or scream. Something. Anything. But nothing would come out.

Then, he came out of the restroom to find Arien waiting just outside the door. Maybe it was the way she looked up at him with her sad, hazel eyes, her wound nearly as fresh as his own, that had him putting his arms around her. Whatever it was, the floodgates opened.

"Oh, Billy, I know what you're feeling." Her voice cracking, she rubbed his back while he wept. "And I know sorry doesn't help much, but I am."

He couldn't say how long they stayed like that. But his eyes burned. Billy opened them to see Tanner, Kellan, and Jake right there behind her. Fitting, since the five of them were all in the same fucked up club.

"It's all my fault."

Arien lifted his chin. "What's your fault, babe?"

"That she's dead."

Jake must've told them what he said.

Justin sat him on the sofa. His brother poured a glass of whiskey and put it in his hand.

Billy chanced a glance at his father as he swallowed it, but he didn't say a word.

Not at first, anyway.

"Talk to me, son." He sounded broken. "Tell me what's goin' on in your head?"

"I broke the rules." Billy finished the whiskey and set down the glass. "Mama died because of me. It's my punishment."

"Is that what you think?" Cocking his head, Victor scoffed.

"Just because you kissed Emily before your birthday that the earth took your mother?"

"I did more than kiss her."

"I don't care if you fucked her."

"Victor." With a hand on his thigh, Justin calmed him.

"Billy, I want you to listen to me." His father sat beside him and held onto his shoulders. "Her death was not a consequence of anything you might've done."

"You don't know that."

"I do know that." Insistent, he raised his voice and then softened it. "We discovered the aneurysm on her CT scan when she had the stroke, but unfortunately, because of its location, surgical repair wasn't an option." He glanced over at Justin. "All we could do was try to keep her pressure down and hope…"

"Are you saying you knew there was a ticking time bomb in her head?"

His eyes filling, he nodded. "Yes."

"Did she?"

And he shook his head. "No, son."

"She didn't need to know." Justin confirmed he knew all along, too. "What good would it have done?"

The fuck?

He wasn't sure how to feel besides sad. Relieved that he wasn't cursed? Pissed they kept it from him? Would he have done anything differently had he known?

"Everything you're feeling is normal, Billy." Justin put his arms around him. "You and your brother just lost the woman who loved you even before you were born. Your father lost his wife. I lost my sister. We're all second-guessing ourselves here. What if I had done this or hadn't done that? I should have said this…I shouldn't have gotten angry. The shit just keeps running through your head. Believe me, I know."

"It's called grieving, son." His dad had one arm around him

and Justin, and the other around Jake. "She loved the two of you more than anything in this world. Even me. And that's how it's supposed to be. Now, it's your turn to pass that love on to Emily and your children, so that one day, they can do the same."

"It's true, you know," Justin said, his head resting on Billy's shoulder.

"What is?"

"Love is timeless, and it's forever." His fingers slipped into his father's hair. "It truly never dies."

Twenty-Four

Emily marked off another day on the calendar with a big red X. *Three more weeks.*

Twenty-one days from today, she'd marry Jake at the courthouse in Jackson, and then afterward, she'd put on Miss Lilly's dress to meet him and Billy at the stones. It's there, she'd become the wife of two brothers, and they'd both become husbands to her.

Perfect.

The only thing putting a damper on the long-awaited occasion was knowing how badly they grieved. And not just Billy and Jake, but Victor and Justin, too. Emily, her mom, and even Grams went over there often, to help out or cook them a meal.

Most days, Victor didn't come home until late. Then, he'd pick

THE Hardest Part | 195

at his dinner, and go straight up to bed. It was a rare occasion to see Justin come out of his studio. He painted in there, night and day. That left Jake and Billy on their own.

Grams told her not to worry. It had only been a couple of months, after all. Everyone processes loss on their own time, in their own way. "Your job is to love them through it," she said.

"I am, Grams." Emily hugged her with a heavy sigh. "I just want everyone to be happy again."

"It's there, dear. You just can't see it right now." She took a step back, and with a tender smile, brushed the hair from her face. "I'm gonna tell you the same thing I told Arien. Life has a way of giving us our joy back."

She wasn't so sure about that. "It hasn't for Mama."

"What makes you say that, honey?"

"I dunno." Emily shrugged. Maybe she shouldn't have said anything. "She pretends to be happy, but when no one's lookin', I think that she's sad—lonely, you know?"

"Hmm." But she was nodding.

"And soon, Mama won't have me here anymore."

"Could be that's exactly what she needs."

Her brow shooting upward, Emily looked into her grandmother's eyes. "What do you mean?"

"Your mother was so young when Timothy and William were killed, but she had you to care for, my dear girl." Grams drew her to her chest and kissed her on the forehead. "Being on her own just might be the kick in the ass she needs to take a chance on life again."

Emily tossed the red marker to her dresser and sighed. "Maybe she's right."

Then, noting the time, she packed up her veil, got in her car, and drove over to the ranch. Emily was taking her cousin up on the offer she made that time they got their picture taken in Jackson. Arien was talented with a camera, so she knew the photos would turn out gorgeous. Jake and Billy were going to love it.

"God, you're huge!" Afraid she might come tumbling down, Emily followed Arien closely up the stairs. Seven months along, it looked like she had a basketball in her belly. "I don't remember Shiloh being this big."

"Well, there are two of them in there."

"I didn't mean for it to sound like that, because you look fucking amazing."

"For a pregnant chick, I guess." She giggled, rubbing circles on her belly. "C'mon, I've got everything set up in my old room."

Emily gazed at the pretty sage walls and fondly remembered going with her mom and Grams to choose the paint. She couldn't believe that it was less than two years ago because it seemed like a lifetime since then. Smiling, she slipped into her lacy white underthings and pinned the veil to her head.

"Oh, Ems, you look so beautiful." Arien adjusted the tulle to frame her face. "Only three weeks to go until the big day. Are you excited?"

"Course, I am. Weren't you?"

She pursed her lips, then grinned, the shutter on her camera clicking. "We were too busy putting a wedding together in only two weeks, remember?"

As if she could forget.

"We pulled it off, though, didn't we?"

"Yeah, we did." Arien kissed her cheek. "And it was perfect."

"You're happy?" It seemed so, but she needed to hear her say it. Emily placed her hand on her cousin's belly, hoping to feel the babies kick.

"So happy, Ems." Arien's soft palm covered her own. "I don't even want to imagine a life without them."

Awestruck, Emily felt life move within her.

"Is everything all right?"

"Yeah." She nodded, swiping wetness from beneath her eyes. "I just feel...I dunno...guilty?"

"Why?"

She hesitated.

"For going ahead with the wedding so soon after losing their mom." *There, I said it.* "They didn't want to postpone it, though."

"And why would they?" Arien looked at her like the thought alone was ludicrous. "They've only been waiting forever to marry you."

"Because they're sad," she reasoned, throwing her hands in the air. "Victor is sad. Justin is sad. Everybody's sad, and I don't know how to make it go away."

"You can't. And you shouldn't even try." Arien took hold of her shoulders and released a sigh. "They're always gonna miss her, Ems. That will never go away, but it doesn't mean they can't feel joy."

Nodding, she bit into her lip.

"Just love them."

"That's what Grams said."

"Listen to her, Ems." Arien winked, and then she grinned. "You know she's always right."

Billy thought he was ready, but nothing could have prepared him for the feelings that bloomed in his chest when he saw her.

In a simple gown of creamy white, he'd never seen her look more beautiful.

The years of waiting had been worth it, and he'd do it all again to have this moment. To share a life with her. To make Emily his wife.

He glanced at Victor and Justin. Billy patted his breast pocket. They smiled and did the same. Jake clasped his hand, and with thoughts of their mother, his vision blurred. Each man carried a square of cloth from her wedding dress, a symbolic way to have her with them. Matthew Brooks gave his father the idea. He gave Arien a ribbon from Jennifer's dress the day she married his sons.

Billy felt her spirit.

The mountain hummed.

In his heart, he knew she was here.

And as Emily walked toward them, glowing in the fiery hues of the setting sun, Billy wiped the wetness from his face. He thought of their first kiss when he was fifteen. Bike rides. Sandboxes. Haylofts and bonfires.

Then her mother placed Emily's hand in his, the other in his brother's.

This was the important part, the moment the three of them had been waiting for, and with the purest intent and absolute love in their hearts, he and Jake took Emily as their wife, and she took them for her husband. Mind, body, and soul. Together, as a triad, they became whole.

It was good.

It was right.

And it was perfect.

Three hours into the party, after dinner, and dancing, and Maizie's lemon buttercream cake, Jake traded a look with him, then he swooped Emily into his arms. She shrieked. "Where are we going?"

"Home."

"Wait." Justin came running after them. He put a wrapped oblong box in his hands and winked. "Happy weddin' day. You can open it later."

Billy tossed the box in the back and opened the door for his brother and his wife. Jake set her down, and while she scooted over, his brother dashed around the truck and got in on the driver's side.

Jake glanced over at him. "Ready?"

He was. "Yup."

They pulled away from the ranch, passed the drive to Kim's Dutch barn, then turned on the road toward town. "C'mon, baby," she said, tugging on Jake's arm. "Where are you takin' me?"

"Told you, wifey." He chuckled, but refused to elaborate. "Home."

"Where's home?"

Wherever you are.

"You'll see." Kissing her on the cheek, Jake nudged his shoulder. "Think we should blindfold her?"

"We could." Billy pictured it in his mind. "Ain't a bad idea."

"You wouldn't."

"Oh, I would, and I think you'd like it if I did." He sipped a sweet kiss from her lips. "But bein' I don't have one handy, I'll just cover your eyes before we get there."

And a few miles later, he did just that.

The late spring breeze rustled through the trees. Flowers in every color filled the porch. And the sound of the creek welcomed them home.

Jake opened his door. "Got her?"

"Yeah." Billy guided her out, holding his hand over her eyes. "No peeking, Em."

How they'd kept this a surprise, he would never know. But they did, somehow. He couldn't wait to see the look on her face.

One.

Two.

Three.

Billy uncovered her eyes, and tucking her beneath his chin, wrapped his arms around her middle. "Open 'em."

Her jaw dropped. Literally. "This is ours?"

"Yeah." With his arm around her shoulders, Jake pulled them both against him. "Billy had a vision."

"We built it together." Billy kissed her crown. "With a whole lotta help."

Family. Friends. Community. It's the heart of Brookside.

Emily twisted in his arms and gazed up at him. "It's the most amazing, incredible, beautiful house I've ever seen."

"Just wait, you haven't been inside yet." And Jake lifted her into his arms. "We should fix that, don't you think?"

"I do."

Miss Kim and their mom, before she died, helped them choose some of the furniture. Justin's paintings graced the walls. They left most of it a blank slate, so they could fill it with the things they loved, and make it their own together.

"Welcome home, beautiful wife." Jake set her down. "We love you."

"That we do," Billy said, putting the box on a table. "There's a greenhouse out back. Ruby, Chaser, and Blaze are in the barn. Tanner brought 'em over this mornin'. I think they already like it here."

"Aren't you gonna open it?"

"What?"

Emily tipped her chin toward the table. "The box Justin gave you."

"Go on." He chuckled, patting her on the behind.

Like a kid on Christmas morning, she tore off the shiny gold paper and lifted the lid. "Look, it's a drawing of our house."

"Justin drew that at dinner the night Billy described his vision for this place." Jake held up the framed drawing. "You see this, bro?"

He saw it.

Charcoal on vellum paper. As if he'd been inside his head, Justin sketched it exactly as Billy had seen it. But he and Jake built more than a house here. Strengthening their bond as brothers, they laid the foundation for the future of their family, for the life and dreams they'd share with Emily.

"I'm so lucky." She stood on her tiptoes to kiss him, then did the same with Jake. "I get to love you both all of my life."

He and his brother exchanged a glance, and Jake hoisted her into his arms. He carried her to their room, and when her feet touched the floor, Billy bent his head and kissed his wife while his brother unfastened her gown.

Jake took his place, and slipping the straps from her shoulders, a cloud of white billowed to the floor. Naked, but for a wisp of lace between her legs, his brother gazed at her, circling her nipples with his thumbs. "We're the lucky ones, *michante*."

After he removed her panties, Jake laid her down on the bed. They each claimed a nipple, sucking, nibbling, and kissing, they worshipped every inch of her skin. They reached the sweet spot between her thighs, and she opened. Her fingers in his hair, Emily yanked his head to her cunt. Hot salted honey. Billy kissed her clit, tasting her sweetness on his tongue, while his brother filled her with his fingers.

"Please." It was a breathless, whimpering plea.

"Don't let her come yet, brother."

He lifted his head from her pussy to see Jake gripping his dick, positioning himself at her entrance. Her body trembled, and her eyes went wide. Billy reached for her hand, and as he held her fingers to his lips, she sucked the air in through her teeth. He didn't have to see it to know his brother was deep inside her.

"Oh, oh, oh."

Billy watched her lips part, the bliss on her beautiful face.

Then, withdrawing from her, Jake tapped his thigh.

He pushed himself inside her, and Christ, he'd never imagined it would feel like this. Tight, wet heat squeezed his cock. So tight he didn't think he could move.

Jake knelt on the bed beside them. His dick, hard and glistening with her sweetness, bobbed between his legs as he rubbed Emily's clit while he fucked her.

"That's it, baby," he praised her. "Squeeze the cum from my brother's cock."

And she did.

Billy thrust inside her faster, fire at the base of his spine. He didn't want to stop, but he couldn't hold on. Sweet fuck, he was burning alive.

Out of breath, he collapsed on top of her. "I love you."

Fingers combed through his sweat-drenched hair. "I love you, too."

"Happy weddin' day." Jake smacked him on the ass.

Same to you, brother.

Billy rolled onto his side.

And Jake took his place inside her.

Twenty-Five

Levi wrapped the cloth around his waist, covering himself as best he could. If he was going to share his blanket tonight, he figured he should at least wash the stink from his skin. After conferring with the others in their party, Cookie's wagon was loaded with their provisions, giving each family more space to pack the supplies they would need to get through the winter.

He had three yokes of oxen, new shoes on the horses' feet, and an unshakeable determination.

A slight chill in the air, gooseflesh prickled his skin. Levi dried off and dressed quickly. What was the date today? *Friday, the first day of October*. It would serve him well to remember it.

With Dalton and his party gone, the circle of wagons appeared woefully small. He would miss the man's camaraderie and hoped they'd make out all right. Perhaps it was best they'd chosen a different path. Fifty was plenty to be accountable for.

Elijah stood with the twins, little Elizabeth, holding onto his leg. "Are you ready, good brother?"

"I am."

"Oh, no, you are not." Victoria turned to her sister. "Get me a comb and the scissors."

She snatched the cloth from his hands, drying his hair while Mary Alice fetched the items she'd requested.

"What in tarnation are you doing, little sister?"

"You look like a shaggy old barn dog." And she went to work with the scissors. "Can't let you get married looking like that, so we're gonna tidy you up a bit."

"What difference does it make?" With a roll of her eyes, Mary Alice shook her head and turned away.

"Pay her no mind, Levi. It's gonna take her some time to get used to the notion, is all." She patted his shoulders and took a step back to appraise her work. "That's much better. All done."

"I cannot believe you're all fine with this." Mary Alice glared at Elijah, then gathering her skirts, she looked at him. "And *you* expect us to be a witness to it?"

"I expect nothing, Mary Alice." Levi took her by the hand, the tattered, mud-stained hem of her dress falling to her feet. "Least of all that you'd understand, but you *will* show Lucy and Fallon all due courtesy and respect. Is that understood?"

She nodded, staring down at her shoes.

"Good." He let her hand go. "You can wait here if you'd rather."

"And go hungry?" Her lips twitching, she glanced up at him. "I'm coming. For the food. Heard you got us a cook. And 'cause I love you."

"I love you, too." Levi drew her to his chest and hugged her, smoothing her long blonde hair down her back.

"We're gonna go to hell for this, you know."

"Hell?" He didn't believe in such a place. Or heaven, either. "I reckon, Mary Alice, we've already been there."

The preacher, if that's what he really was, waited for them in a small room, tucked away behind the counter where they'd purchased their flour and beans. He didn't look like a man of the cloth, but if Levi had learned anything, it's that looks could be deceiving out here. Few folks were what they seemed.

"Name?" the man asked him.

"Levi Gantry."

"And the bride?"

Josiah spoke up and tapped on the good book the man was writing in. "Lucy Fallon Walker."

Well, aren't you a clever one?

It took all of five minutes.

Before he could even kiss his bride—one of them, anyway—Walker tugged on his arm and ushered them all outside. "Now we can have the real weddin'."

"What was that?" Mary Alice pulled her head back and wrinkled up her nose. "Pretend?"

"*That* was your way," Walker said, then a faint smirk curled his lip. "This is ours."

They returned to their camp, where Taghee, Hawkes, Tyndall, and Cookie waited with Archer and the others.

A triangle of stones had been laid out around the fire. The tall Bannock approached Josiah and placed a blade in his palm. Levi swallowed and looked at him. "What's that for?"

"Vows are sealed in blood." Taghee dipped his chin. "Forged in fire."

"I cannot watch this." Hiding her face in Elijah's chest, Mary Alice covered her eyes.

Taghee chuckled and took a step back.

Without being told to, Fallon and Lucy extended their hands

to their father, palm up, so Levi followed suit. Then Josiah cut each of their hands, binding Levi to each of his daughters. Taghee spoke in a tongue he didn't understand, and after he finished speaking, the old man removed the bloodied bindings and tossed them in the fire.

"It is done, husband." Gazing up at him, Lucy ran her fingers through his newly trimmed beard. "We are married now."

Levi supposed he should kiss his wife, but he wasn't sure which one he was supposed to kiss first.

Fallon decided for him. She got on her tiptoes, and bending his neck, she kissed him. When she released him, Lucy was smiling, patiently waiting her turn, so he obliged her.

Cookie slapped his back. "Made us all a nice supper to celebrate your nuptials. Butchered a pig."

"C'mon, everyone gather 'round and eat." Levi waved a bottle in the air. "I've got a lot I need to tell you."

They all sat before the fire, tin plates on their laps. If anyone was put off by what they'd witnessed or disgusted by what he'd done, they didn't show it. Levi got a few curious looks from folks, but he pretended not to notice.

Walker wiped the grease from his mouth with his sleeve, swallowed some whiskey, and stood on his wobbly legs.

"I need y'all to listen up, and listen good." He paused until he had their undivided attention. "I seen all your faces before I ever laid eyes on ya, and I know what's comin'. Came to me in a dream a long, long time ago. Follow the *Seeds-kee-dee-agie*, and when you can't follow it no more, keep going. When you see the lake beneath the three-headed mountain, you will have found your new home."

"He's drunk," someone heckled. It sounded like Clary.

"Maybe I am." And he took another swig from the bottle. "Still, I seen it. Yer gonna build a town there, grow food, and breed cattle. Keep the ways of the people, listen to the mountain, respect the earth, and you will flourish and prosper."

"And if we don't?" Archer asked.

"You'll die."

Clary waved a hand in front of his face and stood. "Take another shot, Walker."

"Mock me all you want." Not bothered in the slightest, Josiah went over to the Bannock. "Taghee and these fine gentlemen are going with y'all 'cause they know what I've seen will come to be. Same as it did with Levi and my girls here."

He swung around toward where they sat and nearly fell over.

Levi and Elijah jumped to their feet, catching him in the nick of time.

"Won't be long, boy. Mark my words. They're gonna see, and they won't be givin' you no shit then." Slinging an arm around his neck, he said, "Yer gonna have a dozen sons, one for each wagon that left you."

Elijah's eyes went wide, and he hid a chuckle behind his hand.

"And you?" Walker poked Eli's chest, his head bobbing. "Yer gonna see yer sister again."

And he stumbled off, taking the bottle with him.

"What the hell?"

"He's drunk, Eli. He doesn't know what he's saying."

"Yes, he does." Fallon rose and went to him. "Come, rest now. We travel again in the morning."

Between his two wives and their impending departure on his mind, he got little.

Cookie woke the camp for breakfast. They all ate in reflective quietude, then lined up the wagons to set off on the last leg of their journey.

After Taghee, Hawkes, and Tyndall on horseback, Coulter's wagon, the coop filled with chickens, was first. His. Elijah's.

Levi called out their names one by one.

"Archer, Jacoby, Keough, Lewis, Quigley, Mathers, Clary, Wilson, Shepard, Edwards."

And each of them answered the same.

"Ready, Gantry."

Walker stood beside him. "Take good care of my girls, ya hear?"

"You already know I will."

"Heh." He clapped him on the shoulder. "That I do."

"Are you sure you won't come with us?"

"It ain't for me to go. Never could stay in one place for too long." Josiah winked. "But don't worry none, I know where to find ya."

"Papa." Hugging him, Lucy wept.

Fallon kissed the old man's face.

"*Abisha'i*," she choked in a whisper.

Goodbye.

Jake closed the cover of Levi's journal.

Arien, with Kellan and Tanner on either side of her, adjusted the pillow behind her back, her mouth hanging open. "You can't do that to me, Jake."

"Do what?"

"End the story like that." She was making these funny motions with her hands, like a hamster running in one of the spinning things. She'd probably be bouncing on her toes if she could. "C'mon, I know there's more."

"They followed the river and found the mountain," he said, teasing her. "You're living on it."

She stuck her tongue out at him.

Victor had Arien on strict bedrest until the babies were born. He, Emily, and Billy came by now and then to keep her company, watch movies, and tell stories.

"I know all those names."

"They're the OG, pretty girl." Tanner slipped his arm around her, tucking Arien beside him. "Didn't I tell you, everyone in Brookside either came from or married into one of those families?"

"Yes, I know that, but he's leaving out parts." She palmed her husband's cheek, but Arien was looking at Jake. "Was the old man, right?"

"About what?"

"Did Levi have twelve sons?"

"He did." Grinning, Jake bit into his lip with a nod. "Six with Lucy and six with Fallon."

"Damn." Her eyes bugged out. "And what happened to Eli?"

"You're married to his great-grandsons."

Kellan and Tanner looked at each other and chuckled.

"Wait." Arien tried her hardest to sit up straighter, but with her enormous belly, she didn't get very far. "Is his sister alive or dead?"

"They're all dead, baby cakes." Kellan helped her up, and giving her a smooch, added another pillow behind her back. "Have been for more than a hundred years. You can pay 'em a visit at the cemetery."

"You're terrible." She playfully smacked his thigh. "I've been meaning to photograph all the old gravestones—preserve them somehow, you know?"

"Oh, I love that idea." Emily grabbed his hand and squeezed it. "After the babies come, we'll go with and help you."

That'd be cool.

"You should write a book of their stories, Jake." Rubbing her hands together like she was plotting, Arien grinned. "I'd read it."

I am.

"I might."

"I need to know what happened to little Elizabeth and the twins. All of them." And she put her hands together as if she were praying. "Please, tell me, did Elijah ever see his sister again?"

Can I get a pretty please with a cherry on top?

"Her name was Amelia. She was to marry Levi's brother, Caleb."

"But she didn't?"

Jake shook his head. "She didn't."

"How come?"

"You're gonna have to wait for the book." He winked. This was too much fun.

"No fair." She threw a pillow at him.

"I'm kidding." He caught it. "But it's a long story, so we should save that one for another day. Deal?"

"Party pooper." Pursing her lips, she tossed her blonde waves and gave in. "Fine. Deal."

"Oh, I brought you something." Jake handed her the manila envelope.

"What are these?"

"Old recipes I found. They were called receipts back then." A few of them had been written in Victoria's own hand. "Thought you could use 'em for your vlog, so I made copies for you."

"This is so cool, Jake." She held the envelope to her chest like a priceless treasure. To Arien it was, he supposed. "Thank you."

Billy, who sat on the other side of their wife, gave him his *'let's wrap this shit up'* look.

"Course, we need to preserve those, too." Jake stood and went over to kiss Arien's cheek. "Well, I need to get my wife home. You get some rest, and take care of those babies, now. Kel, Tanner, you two take care of her."

"Chrissakes, Jake, you can talk for fuckin' ever," Billy said when they got in the truck. "I was dyin' to go home an hour ago."

"What for?"

C'mon, now. You really gotta ask, wild one?

"We got plans for you."

Damn, right.

"You're so bad." She swatted Billy and grinned out the window.

"You complainin', sweet cheeks?"

"Never." And she kissed him.

Jake followed his wife into the house he built with his brother.

They could see and hear that creek from every room in the house. Billy's vision and Justin's sketch ultimately translated into one of the most impressive architectural features he ever could've imagined—their living room, a glass bridge that spanned the meandering creek, with views of Emily's flower garden in shades of ivory, cream, and white.

He smiled and went up the stairs.

Twenty-Six

Married six weeks, and there were still some days Emily had to pinch herself to be sure she wasn't dreaming. But then, she was living one, wasn't she?

The summer sun kissed the mountain's peak, bathing the sky in a beautiful display of colors, pink and orange and red. A shadow crept upward, the light fading from the hillside paddock where the horses grazed.

"Ruby," Emily called out to the dapple gray.

The mare came, with Chaser and Blaze following along behind her. They knew what time it was, and went right into their stalls in the barn for the night, as happy in their new home as she was. And with the horses inside, Emily returned to the house to prepare for dinner and game night.

It was Billy's idea. On Saturday nights, he and Jake went and got takeout from Harry's—the best, and the only, place to eat in town—and they each took a turn choosing which board game to play. Scrabble was Jake's pick for tonight.

He always wins, too, dang it.

Maybe this time she'd get lucky.

After a quick shower, Emily slipped into a pair of striped boy shorts and her cropped cotton cami. She heard footsteps from the kitchen, so she hurried, rubbing the body butter Shiloh made into her skin. Her latest hobby smelled delicious, like oranges and chocolate.

The footsteps faded, and suddenly, the house grew quiet. Too quiet. "Babe?"

But no one answered.

Was she hearing things now?

Figuring she must be, Emily shrugged, pulled her hair into a messy bun, and slathered vanilla gloss on her lips.

Then, she opened the ensuite door, and an arm snaked around her waist. "Gotcha."

She screamed.

"Whoa, Emily, it's me." Jake held her to his bare chest and chuckled.

She held her hand to her rapidly beating heart—not laughing. "You scared me."

"Didn't mean to." Grinning against her forehead, he kissed it. "Just wanted to surprise you."

"Well, you succeeded." Giggling, she twisted his nipple. "Where's Billy?"

"He's coming." His voice, dark and smoky, he walked her backward.

Her legs touched the mattress, and Jake pulled the clip from her hair. He gathered it in his hand, softly tugging as he took possession of her mouth. She allowed it, her body inching its way down to the bed.

"What about dinner?" Her lips skimmed the pulse at his neck. "And game night?"

"It'll keep."

He slipped the thin straps of her cami down her shoulders. With her arms trapped at her side, Jake released her breasts and nuzzled his face between the globes of supple flesh. His dick, hard as concrete in his faded blue jeans, weighed heavily on her thigh.

She shifted against him. "And this can't?"

"No." He kissed her nipple, leaving it with a little lick. "I need to be inside my wife."

He was inside her just this morning. Billy, too. Emily didn't get the chance to remind him of that, though, because her nipple was back in his mouth. As if they hadn't been fucking like bunnies mere hours ago, Jake sucked on it, biting into the tender bud, then soothing the sting with his tongue, while his fingers trailed up and down her neck, across her collarbone, and down again to caress her breasts.

With the ache in her pussy flaring, Emily lifted her hips. She wanted him. She always wanted him. And his brother. "I need you, too."

Jake pulled the boy shorts down her legs and freeing her arms, the cami remained around her waist. He held onto her breasts, squeezing them as he made his way down her tummy. His teeth grazing her skin, she fisted his hair, anticipating the moment she'd feel his lips on her clit and his fingers in her cunt.

A husky chuckle fanned her pussy.

Emily pulled on the long sable locks.

And his tongue swiped up her slit.

Fucking hell.

That first touch sent the heat of a million tiny stars shooting through her body, the same as it always did.

The man knew just how to make her crazy. Tantalizingly slow licks, fast flicks, and pointed circles with his tongue turned Emily into a whimpering, quivering mess. And it never failed. At the very moment she thought she'd die, Jake filled her with his fingers, fucking her while he sucked on her needy little clit until she screamed.

He knelt between her legs, licking up the copious wetness that coated his fingers. And when he was finished, he stood, popping the buttons open on his jeans. Thick and hard, his cock sprang free, bobbing between his legs as if calling to her.

She reached for him, and wrapping her fingers around his length, Emily kissed the precum from its tip. His head thrown back, Jake hissed, sucking the air in through his teeth. She loved knowing she had that effect on him, and swirling her tongue around the head, she took him into her mouth.

"Fuck." His fingers dragging through her hair, he yanked on the ends. "I'm gonna come."

She sucked harder, craving the taste of him.

In a quick maneuver, Jake pulled her off his dick and sat her on his thighs. He nipped at her nipple, probing her hole with his finger. "And when I do, baby, it's gonna be right here."

That's all he had to say.

Straddling him, Emily lowered herself onto his steely dick with a sharp intake of breath. She loved the way he filled her, how the initial penetration stretched her open to accommodate him.

He kissed her. "Lean back on your hands, now."

Emily complied. It put her at an odd angle, but Jake felt incredible inside her.

Her head tipped back, she closed her eyes, enjoying the unfamiliar sensation.

Warm, wet lips tugged at her nipple. Long hair tickled her skin. Emily smiled, and reaching for Billy, she almost toppled off of Jake, but he caught her. Holding her in position, he fed at her breast and watched his brother fuck her.

As he drifted in and out of her, Jake rubbed her clit with his thumb. Too much, and not enough, she whimpered. "Please."

"More, wife?" And with his dick already filling her, he slid his fingers inside.

"That's our girl." Billy pinched her nipple while Jake stroked his cock inside her pussy. "I love watching my brother fuck you, baby."

I know you do.

"Kiss me, Billy."

And he did. Twisting her nipple, Billy fucked her mouth with his tongue while Jake fucked her cunt with his fingers on his dick.

"Suck him," Jake commanded.

Billy's dick tapped her lips, and she opened.

Gladly.

"Yeah." And fucking her throat, he groaned. "She ready yet, brother?"

"See for yourself," Jake said, withdrawing his fingers. He left his cock inside.

Billy replaced them with four of his own. Brushing past his brother's dick, his fingers grazed the wet walls of her pussy, his thumb pressed into her clit.

"Ready for what?"

Jake lapping at her nipple, Billy pulled his hand out. "For your dream to come true."

Oh, yes, I'm ready, and I want it so bad. Please, please, please.

She'd had them fuck her together before, one in her ass and the other in her cunt. She'd taken Billy's fist inside her, all the way to the wrist, and then Jake's. Christ, there was nothing else like it. Emily begged for it often, and her husbands enthusiastically obliged her.

"We always know what you need, baby."

I need to you to stuff your big dick inside me.

She leaned forward onto Jake, biting at his lips. "I love you."

"We're gonna breed you together, *michante*." He thrust his hips up. "Put our baby in your belly."

"You wanna get me pregnant?"

"You wanna be?"

"I do."

Jake glanced over at his brother. Billy positioned himself behind her on the bed.

"Can't wait to fuck you when you're big and round." He grasped her nipples between his fingers. "And drink milk from these pretty tits."

Fuck.

The head of Billy's cock prodded at her opening, already filled with his brother's dick. He pushed forward, and it burned, the thin tissue stretching even further.

She must've cried out because Jake was stroking her hair and kissing her lips. "Relax, baby. Let him in."

"I'm trying." *But it hurts.*

"Shhh, you can do this." Jake rubbed her clit and Billy pushed in farther. "Take my brother's cock with mine."

Then he sucked her nipple into his mouth and Billy went all the way in.

Even if Emily could speak, and with the air locked in her lungs, she couldn't, there were no words to describe what she was feeling. But if there was a heaven, she was in it. These men, she was lucky enough to call hers, took her far beyond her wildest dreams.

Billy gripped her chin and, turning her face toward his, he kissed her. "I love you, Em."

"So beautiful." Jake held onto her hips, his lips brushing hers. "And perfect."

Everything that comes in threes is.

Emily had always known that together they would be.

And there'd always be something else to wait for, something more to look forward to. Becoming a mother someday. A teacher.

But the hardest part was behind her now, and with their love made even stronger for it, she'd learned to cherish every fucking moment of today. Even the waiting. Because too soon, tomorrow becomes yesterday.

She reached out to touch Jake's hair.

He held her hand to his face. "I love you with every breath, *michante*."

My heart.

Everything she ever wanted and dared to dream of was right here.

"I feel it in my bones." Stroking his cheek, Emily smiled. "And I love you both."

I always have and I always will.

Twenty-Seven

Billy led Airdrie's Christmas filly around the paddock. He and Tanner had been loving on her, physically holding her, and petting her all over from day one, so she was comfortable with human touch. Now, almost nine months old, Noëlle was a trainer's dream. Smart and sweet, she already knew some commands.

"Whoa." She stopped.

"Walk." She went.

They wouldn't start groundwork until she was a yearling, though.

Since Arien had the babies, Tanner left more responsibilities with him. He figured that was to be expected. When the time ever came, Billy wouldn't want to be away from Emily and his child for too long, either.

Kellan and Tanner took turns. Unless Grams, Miss Kim, or Matthew were up at the house, one of them was always with her.

Billy understood that, too. No one ever mentioned it, but despite Justin's sound logic, Jacoby's empty grave left some folks wondering.

He didn't believe it was possible, though. There's no way anyone could have survived that fall. Besides, the dream never came to him again. But better safe than sorry, he supposed.

Given time, Jacoby, the man, would be forgotten. Reduced to nothing more than a ghost story told around the campfire. Billy chuckled. The old loon probably would've liked that.

Instead of opening the gate like a normal person, Tanner hopped the paddock fence. "What's so funny, Billy boy?"

He stifled a smirk. "Uh, just thinkin'."

"How's our little lady here doin'?" Tanner asked. Offering her pieces of apple, he patted the filly's flank.

"Good," Billy said with a nod. "I was just gonna take her in and rub her down."

"I'll do it." And lifting his chin, he grinned. "You should go on home and see Ems, get busy makin' Harper and Cayden a little cousin or somethin'."

"Maybe we already have."

"Yeah?"

"Well, I'm hopin' so." He shrugged. "She ain't said nothin' yet."

It's not like Billy had any real reason to suspect Emily might be pregnant, except they'd been married nearly four months now. Chrissakes, how long does it take? Between him and his brother, one or the other, if not both of them, was always there loving on her. The cattle round-ups were starting up again soon. Then, sorting and fall market. Days and nights spent away from her. They'd have to wait again.

"I see you, and I know what you're thinkin'." Tanner did that thing where he pointed to Billy's eyes, then his own. And he winked. "That homecoming will be somethin' else, trust me. Of all people, you should know, it's the waitin' that makes everything so fucking worth it."

Yeah, he knew.

"You'll be all right."

He would, because Emily would be there waiting for him.

"I know."

Taking the lead from his hand, Tanner clapped his shoulder. "Now, go. Get on home to your wife."

Billy found her out on the back patio. Eyes closed, a textbook resting open on her chest. But it didn't look like she was sleeping.

"Hey." He kissed her brow and her beautiful green eyes opened. "Whatcha doin'?"

"Enjoying the sun." Emily sat up, tossing her book onto the table. "This could be one of the last warm days we've got left."

You're likely right.

"Think of how pretty it's gonna be, sittin' here, watchin' the snow fall."

"And cold." Drawing her knees to her chest, she hugged herself as if the December winds were already blowing. "Me and winter ain't friends."

Emily got a little blue, then, didn't she?

"This one'll be different." *And every winter after that.* "You've got me and Jake to keep you warm."

"That I do." She let go of her knees and glanced up at him, shielding her eyes from the afternoon sun. "How come you're home so early?"

"Missed my wife," Billy said, getting on the lounger beside her. It was the truth, after all, so he didn't bother telling her Tanner sent him home with instructions.

"Yeah?"

"Always." His thumb skimming her cheek, he tasted her lips. "So, what'd you do today?"

"Did some studyin'. Mulched the flowers. They're all gonna die soon." She looked out at her white garden and shrugged with a sigh. "Bein' I got ditched twice."

Huh?

"First, I was supposed to meet Mama for breakfast. Last minute, she texts me to say she's sorry, but something came up." Her hair lifted in the breeze, a piece of it sticking to her lip.

"Maybe somethin' did." Gazing into her eyes, Billy freed the strand. He was dying to kiss her again. Half-listening, he dipped his head, brushing his lips along her jaw.

"Like what?"

"Hell, I dunno."

"She sits in her house playin' with numbers all damn day."

Maybe she found somethin' else to play with. Or someone.

He wasn't about to say that, though.

"And then, Shiloh? She bailed on me, too." Emily rolled onto her side and snuggled up against him. "Did you see Archer today?"

"Nope." Funny, because he usually did. "Why?"

"Just wonderin'."

"I'm sorry you got ditched." He pulled her close against him and hiked her leg across his hip. "But then I ain't 'cause you're here, and bein' I'm home early, I get to love on my beautiful wife some more."

"Yeah?"

His fingers strummed over her nipples. Billy watched them bead beneath her shirt.

Fuck, yeah.

"Nothin' else I'd rather do."

"Right here?" She bit into her lip, a wicked glint in her eyes.

Billy glanced up at the mountain and the cloudless Wyoming sky. A gentle breeze rustled through the pines, tall grasses swaying with the horses in the pasture. Was there a better place to make love to Emily than this magnificent place they were lucky enough to call home?

He kissed her. "Right here, baby."

"I love you, cowboy."

"I love you."

But then, he always had.

And under the warmth of a golden sun, he made love to his wife.

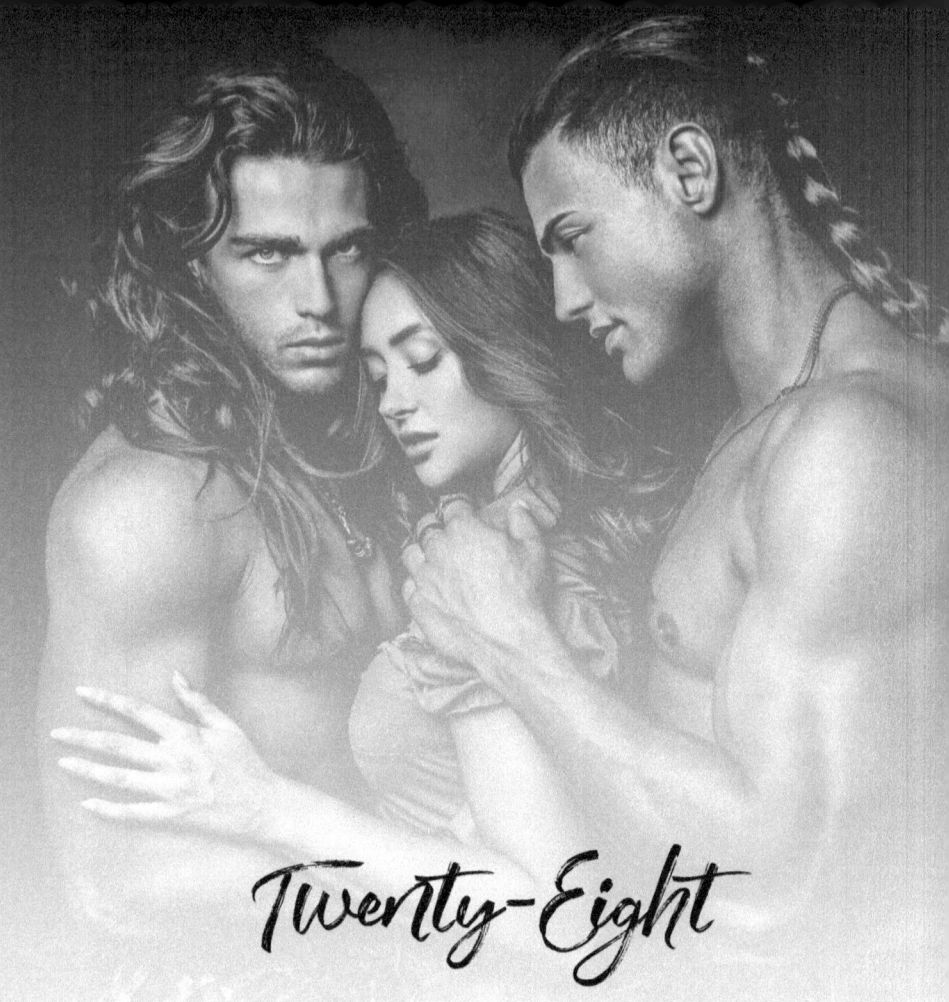

Twenty-Eight

T hree weeks.

That's how long they'd been following this goddamn river. With October nearly gone, the days were cold, and the nights even colder. Crystalline ice and snow clung to the faces of the rugged peaks surrounding them. Majestic as it was, Levi wondered how the fuck they could ever survive in a land such as this.

The river corridor came to its end, and they gazed out on the edge of the wilderness. Water trickling through the scree fields gathered into a stream at the bottom of the V-shaped valley. A vast blue lake fronted a square-top mountain, and tucked between two ice-covered canyons, stood to the north of them.

"Now what?"

Follow the Seeds-kee-dee-agie, and when you can't follow it no more, keep going.

"We'll camp here for the night, Elijah." He squeezed his friend's shoulder, hoping to reassure him. "And tomorrow, we keep going."

"To where, brother?" He threw his hands up. "This is as good a place as any to settle."

This isn't our home.

Levi refused to give up. Somehow, they would get there.

"We keep going."

The girls gathered wood, and he built a large campfire to warm them. Coulter served up a generous rabbit stew with biscuits. *Sure beats hardtack, beans, and bacon.* He was grateful for the bounty. Taking on Cookie had proven to be a wise decision. He looked out upon the lake and, sopping up the gravy with his bread, Levi couldn't help but wonder if perhaps Elijah was right.

"Should we stay here, Taghee?" He turned to the Bannock eating beside him.

Taghee licked gravy from his fingers. "What does your heart tell you?"

"No."

With a tip of his chin, the man smiled. "Then we don't."

"Do you believe Josiah's visions?"

"Do you have faith in yours?" He picked up his plate and stood then. "We all have them, my friend, but most of us don't listen."

Levi had faith, but he worried for Lucy, Fallon, his sisters, and young Elizabeth. For all of them. They trusted him enough to follow him here, and that made him responsible for their welfare.

Since the wagons were packed with no room to spare, they slept on blankets spread atop the cold, hard ground underneath the box of the wagon. They hung canvas cloth or blankets from the sides to afford them some protection from the elements. Four feet wide and nine feet long, it made for cramped quarters in which to rest, but it was something.

Victoria and Mary Alice came around from the back, bundles of blankets in their arms. "We're going to stay with Elizabeth tonight. She's frightened and cold. We can care for her."

"And Elijah can't?" He cocked his head at the younger twin.

"He has no one, Levi." Her pert brows drawing together, Mary Alice stomped her booted foot. "Besides, you'll have some privacy without us. I'm tired of hearing you rutting under the blankets."

"Mary Alice," Victoria nudged her sister, muttering under her breath.

"Like you're not?"

"Fine." And here, he thought, they'd been discreet. "Go on, then."

It's not like they were going very far. Elijah's wagon sat right next to his.

Lucy held the blanket open, ushering him inside. "What's troubling you, husband?"

"Nothing, love."

"Spread your legs for him, sister." With a soft chuckle, Fallon winked at him. "That will ease the worries from his mind."

It did for a time, but his slumber was fitful. He woke up tired, and just as troubled as he'd been the day before.

After breakfast, the camp packed up in silence. Too weary, no one chattered as they resumed the grueling journey. Without the river to guide them, Taghee, Hawkes, and Tyndall scouted out their route up ahead.

They'd just stopped for a brief nooning when Cooper came racing back. "Hurry and eat your damn beans, you're all gonna wanna see this."

A mile ahead, maybe two, an alpine lake fed a clear-running stream. A green, fertile valley lay below them, and a mountain with three peaks loomed above their heads.

"It's just as my father saw it." Tears ran down Lucy's beautiful face. "I told you, husband."

It seemed as if no man before them had ever set foot upon this earth.

"This is the place," Levi shouted, a jubilant fist in the air.

He kissed Lucy, then gathering Fallon to his chest, he kissed her, too.

Elijah picked up Elizabeth and, spinning in a circle, hugged the child who still hadn't cried for the mother she lost, her sister, or her father. He held her tightly to his chest, the twins hanging onto his arms. Victoria glanced up at him. Lifting her chin with his finger, he lowered his lips to hers.

Ha! I knew he was sweet on her.

But then, he bestowed a kiss upon Mary Alice, too.

His lips twitching, Taghee tried to hide a smile.

Behind their hands, Lucy and Fallon just giggled.

He gave them a pointed look.

"Didn't I tell you?" Lucy kissed his cheek and grinned. "Everything that comes in threes is perfect."

"Look at this place. We have been generously favored. The earth has given us its blessing." Her arms wrapped tightly around him, Fallon laid her head on his shoulder. "Don't fret, husband. All is as it should be."

Levi glanced at Elijah. He'd have a word with him later. Right now, they had to prepare for winter. And after that, a town to build, crops to plant, and cattle to breed.

"Welcome home, Levi Gantry." And she kissed him. "I love you."

"I love you." Gazing into her warm chocolate eyes, his fingers caressed her cheek. He reached for Lucy, and holding the sisters close, he whispered, "My bluebird and my butterfly."

The West was a place where their dreams had been tested, where the land itself seemed to challenge every one of them who'd been brave enough to cross it. But the journey wasn't just about reaching a new home, it was about discovering the strength they didn't know they had. They lost everything they thought they could never live without, but they gained something far greater: resilience, trust, and a bond that defied the world's expectations. The frontier wasn't just a place; it was a test of will, and for them, the rewards weren't just land or riches, but the unshakable knowledge that not only had they endured it, they had survived.

The blood, sweat, and tears—the love—of those who came before them is the reason they were all here. Levi, Elijah, Taghee, Archer, Cookie, together with every man, woman, and child worked to build a place that not only sustained itself but thrived. All because they heeded the words of a crazy old mountain man.

He told them if they kept the ways of the people, listened to the mountain, and respected the earth, that they would flourish and prosper.

They shouldn't have survived, but they did.

Prosperity, which continued to this day, had been granted to all of them.

An outsider, someone who didn't know their history, would never understand, but for nearly two hundred years, their ways had served them well.

Jake got out of the truck and breathed in deep. The scents of clear spring water, wild meadows, earth, ozone, and pine reminded him how favored he was, and how lucky they all were to belong to this place.

Brookside might not be Eden, but it was pretty darn close as far as he was concerned. The world outside the gate could keep their bullshit. He wanted no part of it. Here, at least, they could live a life filled with abundance, absolute love, and the purest joy.

His wife stacked foil-wrapped aluminum pans in his arms. "Got it?"

"Yeah, babe." Emily looked a little peaked. "You okay?"

"What do you think? I've only been cooking since five o'clock this morning."

Thanksgiving at the ranch. Despite the loss of his mother, Jake had so much to be thankful for. They all did.

"Wait, Billy." She placed a casserole dish in each hand. "Okay, I think that's everything."

"You sure?"

"Yeah, c'mon."

They followed her into the kitchen, where Arien, Grams, Shiloh, and his mother-in-law prepared the feast while sipping on Melinda's hard apple cider. The stuff was potent, too. It could grow hair on your chest.

Well, not exactly.

"Ladies, you're all beautiful. Happy Thanksgiving. Where do you want these?"

"Here, honey." Grams kissed his cheek. "I made you some room."

Jake relieved himself of six aluminum pans, and Billy dropped off two casserole dishes.

"I guess we'll leave y'all to it." He waved to the ladies, laid a smooch on his wife, and then he and his brother got out of the kitchen.

The living room looked like a daddy daycare. Matthew Brooks had Benjamin playing with blocks on the floor at his feet. Griffin entertained eight-month-old Jaxson on his lap, while the twins napped on Tanner and Kellan.

A childless Justin looked up at him, and pursing his lip, he shrugged.

"Dad, what the fuck did you do?" Billy's hand covered his mouth, no doubt concealing his hanging jaw.

"He cut all that glorious hair off, that's what he fuckin' did." And judging by the pout, his father's husband wasn't at all happy about it.

"Why?" Jake asked, even though he knew. *You miss her.*

"It was time. I'm almost fifty." Victor ran his fingers through his newly shorn scalp. Short on the sides, he still had some length on top. "Besides, I only kept it long for your mother."

"What about me?" Justin protested.

"I didn't think it mattered to you."

"It did." He crossed his arms over his chest.

"I'm sorry. Shall I grow it back?"

"Yes."

Kim came waltzing through on her way to the dining room. "I'll never understand why y'all think it's a good idea to cut off your hair."

"I ain't cuttin' mine." Billy held onto his chest-length mane as if it might disappear.

"Smart boy," their mother-in-law said over her shoulder. "Your wife would never forgive you if you did."

Noted.

Not that Jake had any intentions of cutting his, either. Hair is sacred, a symbol of strength and pride. Cutting it is a sign of grief and mourning.

"Ems," Arien called out from the kitchen. "What's the matter?"

Holding both hands over her mouth, she tore through the living room.

He jumped up and ran after her.

"I got you." Rubbing her back, Jake held up her hair while Emily vomited, holding onto the commode for dear life. "It's okay."

"It's not." She threw up some more. "Ugh, this is so gross."

Billy knocked on the door. "She all right?"

"Yes," he said.

"No," she countered.

"C'mon, let's get you over to the sink." Jake helped her rinse out her mouth, and after looking through the vanity drawer, he handed her a toothbrush and smoothed her hair. "Emily, do you think you might be—"

"No, I'm not pregnant." She sniffled, wiping off mascara from her face. "I had my period a couple of weeks ago, remember?"

He did.

"Must be Grams' cider or maybe it's all the shit I ate making the food this morning."

"You feel better now?" Jake held her and kissed her forehead.

Blowing out a breath, Emily nodded. "I'm sorry."

It's going to happen soon, michante. I feel it in my bones.

He'd dreamt of a little girl with long, dark hair and golden eyes. They called her Lucy.

"Did I ever tell you which story is my favorite of them all?"

"No." She shook her head.

"Ours." He gazed at the woman he'd love for the rest of his life. "And it isn't over yet."

Epilogue

A few weeks later.

S he was going to absolutely burst.

Emily scrambled to her car, squealing like a kid on Christmas morning, and Christmas was still a week away. She had to tell someone besides Billy and Jake. They already knew, of course, but she wasn't ready for anyone else to know yet except her mama.

Or it could be bad luck, right?

Maybe not, but she wasn't going to take any chances.

By the time Emily pulled into her mother's driveway, she was practically bouncing in her seat.

She skipped up the familiar porch steps, shaking her head at the pots of dead flowers flanking the doors. Next spring, she and Billy would plant her new ones. Because sure as shit, she knew her mama never would.

In every color of the rainbow, Mama. You gotta have some in your life.

Emily worried about her, especially now that she was married and her mother was alone.

The living room was empty. No laptop. No ledgers strewn about the coffee table like she'd expect to find. She checked her mom's office, which she rarely used. The kitchen. If it weren't for her Jeep in the driveway, Emily would have thought she wasn't home.

"Mama?" She tiptoed down the hallway. It didn't feel right to make noise with the house being so quiet.

The bedroom door was ajar.

Her hand poised, Emily was just about to knock when she heard it.

The rhythmic creaking of mattress springs. Muffled groans. Breathless whimpers.

"Does that feel good, baby?"

She scrunched her eyes closed.

Don't look. You'll be scarred for the rest of your life.

But in the end, curiosity got the best of her. Emily just wanted to know who it was.

Muscular, sculpted body. Ass high and taut. Golden skin.

She shouldn't have looked.

As quietly as she did when she came in, Emily tiptoed down the hall.

She ran to her car, not believing what she saw.

"Oh, yeah, I'm scarred for life, all right."

Holy fucking hell.

The End...until *The Distant Thunder*

Acknowledgments

Kickin' off my damn boots

Between two hurricanes, evacuating 120 patients, repopulating nearly three weeks later, signings, football, and cheer competitions, sometimes I thought I'd never get this story written. But when we left Arien, Kellan, and Tanner, didn't I tell you I had a feeling we'd be headin' on back to the ranch someday? *The Third Son* was supposed to be a *'one and done'*, but those cowboys had other ideas, and here we are. Just like Emily, Jake, and Billy, we've known from the start they'd end up together. What we didn't realize was how hard it would be for them to get to their happy ending—not that their story is over. Far from it. I've always loved historical novels, so I was thrilled to incorporate some history into this book. While I've taken some creative liberties, the emigrant experience on the Oregon Trail and Brookside's "ways" are based on fact. There are so many stories still to be told, and since y'all seem to love that strange little town in Wyoming, I can tell you we're going back again, and soon.

The Pinterest board and the playlist for *The Hardest Part* on Spotify and YouTube are open. Matt's story, *Rhythm Man*, Book 7 in the *Red Door* series, is coming next. It's time to play with the Venery boys. And after that? I haven't decided yet. We'll see where the muse takes me. You know I get ahead of myself, so let's just leave it at that.

As always, there are so many people to thank. I couldn't go on this journey alone, you know. And yes, I say it every time, I'm going to keep it short and sweet. After doing this ten times (and that blows my mind), you'd think I'd have figured out how to do it by now. I haven't.

My loves—**Michael** and **Raj, Charlie, Christian, Josie Lynn** and **Josh, Zach** and **Sam, Jaide, Julian, Olivia, Jocelyn,** and baby **Jalina.** I love you with every breath. Always have. Always will.

My ride-or-die, **Linda Russell,** and her fantastic team at *Foreword PR.* She loves cowboys and whips, and I love her. Thank you for having faith in me even when I didn't! xoxo

My Cover Queen of Hearts, and my beautiful Aussie friend, **Michelle Lancaster,** *Lanefotograf.* I love you so, so much! It took a Dream Team to bring you this cover, and when I tell you Michelle went *wayyy* above and beyond to capture the perfect image for it, I'm not even kidding. Between transforming Tristan and Andy into Billy and Jake with hair extensions and shooting in the heat of an Australian summer—she sent me a gallery of over 500 images. Do you have any idea how hard it is to choose just one? **Andy Murray, Tristan Pons,** and **Verity Runje** are so incredibly beautiful and portrayed the characters of Jake, Billy, and Emily to perfection, so it was *really, really* hard. My deepest thanks and much love to all of you! Pssst…Boys, I just gotta say this, the hair looks amazing on you! Xoxo

Lori Jackson, *Lori Jackson Design.* Dream Team Designer. Magic Maker. Gosh, I adore you! I keep telling y'all she makes magic. It has to be, right? She takes an image of three people squished together in a box and transports them to a ranch in Wyoming at sunset—there's no other way to explain it. From the initial concept to the final cover, working together with Lori and Michelle is such a joy and a helluva lot of fun. I love you, beautiful, and I can't wait for us to do the next one! xoxo

Ashlee O'Brien, *Ashes & Vellichor.* My girly. Book Daughter. Dream Team Graphic Designer. Trailer Maker. Alternate Cover Goddess. Alpha Reader. She named our Brooksiders the *Cowboy Cult Triad* (I love that!) and gave me the idea for Emily's white garden when we were talking about Sissinghurst Castle's garden one day. Told you, we have some strange conversations. Remember crying grass? She's been my right hand and my voice of reason from the very beginning. A perfectionist, her attention to detail, talent, and creativity know no bounds—she's always surprising me. And Ashlee, I love you the mostest! xoxo

Stacey Blake, *Champagne Book Design*. Look at that gorgeous interior!!! She's the one who makes the pages inside as beautiful as the cover, and no one does it better than she does. Thanks so much for everything you do, Stacey—I love you! xoxo

My Beta Team—**Charbee Balderson, Jennifer Bishop, Heather Hahn, Kim Lannan, Marjorie Lord, Lee Ann Mathis, Anastasia Meimeteas, Melinda Parker, Sabrena Simpson, Trisha Sparks, Rebecca Vazquez**, and **Staci Way**, together with my **ARC Team**—as always, thank you for jumping in the saddle and coming along for the wild ride! Y'all are amazing and I love you! xoxo

Bloggers, Bookstagrammers, and **Booktokkers**—I appreciate everything you do, every day, and not just for me, but for every indie out there. Your dedication to the book world is invaluable—none of us would be here without you. So, to say thank you isn't nearly enough, but thank you!

My **Redlings**, who hang out with me *Behind the Red Door*. Y'all know how to hype a girl up and I love you for it! If you'd like to hang with us too, you can find the group on Facebook. They're truly some of the most wonderful humans on the planet. We'd love for you to join us!

And, as always, my lovely **readers**. Thank you for being here and loving that strange little town in Wyoming. Your messages and emails make my day—I appreciate every one of them. *Brookside* didn't start as a series, but it sure is one now, so thank you for that, too. I hope you enjoyed your time at the ranch. Keep your boots handy, you're gonna need 'em again. But first, there's a bass player we all know who's been waiting for his story to be told, so I'll be seeing you at the *Red Door*—real soon.

Until The Distant Thunder...

Much love,

Dyan
xoxo

The doorbell rang.

"About time."

After a late night at the club, he was fucking starving.

Wearing only a pair of grungy, old sweats, Matt opened the door. A girl stood on the other side of it. Long dark hair in a ponytail, her eyes a mix of sable and green, she cocked her hip, his pizza in her hand.

He licked his lips. "You're not Luca."

"Nope." Shifting her eyes, she scanned his bare torso and made a face.

"Who are you?"

"The pizza girl." She smirked, shoving the box into his hand. "It's gonna get cold."

Then turning around, she skipped down his porch steps.

He was tempted to chase after her, but he didn't.

"Hey, you got a name, pizza girl?"

"Doesn't everyone?"

What the hell?

Her ponytail swinging, she glanced back at him from over her shoulder. Shaking his head, Matt took a step back inside the house.

"Gina."

She'll be back.

And closing the door behind him, he grinned.

Books by

DYAN LAYNE

Red Door Series
Serenity
Affinity
Maelstrom
The Other Brother
Drummer Boy
Son of a Preacher Man
Rhythm Man (coming 2025)

Brookside Series
The Third Son
The Hardest Part
The Distant Thunder (coming soon)

Standalones
Don't Speak
Whiteout

About the Author

Dyan Layne is a nurse boss by day and the writer of edgy sensual tales by night—and on weekends. She's never without her Kindle, and can usually be found tapping away at her keyboard with a hot latte *and* a cold Dasani Lime—and sometimes champagne. She can't sing a note, but often answers in song because isn't there a song for just about everything? Born and raised a Chicago girl, she currently lives in Tampa, Florida, and is the mother of four handsome sons and a beautiful daughter, who are all grown up now, but can still make her crazy—and she loves it that way! Because normal is just so boring.

Character Index

In alphabetical order by first name

Airdrie—Friesian mare

Amanda Jacoby Brooks *(deceased)*—wife to Matthew, mother to Kellan, younger sister to Heather

Arien Brogan Brooks—daughter of Jennifer *(deceased)*, stepdaughter/daughter-in-law to Matthew Brooks, wife to Kellan and Tanner

Benjamin Brooks—infant son of Matthew and Jennifer

Blaze—Jake's sorrel gelding

William "Billy" Gantry—younger brother of Jake, husband to Emily

Brigham Young *(1801-1877)*—American religious leader and politician, second president of the LDS (Mormon) Church from 1847-1877. A polygamist, he had 56 wives and 57 children.

Caleb Gantry *(1826-1847, deceased)*—brother of Levi, Victoria, and Mary Alice

Carrie Sawyer Gantry *(deceased)*—elder sister to Justin, wife to Victor, mother to Jake and Billy

Cassandra "Cassie" Lewis Archer—elder sister to Shiloh, wife to Griffin

Cayden Elijah Brooks—Harper's twin brother

Charlie Tyndall—ranch foreman

Sunchaser "Chaser"—Billy's chestnut mustang

Cooper Hawkes—cowboy from Kentucky, 1847

Daisy—Arien's American quarter horse

Deacon "Deke" Clary—tends bar at the bonfire parties

Elijah Brooks *(1826-unknown, deceased)*—one of the original settlers of Brookside, great-grandfather to Kellan and Tanner, elder brother to Elizabeth

Elizabeth Brooks *(1841-unknown, deceased)*—youngest sister of Elijah

Emily Keough Gantry—daughter of Kimberly, Timothy, and William *(deceased)*, wife to Jake and Billy

Everleigh Clary—sister to Deke, Jake's first kiss

Fallon *"Kimana"* (Butterfly) Walker Gantry *(1829-unknown, deceased)*—elder sister to Lucy, wife to Levi

Garrett Brooks *(deceased)*—father to Matthew and Kimberly, grandfather to Kellan, Tanner, Emily, and Benjamin

George Dalton—19th century pioneer (appears in *Whiteout*)

Griffin Archer—younger brother of Reed, husband to Cassie and Shiloh

Gunner—Kellan's Friesian stallion

Henry "Hank or Cookie" Coulter—chuckwagon cook, 1847

Harper Elizabeth Brooks—Cayden's twin sister

Harry Coulter—proprietor of the diner

Heather Jacoby Brooks *(deceased)*—wife to Matthew, mother to Tanner, elder sister to Amanda

Jacob "Jake" Gantry—elder brother to Billy, husband to Emily

Jaxson Archer—infant son of Griffin and Shiloh

James Felix "Jim" Bridger (1804-1881)—American Frontiersman, established Fort Bridger in 1843

Josiah Walker (*deceased*)—mountain man, father to Fallon and Lucy

Jennifer Brogan Brooks (*deceased*)—mother to Arien and Benjamin, third wife to Matthew, stepmother to Kellan and Tanner

John Jacoby (*presumed deceased*)—father to Heather and Amanda, grandfather to Kellan and Tanner

Justin Sawyer—younger brother of Carrie, husband to Victor

Kellan Brooks—firstborn son of Matthew and Amanda (*deceased*), brother to Tanner, husband to Arien

Kimberly Brooks Keough—widow, sister to Matthew, mother to Emily, aunt to Kellan, Tanner, and Benjamin

Leonard "Lenny" Quigley—the butcher

Levi Gantry (*1825-1906, deceased*)—one of the original settlers of Brookside, great-grandfather of Jake and Billy, elder brother to Caleb, Victoria, and Mary Alice

Miss Lilly—dressmaker, sister to Victor, aunt to Jake and Billy

Lucy "*Chosro*" (Bluebird) Walker Gantry (*1831-unknown, deceased*)—younger sister of Fallon, wife to Levi

Maizie Jacoby—baker, wife to John, mother to Heather and Amanda (*deceased*)

Mary Alice Gantry (*1831-unknown, deceased*)—younger sister of Levi and Caleb, identical twin to Victoria

Matthew Brooks—father to Kellan, Tanner, and Benjamin, husband to Jennifer (*deceased*), stepfather to Arien, brother to Kimberly, uncle to Emily

Melinda Brooks—mother to Matthew and Kimberly, grandmother to Kellan, Tanner, Emily, and Benjamin

Noëlle—Airdrie's foal, sired by Gunner

Oliver Tyndall—cowboy from Texas, 1847

Paul Brooks (*deceased*)—father to Matthew and Kimberly, grandfather to Kellan, Tanner, Benjamin, and Emily

Reed Archer—Griffin's older brother

Ruby—Emily's dapple gray

Samantha Quigley—the butcher's daughter

Savannah Mason—classmate of Arien's in Denver

Shiloh Lewis Archer—younger sister of Cassie, wife to Griffin, mother to Jaxson

Sunday, Monday, Tuesday, Wednesday, Friday—Brooks Ranch border collies

Taghee Smith—member of the Bannock tribe, 1847

Tanner Brooks—son of Matthew and Heather (*deceased*), brother to Kellan, husband to Arien

Timothy Keough (*deceased*)—elder brother to William, husband to Kimberly, father to Emily

Tux—Tanner's Shire stallion

Tyler "Smitty" Smith—electrician

Victor "Doc" Gantry—physician, husband to Carrie (*deceased*) and Justin, father to Jake and Billy

Victoria Gantry (*1831-unknown, deceased*)—younger sister of Levi and Caleb, identical twin to Mary Alice

Wade Mathers—Billy helped build his barn.

William Keough (*deceased*)—younger brother of Timothy, husband to Kimberly, father to Emily

One

'm going to fuck you. You may not know it yet, but I do. It's only a matter of time. I've been watching you. I swear that you've been watching me too, but maybe it's all in my head. No matter. Because I've seen you, I've talked to you and I've come to a conclusion: You are fucking beautiful. And I will make you lust me.

The words danced on crisp white paper. Her fingers trembled and her feet became unsteady, so she leaned against the wall of exposed brick to right herself, clutching the typewritten note in her hand. She read it again. A powerful longing surged through her body and her thighs clenched.

Who could have written it? She couldn't fathom a single soul who might be inspired to write such things to her. Maybe those words weren't meant for her? Maybe whoever had written the note slid it beneath the wrong doormat in his haste to deliver it undetected?

Linnea Martin, beautiful? Someone had to be pulling a prank. *Yeah. That's more likely.*

She sighed as she turned and closed the solid wood front door. She glanced up at the mirror that hung in the entry hall and eyes the color of moss blinked back at her. Long straight hair, the color of which she had never been able to put into a category—a dirty-blonde maybe—hung past her shoulders, resting close to where her nipples protruded against the fitted cotton shirt she wore. Her skin was fair, but not overly pale. She supposed some people might describe her as pretty, in an average sort of way, but not beautiful.

Not anything but ordinary.

Linnea slowly crumpled up the note in her hand. She clenched it tight and held it to her breast before tossing it into the wastebasket.

Deflated, she threw her tote bag on the coffee table and plopped down on the pale-turquoise-colored sofa that she'd purchased at that quaint secondhand store on First Avenue. She often stopped in there on her way home from the restaurant, carefully eyeing the eclectic array of items artfully displayed throughout the shop. Sometimes, on a good day when tips had been plentiful, she bought herself something nice. Something pretty. Like the pale-turquoise sofa.

Linnea grabbed the current novel she was engrossed in from the coffee table and adjusted herself into a comfortable position, attempting to read. But after she read the same page three times she knew she couldn't concentrate, one sentence blurred into the next, so she set it back down. She clicked on the television and scrolled through the channels, but there was nothing on that could hold her interest. The words replayed in her head.

I'm going to fuck you.

Damn him! Damn that fucker to hell for being so cruel to leave that note at her door, for making her feel…things. The words had thrilled her for a fleeting moment, but then the excitement quickly faded, replaced by a loneliness deep in her chest. Love may never be in the cards for her, or lust for that matter, as much as she might want it to be.

Once upon a time she had believed in fairy tales and dreamt of knights on white stallions and handsome princes, of castle turrets shrouded in mist, of strong yet gentle hands weaving wildflowers in her long honeyed locks—just like the alpha heroes in the tattered paperbacks she had kept hidden under her bed as a teenager.

She thought if she was patient long enough, her happily-ever-after would come. She thought that one day, when she was all grown up, that a brave knight, a handsome prince, would rescue her from her grandmother's prison and make all her dreams come true.

Stupid girl.

Her dreams turned into nightmares, and 'one day' never came. She doubted it ever would now. It was her own fault anyway. She closed her eyelids tight, trying to stop the tears that threatened to escape, to keep the memories from flooding back. Linnea had spent years pushing them into an unused corner, a vacant place where they could be hidden away and never be thought of again.

It was dark. She must have been sitting there for quite a while, transfixed in her thoughts. The small living room was void of illumination, except for the blue luminescence that radiated from the unwatched television. Linnea dragged herself over to it and clicked it off. She stood there for a moment waiting for her eyes to adjust to the absence of light and went upstairs.

Steaming water flowed in a torrent from the brushed-nickel faucet, filling the old clawfoot tub. She poured a splash of almond oil into the swirling liquid. As the fragrance released, she bent over the tub to breathe in the sweet vapor that rose from the water and wafted through the room. Slipping the sleeves from her shoulders, the silky robe gave way and fell to a puddle on the floor.

Timorously, she tested the water with her toes, and finding it comfortably hot, she eased her body all the way in. For a time serenity could be found in the soothing water that enveloped her.

You may not know it yet, but I do. It's only a matter of time.

At once her pulse quickened, and without conscious thought her slick fingertips skimmed across her rosy nipples. They hardened at her touch. And a yearning flourished between the folds of flesh down below. Linnea clenched her thighs together, trying to make it go away, but with her attempt to squelch the pulsing there, she only exacerbated her budding desire. And she ached.

Ever so slowly, her hands eased across her flat belly to rest at the junction between her quivering thighs. She wanted so badly to touch herself there and alleviate the agony she found herself in. But as badly as she wanted to, needed to, Linnea would not allow herself the pleasure of her own touch. She sat up instead, the now-tepid water sloshing forward with the sudden movement, and reaching out in front of her she turned the water back on.

She knew it was wicked. Lying there with her legs spread wide and her feet propped on the edge of the tub, she allowed the violent stream of water to pound upon her swollen bud. It throbbed under the assault and her muscles quaked. She'd be tempted to pull on her nipples if she wasn't forced to brace her hands against the porcelain walls of the clawfoot tub for leverage.

Any second now. She was so close.

I'm going to fuck you.

And he did. With just his words, he did.

Her head tipped back as the sensations jolted through her body. The sounds of her own keening cries were muffled by the downpour from the faucet. Spent, she let the water drain from the tub and rested her cheek upon the cold porcelain.

Prologue

"Aidan, baby."

His mother took him by the hand and pulled him along behind her as she hurried out of the kitchen. He'd only eaten half of his grilled cheese sandwich and some grapes when the banging started. It startled him and he knocked over his juice. By the time she went to the front door to see who it was, the banging noise was coming from the other side of the house.

"You can't keep me out, bitch."

It was a man. He was yelling. He sounded angry. Aidan didn't recognize his voice.

His mother seemed to, though. Her eyes got real big and she covered her mouth with her hand. It was shaking.

There was a hutch in the living room that the television sat on. It had doors on the bottom. He hid in there sometimes. His mother opened one of the doors, and tossing the toys that were inside it to the floor, she kissed him on his head and urged him to crawl inside.

"We're going to play a game of hide and seek from the loud man outside, okay, baby?" his mother whispered.

Aidan nodded.

The banging got louder.

"You have to be very, very quiet so he doesn't know you're here."

It sounded like she was choking and tears leaked out of her eyes, but she smiled at him.

"Like at story time?"

Aidan's mother took him to story time at the library every Saturday, and afterwards if he'd been a good boy, she would let him get an ice cream.

"Yes, baby. Just like that." She nodded with tears running down her face. "Now stay very still and don't speak a word until I tell you to—no matter what, okay?"

He nodded again. "Okay, Mommy."

"I love you, Aidan."

"I love you, Mommy."

Everyone said the place was haunted. The kids at school. The people in town. It didn't look scary, but nobody ever went anywhere near the two-story white clapboard house that was set off by itself on the cove.

It was to be her home now.

Molly stood at the wrought-iron gate with her mother, holding onto her hand. She clutched her *Bear in the Big Blue House* backpack, that she'd had since she was four, with the other. A boy with sandy-blond hair sat on the porch steps. Aidan Fischer. He didn't pay them, or his father unloading their belongings from the U-Haul, any mind. He had a notebook in his lap and a pencil between his fingers. It looked like he was drawing.

The boy chewed on his lip as he moved the pencil over the paper. Even though he was in the fifth grade, and three years older than her, Molly knew who he was. Everybody did. He was the boy who didn't talk. And six days from today, when her mother married his father, that boy was going to be her brother.

Preview of *The Third Son* (Brookside #1)

One

Coming out of the bathroom, Arien stubbed her toe, close to taking a tumble over a stack of forgotten boxes in the hallway. "Ouch. Motherfu…"

She held onto her foot, hopping the rest of the way to her bedroom in the small townhouse apartment she shared with her mom. It was all packed up, cartons neatly labeled, identifying the contents inside. Bed stripped. Closet and drawers emptied.

It wasn't like she had a choice.

A moving van was parked outside.

Holding her towel closed, her back against the wall, Arien sat cross-legged on the bare mattress. She had exactly thirty minutes to put on some makeup and get dressed. It should only take her ten.

This is so not fucking fair.

She blew out a breath. A week ago, her room was pretty and her life wasn't packed away in cardboard boxes. That all changed when her mother and her boyfriend—if that's what you call a man in his forties—took her out with them to dinner.

And that alone should have told her something was up.

Jennifer Brogan had been dating Matthew Brooks for about six months now, but Arien didn't know him all that well. A real cowboy, her mother said. He had two sons and lived on some ranch up in Wyoming, an eight-hour drive from Denver. He'd come into town for business, and to see her mom, a few times a month.

He was the one to break the news to her. "Arien," he said with a smile, taking her mother's hand in his. "First off, I need you to know I love your mama very much. So much, that I've asked her to marry me."

She about choked on her green chili cheeseburger.

Her mom held up her left hand, waving the huge diamond glittering on her finger. "I said yes."

Okayyy.

Arien was seventeen, soon-to-be eighteen. She'd be going away to college at the end of summer anyway. Her mom deserved some happiness, right?

Swallowing down the cheeseburger, she put on a smile. "At least you won't have to change your monogram. When's the wedding?"

"Next week," her mother announced, biting her lip. "I'm pregnant."

"Three months already," Matthew said, like he was proud of the fact, patting his new fiancée on the shoulder. "I'm coming back with the boys. We'll get married and have you all moved in before Thanksgiving."

What? To Wyoming? Nope. Not happening.

"Wait. You want me to move, to change schools during my senior year?"

"I'm sorry, sweetie."

"You're going to love Brookside." Her soon-to-be stepfather patted her on the hand. "We have a superior private school there. The ranch. The mountains. You can take lots of pictures."

"There's mountains right here."

Isn't thirty-six too old to have a baby anyway? Apparently not.

And what happened to all those lectures her mother gave her about having sex, taking precautions, and all that stuff? Mom should've listened to her own advice. If she had, Arien wouldn't be going to a courthouse wedding to leave Denver, and the only life she'd ever known, behind.

Only for a little while.

True. She already had her acceptance letter to UC. She'd be back.

"Sweetie, are you ready yet?" her mother asked from downstairs. "Matt and the boys are here."

Dammit.

"Almost," she answered, plucking through her makeup bag.

Clearly a lie. She hadn't even begun.

Holding a compact mirror in one hand, Arien applied mascara with the other, the towel slipping away from her.

She couldn't say for sure what made her look up. A feeling she was being watched, maybe.

Two boys—no, these were not *boys*, they were hot-as-fuck men—stood smirking in her doorway.

"Who the hell are you?"

"I'm Tanner." The darker one smiled, and taking a step inside her room, he hitched a thumb behind him. "That's Kellan."

"And I'm naked." She snatched up the towel, covering herself.

Kellan snickered.

Tanner came closer. "Well now, that's a mighty fine hello, little sister."

You've got to be friggin' kidding me.

Her eyes darted between the inked brother looming right in front of her to the blond one leaning against the doorframe behind him. Both of them tall, gorgeous, and ripped, they were hardly the annoying prepubescent boys she'd presumed Matthew's sons to be. Not that she'd bothered to ask about them. And why hadn't she?

Too caught up in her *poor, poor me* shit, Arien had been too angry to care. In the space of a week she'd packed up her life, said goodbye to all her friends, and for what? So her mom could get married to some dude who knocked her up. Were these two "Save a Horse, Ride a Cowboy" poster boys supposed to be like a consolation prize or something?

"She's even prettier than her picture, ain't she, Kel?"

"Hmm." Kellan rubbed his finger back and forth over his upper lip. "I reckon."

"Do you mind?" Arien pulled the towel tighter. "Naked here."

With a chuckle, Tanner leaned down and kissed her cheek. "We don't mind at all."

The wedding went off without a hitch. Her mother in a short ivory dress and Matthew in a navy-blue suit, Arien and her new stepbrothers stood as witnesses to their parents' nuptials. It took all of five minutes. She took their photos on her Nikon Z50 she'd spent years saving up for. The Denver County Courthouse, a magnificent example of neoclassical grandeur, made for a gorgeous backdrop. Its three-story portico of columns, the wide staircase, and ironwork lanterns gave her some amazing shots.

Matthew tapped her on the shoulder. "Can I see, honey?"

"Oh, yes, of course." And she handed him her most prized possession.

"These are really good."

"Thanks."

He glanced at her. "There's only one thing wrong."

"What's that?"

He smiled. "There aren't any of you and the boys."

They went to Benzina, a trendy new Italian place nearby, after. Sadly, green chili cheeseburgers weren't on the menu, but the coconut macaroon panna cotta wedding cake came pretty darn close to making up for it.

Sandwiched between the two brothers, each nursed a beer on either side of her. Arien assumed then, they were at least old enough to drink legal. Or perhaps their dad simply allowed it? She glanced over to Tanner, since he seemed more approachable. "How old are you anyway?"

"Old enough." He winked. "I'll be twenty-two on Thursday."

"Your birthday's on Thanksgiving?"

"This year."

Appraising her from the corner of his eye, Kellan raised his beer to his lips, draining the glass.

"Are you older or younger?"

"Older," he clipped. Then Kellan addressed his father. "We leavin' tonight or waitin' 'til mornin'?"

"I figured we could load up the truck tonight, get a good night's sleep, then hit the road first thing in the morning." With a wink, Matthew threw an arm around his bride. "That okay with you, son?"

"Yeah, sure." Kellan glanced at his brother, the corner of his mouth ticking upward. "Suits us just fine."

Tonight. Tomorrow. What's the difference? She'd still be leaving in the end, so to Arien it didn't matter either way.

"I think I'm gonna have another piece of cake." Yeah, because sugar can fill up the hollow pit inside, at least for a little while. Not to mention, she had the feeling there probably wouldn't be desserts that came anything close to this where she was going.

"Arien," her mom began to protest, but Matthew covered her hand with his and stopped her.

"I love me a pretty girl with a hearty appetite." Kellan slapped a huge slice on her plate. "No need to be counting all those calories there. We'll be workin' 'em right off you, won't we, brother?"

"Do I look like a cowgirl to you?"

"Not yet." And he grinned.

Leaning into her ear, Tanner squeezed her knee beneath the table. "He's just trying to get a rise out of you."

Arien looked at Kellan, and giving him the most saccharine smile she could muster, lifted a forkful of cake to her mouth. "Mmm." She licked panna cotta filling from her lips. "So good."

"Eat up, baby cakes." His wicked gaze fixed on her. "We got things to do."

She stood with her mother in the living room, watching the new men in their lives cart boxes stacked three high down the stairs, as if they weighed nothing at all. Being these boys probably threw bales of hay around all day long, moving their stuff must be an easy breezy walk in the park. Admittedly, Arien wasn't exactly sure what cowboys, ranchers, or whatever they called themselves did. Except for what she'd seen on TV, and even that wasn't very much.

Her mattress went out the front door. "Mom, they can't take that. Where am I supposed to sleep?"

"The pullout sofa isn't going anywhere—not until Goodwill picks it up tomorrow."

"Okay, what about them?"

"Recliners?" Jennifer shrugged, then pulled her into her side. "It's one night, Arien. Just make do. Tomorrow you'll be in your beautiful new room, in a big, beautiful house, breathing the fresh mountain air."

"Great."

"Listen, sweetheart, I know this is a huge adjustment for you." Her mom squeezed her tight. "It is for me, too, but Matt is so good and the boys are nice, young men…we have a family now, baby. Life is going to be wonderful, you'll see."

Biting her lip so she wouldn't cry, Arien nodded. She'd never seen her mom this happy, and dammit, she deserved to be. So, she was going to suck it up and put a smile on her face. For Mom. It was only nine months out of her life, right?

An hour later, with the truck loaded up and their parents tucked away upstairs, the boys kicked back in front of the TV. Kellan aimlessly scrolled through the channels. Tanner patted the empty space between them. Armed with her pillow and a blanket, Arien took it.

"What are we gonna watch?" Making herself comfortable, she folded the old, lumpy pillow in half and tucked it under her arm.

His gaze remaining on the screen, Kellan shrugged a shoulder and passed her the remote. "Pick somethin'."

"Fine, Hallmark Christmas movie it is."

Kellan snatched the pillow from her, playfully swatting her with it. "See if I ever let you have the remote again."

"Hey," Arien squealed, looking from one brother to the other. She couldn't help but compare the two. Their subtle similarities. The stark differences. Her fingertips brushed the dirty-blond strands that had fallen into his brown eyes. "You must take after your mom."

"Guess so." His gaze returning to the TV, Kellan tossed the pillow to her lap.

Tanner leaned in against her shoulder. "She died when he was just a baby."

"Oh, God. I'm so sorry, Kellan." Arien took his hand and squeezed it. His calloused thumb, sandpaper on petal-soft skin, slowly traced the pulse at her wrist. She turned her head toward Tanner. "Wait a minute…"

"Kellan and me don't have the same mama."

"Oh, you're half-brothers then."

"Brothers." His thumb stopped moving. Kellan didn't look at her when he said it, "End of story."

"Where we come from…" Tanner slung his arm around her shoulder. "…there's no such thing as half, little sister."

"Okay, you're close. I get it." Resuming their movement, Kellan skimmed his fingers along the back of her hand. "Where's your mom, Tanner? Did she and your dad get divorced?"

"No."

"Oh, they were never married?"

"They were married."

"She's dead." Kellan turned the TV off. "Buried in the family plot next to mine."

"Fuck." Her hand flew to her mouth.

"I was three days old." Tanner hugged her to him closer. "Weak heart, they figured, bein' that's what took his mom too."

"Why would that matter?"

"Because they were sisters," Kellan said, matter-of-factly. "I say we get some sleep. We've got a long drive and a truck to unload tomorrow."

Scrunched together, the three of them made themselves fit on the pullout sofa. Kellan faced one way, and Tanner the other, while Arien stared up at the ceiling. She thought of two little boys growing up without a mother. Two sisters lying side by side in the ground. The man who had been married to them both. How tragically sad.

Something woke her. Tanner softly snored behind her, his tattooed arm thrown across her middle. It was heavy.

She gasped.

Moonlight illuminated the piercing eyes that studied her.

Kellan held a finger to her lips. "Shhh."

Chapter One

F ive hours.

That's how long she'd been driving already, and Breanna hadn't even reached the state line yet. Maybe she should've stayed on I-5 instead of cutting over to Route 39, but that's the way her GPS sent her, so she took it. Cranking up the tunes, she passed Klamath Falls and grinned. "Seventeen more miles."

With her Spotify playlist blasting, she excitedly waved goodbye to Oregon as the 'Welcome to California' sign appeared. The state of her birth, though she would be nowhere close to her family in LA. She hadn't even told her mom she was making the trip. She'd only worry. Besides, just hearing the name Dalton made Sarah Benjamin sad. It surprised Breanna she got to keep her dad's last name.

Bad blood between her mother and her late father's family. Namely, her grandmother, Valerie Dalton, whom Breanna had never even met. She'd never met Shane Dalton either—not that she could remember, anyway. He died when she was just a baby.

So when she received an official-looking letter from St. John, Maynard & St. John, Attorneys at Law, on her grandmother's behalf, requesting her presence at Dalton House, it aroused her curiosity. What did Valerie Dalton want? Breanna doubted it was a desire to meet her son's only child after twenty-one years. But it could be, right? The woman had to be in her seventies now. Maybe she'd had a sudden change of heart in her old age.

Yeah, and maybe shit doesn't stink.

The correspondence, signed by one Derek St. John, said little.

No clue why she was being summoned. He only stated he was following the wishes of his client and advised Breanna to plan to get there before the Thanksgiving holiday—and the arrival of winter weather in the Sierra Nevada. Mountain roads can be treacherous when the snow comes.

Did he think she was an idiot?

Chrissakes, just because she was a California girl, didn't mean she'd never driven in snow before.

After marinating on it for a week, she left word with the lawyer's secretary to let him know when to expect her. The week of Thanksgiving break would have to do, and too bad if Derek St. John or her grandmother didn't like it. Breanna had friends to see, parties to go to, and classes to attend. Okay, she was on the flexible undergrad track for her BA in English. If she wanted to, she could log into lectures on her laptop, comfy in her pajamas, from the sofa in her apartment—or from anywhere, for that matter, but the old lady didn't need to know that.

Her gaze flicked over to the snow-capped range of peaks to the east. Overcast, the midday sky looked dreary, but the clouds weren't ominous. *Yet.* She'd be fine. But Breanna still had five hundred miles, some seven hours of driving left before she reached her destination, and her ass was already numb.

A hundred and forty miles later, her bottom screaming at her to get up and stretch, gas gauge down to a quarter tank, she got off the highway. Refuel. Restroom. Coffee. There was no time to waste if she wanted to reach Dalton House before dark. Estimating she'd only need to make one more stop after this one, Breanna stood in line, Styrofoam cup in hand, rubbing circulation into her aching backside with the other. As long as the weather held, and barring any unforeseen hazards on the road, she should be good.

Her ass protesting once more, she sat back down behind the wheel, burning her tongue on the steaming hot battery acid that passed for gas station coffee. *Yuck.* Breanna grimaced into the cup, her phone vibrating on the center console.

"Hey, Kay," she answered.

"Just checking on you. You there yet?"

Kayleigh, her closest friend at college, and her roommate, was a worrywart. An old mother hen in a twenty-year-old body. She was the girl who forbade the consumption of jungle juice at parties—especially those held on Greek Row, cockblocked the fuckboys, and forced her to eat something besides cheap ramen noodles for dinner. And Breanna loved her for it. God only knows just how many bad decisions she'd saved her from.

"Hell, no." She expelled some air, tipping her head back against the seat. "Just made it to 395."

"You're not being safe." Breanna could just picture Kayleigh shaking her head. "You should stop. Get a room and rest for the night."

"No, I'll be fine," she assured her. "It's only a few more hours."

"Stubborn." Kayleigh sighed through the phone. "Have you even bothered checking the weather, Bree? They're predicting—"

"Snow. I know." Swallowing a sip of the putrid battery acid, she glanced up at the sky. "I'll be there long before it gets here, so don't worry, okay?"

"Yeah, I bet that's what the Donner Party said too, and look what happened to them."

"So dramatic," Breanna said, chuckling at the historical reference. "I think it's pretty safe to assume no one's going to be eating me—dead or alive."

Kayleigh giggled. "Well, should that lawyer guy or Grandmama serve fava beans and a nice chianti at dinner? Run. Fast."

"Will do." And she started her car. "I'll text you when I get there."

The cloud cover grew more dense the farther she drove. No longer merely overcast, the sky appeared heavy, saturated in a deepening gray. Breanna wasn't too concerned, though. According to her GPS, Dalton House was less than an hour away.

Like a good, obedient girl, she exited off the highway as the robotic British male voice instructed her to. She preferred him to the Siri-sounding woman. A checkpoint was set up on the road in front of a mom-and-pop store. Coming to a stop, Breanna lowered her window.

"Evening, miss."

She tipped her chin. "Hello."

"You're gonna need to get chains on those tires before I can let you through. We're expecting a doozy of a storm. Can't have you getting stuck out there on the pass."

"But—" *It's not even snowing yet.*

"Sorry, miss." He pointed toward the little store. "Hank's got 'em if you're needing some. Seventy-five bucks and he'll put 'em on for you too. Have you back on the road in a jiffy."

"Okay, thanks," Breanna assented, raising the window. "This is some bullshit. Hank must be raking it in."

Figuring she might as well top off her tank before heading inside the store, Breanna pulled up to the gas pump. A cold gust slapped her in the face as she exited the car, making her clench the unzipped jacket tightly around her middle. Trees danced on either side of the road, their naked branches bending to the will of the wind in the thickening darkness. Gazing heavenward, the slate-gray altostratus ominously churned.

Triggered by a familiar tickle in her nose, she sniffed the air. The scent of an approaching storm mingled with sweet benzene. Breanna zipped her worn, black leather bomber, and winding a scarf around her neck, made her way across the small parking lot. Bells attached to the door clanked into the glass as she wrestled with it, a sudden squall pushing her inside.

It was as if the passage of time had forgotten this place. To her left was a small diner with a checkered floor, red vinyl seats, and an old-fashioned soda fountain. To her right, a counter with rows of penny candy—cost twenty times that now—and a cash register. In front of her were several aisles of grocery essentials and sundries.

A balding head popped up from behind the counter. "Need something, miss?"

"Yes. Yes, I do. Chains." Behind her, the door burst open again. Breanna shivered, tingles creeping down her spine. "The officer at the checkpoint told me to see Hank."

"That's me." Pointing a thumb backward at his chest, he cracked a crooked grin, revealing a crooked front tooth. "I'm Hank."

"Can you put them on for me?"

"Be happy to." His head bobbed. "Where's your car?"

"Right outside," she said, handing him the keys. "The white Miata."

Breanna heard a snicker at her back. A voice, smooth and deep, muttered low, "Figures. Damn girly car."

She whirled around to find six feet of rugged man standing behind her. Bearded. Suede coat lined with sheepskin. A black Stetson on his head. Dark hair brushed his shoulders. Eyes the color of whiskey. "Yeah, well, I *am* a girl."

"I can see that." Smirking, he dropped his head to the side and winked.

Probably drives one of those big-ass pickup trucks to compensate for having a tiny dick.

Flustered by the stranger's boldness, Breanna turned back to Hank. "How long will it take?"

"Not too long," he assured her. The crooked grin fixed on his face, he bobbed his head to the left. "Why don't you get yourself a cup of coffee while you wait? Have a piece of banana cream pie. My wife makes it. Best damn pie in the world, trust me."

"Can't pass that up, now can I?" She smiled at Hank, side-eyeing the tall, dark, imposing stranger. Brushing past him, Breanna took a seat on a vinyl-covered stool at the end of the counter.

Sweet on her tongue, she licked thick, whipped cream from her lips. Hank did not exaggerate. The pie was chef's kiss, and the coffee sublime, especially after the gas station sludge she'd been existing off of.

Rubbing his hands together, cheeks reddened, Hank came behind the counter as she washed down the last of her pie with a sip of coffee. "You're all set, miss."

"Great, thanks." Breanna handed him her credit card.

He just held it in his hand, staring at it. "Dalton, huh? You any relation to Valerie?"

"Yeah, she's my grandmother. Why? You know her?"

Tucking his tongue into the corner of his lip, Hank nodded. "Well, I'll be goddamned. I had no idea. You'd have to be Shane's girl then."

"That's right."

Brows cinching together, his eyes flicked to the windows behind her. "It's startin'. Best get you on your way."

The bold one sat in a booth. Hat on the table, a mug of coffee poised at his mouth, he shook his head. "Suicide. Chains or no chains, she's gonna slide right off the mountain in that thing."

Standing up from the stool, Breanna sniggered. "It's just a few snowflakes."

Slowly, he swiped his tongue across his lip and grinned.

"And every storm starts with just one."

www.ingramcontent.com/pod-product-compliance
Lightning Source LLC
Chambersburg PA
CBHW050035120726
47903CB00006B/2050